MARCIA ARMANDI

AWAKEN

SHADOWS OF A FORGOTTEN PAST

PART ONE

AWAKEN

SHADOWS OF A FORGOTTEN PAST

MARCIA ARMANDI

CITY OWL
PRESS

AWAKEN
Shadows of a Forgotten Past, Part One
By Marcia Armandi

CITY OWL PRESS
www.cityowlpress.com

Cover Design by MiblArt. All stock photos licensed appropriately.

Edited by Lisa Green.

For information on subsidiary rights, please contact the publisher at info@cityowlpress.com.

Print Edition ISBN: 978-1-64898-450-1

Digital Edition ISBN: 978-1-64898-449-5

Printed in the United States of America

For my grandmother, Lola, who taught me to be strong and to believe in myself.

CHAPTER 1
~ OBSCURE REALITY ~

GENEVA, WESTERN NEW YORK, 1937

A meal of three-day-old bread crust and watered-down milk hardly stoked the flames of courage, and standing on the steps of Oak's Place in the drizzly rain, I needed every spark of spirit I could gather. Usually, a teeth-baring gothic door knocker would not give me goosebumps. Neither would unpredictable weather, let alone applying for a job, even at a house whose mysterious owner fueled the town's gossip storm. But hunger could wear down even the bravest heart, and a job opening was a miracle never to be slighted.

I stepped back and gazed up at the high brownstone walls and mortar chimneys of the house, its gables filled with ivy and signs of disrepair. Last summer, the estate fell into the hands of a retired British general. Who was he? And why select this part of the world in which to retire? No one knew. No one ever saw "the Shadow," as people called him, locked away in his mansion in the woods.

Naturally, my imagination went wild. Although Granny—Sister Dolores to the rest of the world—vehemently disapproved, I often tuned into the *Detective Story Hour* after supper, imagining the new owner of Oak's Place a silent yet fierce vigilante. A childish game to play, perhaps, but understandable when I'd spent my twenty years of life with my adopted granny—a saint at heart but devoted to making my life as dull as only a nun could.

A rustling brought my attention to the scrub where the trees clumped together, their branches twisted in serpentine patterns. There. Something moved but disappeared before I could make it out. I told myself it must be some creature of the woodland realm but then got the strange feeling that unseen eyes watched me closely. I quickly grabbed the door knocker as a wind rose, rushing through the ancient trees. Almost as soon as the metal collided with the wood, a gray-haired woman in a black dress opened the door, her catlike eyes gleaming from within the gloomy interior.

"May I help you?" The sharp British voice sounded oddly... familiar.

"Good morning," I said promptly. "I telephoned about the ad in the paper."

Her eyes quietly assessed me for a moment, and I wondered if she would invite me in. Just then, another gust of wind whipped around the yard and shook the door. "Come in. Come in," she said hurriedly as if compelled by the elements.

Brushing my fingers through my hair, I stepped into the unlit foyer and immediately noticed the thick silence. It greeted the tapping of my heels with a faint echo, as if someone invisible walked the long corridors. Yet I detected no one besides the dreariness residing there, the passages I could see beyond the foyer as labyrinthine as one could hope for so mysterious an owner.

Entirely lacking in furnishings, the foyer offered little in the way of color or encouragement, as inviting as the woman who had answered the door. And as she came up beside me, fresh goosebumps prickled my arms. The sensation told me that anything or anyone lurking in the forest would be a welcome companion compared to what might lay ahead in the shadows of the house. But instead of urging me to run, my fears kept me rooted in place.

"I am the housekeeper, Mrs. White."

Her voice brought me to my senses. "Florence Contini. It's a pleasure to meet you." I caught sight of the only glimmer of personality about her

—the black rosary around her neck. Where had I seen this woman before? In the monastery chapel? Perhaps. But when?

I extended my resume, which she took with a slight tremor in her hand. She gazed at the print for a long while, a wave of confusion veiling her features.

"You are too late. Too late indeed." Her fingers trailed the beads of her rosary as if in silent prayer.

"Late? How can I be late? I drove here as soon as we hung up." I hesitated, hoping she said something encouraging.

"You can leave your resume. I'll make sure to speak with Mr. Sterling about it."

My stomach heaved as I desperately searched for the words to convince her I was right for the position.

"What's the matter, Deborah?" a man spoke, his voice blending with the bleakness of the passage ahead.

"Mr. Vines! Why the devil do you creep around the house?" Mrs. White shrieked, undermining the image of self-control she'd projected.

Mr. Vines stood a good foot taller than me, with an olive complexion and dark eyes that left me feeling disquieted.

"Me?" He laughed. "No one knows the art of creeping around more than you, Deborah."

"For goodness' sake, Mr. Vines, watch your tongue."

Mr. Vines laughed again, though it sounded more ill-tempered than merry. Then he contemplated me with such intensity I wondered if he also remembered some common past, a long-forgotten meeting of our paths.

"This is Florence Contini," the housekeeper offered.

"Florence Contini, indeed." He extended his hand. "I'm Mr. Vines, the chauffeur."

"Nice to meet you." I met his firm grip with my own, then swiftly let go.

"I hope you've come to stay this time," he muttered.

Come to stay this *time*? I opened my mouth to question him, my sudden courage more likely drawn from *Detective Story Hour* than my present reality, but Mrs. White quickly intervened.

"Actually, she was just leaving." The housekeeper reached for the doorknob.

"Oh, but she can't leave." Mr. Vines spoke with the same resolution that marked his British accent. "Mr. Sterling would like to meet with her."

"Of course he would." Mrs. White pursed her lips, the same thing Granny did on occasion, but I had the distinct impression she summoned a great deal of restraint not to snap at Mr. Vines. "Well, then." She returned the resume to me and gestured to the first room off the foyer. "Have a seat. I'll check with Mr. Sterling."

"What's there to check?" Mr. Vines objected.

"Do hush." Her gaze fell upon him like a sharpened blade. "Come now."

I stared into the passageway where the couple vanished into blackness, amazed at how masterfully they kept courtesy to its minimum requirements. I wondered if the housekeeper's neglect marked the waiting room also, but as I entered the space, the blush of something different met me.

Faint daylight came through a window overlooking the woods, and in the gray softness, I discovered paintings of European architecture, pastoral landscapes, and vibrant forests. A mahogany desk with a wooden chair, a flowery armchair, and a grotesque armoire with heavily carved doors completed the decor. As I settled in the armchair, I again felt the urge to flee, but the memory of Granny using the same tea bag three days in a row encouraged me to stay.

That very morning, I could not have expected the secretary position in the employment column of the newspaper. Now, I believed it with the full force of the gossip that surrounded this place—gossip that placed Mr. Sterling as a mercenary, fugitive from justice, wartime spy, or, worse yet, some obscure creature who hunted the woods for his victims.

Despite the tales being so far-fetched, I couldn't blame the townsfolk for speculating. It was easy to feel resentful when our nation experienced the worst poverty in its history. The sudden fall of the stock market spared few, not the least the monastery. Granny's soup kitchen, the school for girls, the sisters, the trips—all lay desolate. And here was Mr.

Sterling, uncaring and distant, hidden away with all his money. No wonder they disliked him. But idle prattle wouldn't put food on the table. I needed a job and was determined to see it through.

"Follow me, please." I jumped to my feet as the housekeeper approached, Mr. Vines's words ringing in my head. *"No one knows the art of creeping around more than you, Deborah."* I realized his statement was verified in every particular—the more so as I followed her into the corridor. Only the shifting of her beads and her quiet muttering broke the silence.

At a bend, we turned into another dimly lit corridor and followed the sconces to a door at the far end. Before knocking, Mrs. White ran her hands over her well-pressed dress. Instinctively, I looked at my blue blouse and skirt, leftovers from the monastery's charity chest, feeling too plainly dressed.

"Come in," a voice said in response to her knocking.

Mrs. White pushed the door open and signaled me to enter first. "Miss Contini, sir."

Mr. Sterling stood before the window in a swath of diffused light that spilled through the glass, his back to me. He appeared to be over six feet tall, with broad shoulders and black hair—not what I imagined.

When he didn't respond, Mrs. White said, "Very well. I'll leave you to it," then left, closing the door behind her in a way that transmitted her displeasure.

I glanced around at the wood-paneled walls, brown sofa, brick fireplace, pile of books on the floor, and large desk with leather chairs.

The motionless Mr. Sterling could have simply been one more furnishing. Wondering if I should say something, I looked past him into the yard, catching sight of a statue of a woman embracing a child. At that instant, time stood still, as if I had stepped into a dream—a forgotten dream that called to me from another world.

"Good morning, Miss Contini." Surrounded by the daylight, his face remained in shadow as he turned, his British accent calm and reassuring.

"Good morning."

My heart skipped a beat as he crossed the room. He was neither young nor old. In his early forties, his features bore witness that he had been remarkably handsome in his youth, and still was. The odd sense of familiarity rushed back with renewed intensity. Somewhere, I had seen those deep-blue eyes, dark brows and eyelashes, fair skin, and almost intimidating presence. No. How could it be? I hadn't seen him or his staff before. I had only envisioned him while bemusedly listening to the local gossip, but that man stood worlds apart from the one holding my gaze.

"I'm Alexander Sterling," he said brusquely, showing no inclination to shake hands.

"Pleased to meet you, sir." I suddenly became aware of my looks. The rain and wind had done a number on my hair, several strands escaping from their clips. At least my outfit complemented my auburn hair and brown eyes, or so I hoped. But under Mr. Sterling's silent judgment, I felt gauche and awkward. How on earth would I convince him I could handle the job so windblown and pale with nerves?

He pulled a chair from the desk. "Please have a seat."

"Thank you."

He strolled to his chair on the opposite side.

"Here is my information." I placed the paper on the neatly arranged desk.

Mr. Sterling retrieved it and began reading. Meanwhile, the morning grew darker, and soon the heavy clouds unleashed a torrent of rain that pounded against the window as if wanting to break through it. Though we were surrounded by bodies of water in the Finger Lakes region, precipitations like this were sporadic. And it didn't seem to bother Mr. Sterling one bit as he inspected my resume with a curious intensity. Was there something wrong with it—something wrong with me?

A minute or two later, his voice sounded above the drumming of the rain. "Have we met?" His eyes flitted from the paper to mine.

I had no intention of appearing weak, but I felt captured by his eyes and had to force myself to look away, unable to hold his gaze. "I don't believe so." *Interesting. He, too, feels a sense of familiarity.*

"Are you sure? Maybe not here, but in England?"

"I'm afraid not. I've never left New York."

"Your name is Florence Contini."

"Yes."

"You were raised by Sister Dolores Perkins—a nun?" he asked, a brow raised.

"Yes."

"What about your parents?"

"My parents?" I shook my head, disconcerted. The resume stated it clearly—I'd been orphaned, and his question, if not intrusive, was irrelevant. At any rate, I clarified, "I know nothing about them. They left me at the monastery when I was but a baby."

"It says here you were trained at Higher Grounds, a private school for girls. Where is that?"

"It belonged to the monastery, several miles north of town. But it closed after I graduated two years ago."

"You were born in 1917. How can that be?" His gaze drifted as if he'd been transported to another place, another time. "Twenty years ago . . ."

Did he think I was too young for the job? I had to reassure him—convince him I could be his secretary. "After I graduated, I became the monastery's accountant and record keeper. So, in that regard, I'm confident I can manage your business affairs in a satisfying manner."

"You already have a job, then?"

"Not anymore. With the economy as it is, the church stopped funding the monastery and effectively eliminated my job."

"I see."

A loud crash came from the corridor, my ears ringing with the intensity of the sound. Again. Another blast. This time, I surmised that it must be an object being overturned.

"Excuse me." Mr. Sterling rose, visibly annoyed by the disturbance.

I nodded.

He stepped into the hallway, leaving the door ajar. After a moment of silence, I heard him and Mrs. White arguing in hushed voices. To my disappointment, I couldn't make out their conversation, but I feared I wouldn't get the job. It seemed both scrutinized me with an edge of distrust.

My mind raced, my hands compulsively opening and closing. Granny and I needed the income. She tried hard to conceal her anxiety about our financial state, but I had seen the stack of bills, overdue notices, and the multiplying payment plans. Thankfully, Mr. Sterling didn't take long to return and settled back into his seat. Distress accentuated his features.

"Miss Contini, I have one more question for you."

I braced for the worst.

"When can you start?"

I almost fell off the chair. Had I heard correctly?

"Miss Contini? When can you start?" he repeated.

"Right away." The words tumbled out of my mouth.

"It's settled, then." He smiled faintly. "Mrs. White will explain your tasks. She knows more about my affairs than I do."

"Thank you, Mr. Sterling. I won't disappoint you." My thoughts continued to race. I had a job, my first real job. I wouldn't mess it up, hopefully.

Like an unexpected whirlwind, Mrs. White burst into the room. Had she been eavesdropping?

"Welcome aboard, Miss Contini," she said, confirming my suspicions. "Please, follow me."

I started after her, feeling Mr. Sterling's eyes on my back.

"I'll introduce you to Zaira, our cook, and Mr. Snider, the groundskeeper, tomorrow. People in this house tend to vanish when one needs them," Mrs. White grumbled, moving briskly down the hallway.

A domestic issue could account for the tense atmosphere. It was a comforting thought. However, the word *vanish* didn't sit well with me.

We entered the room where I first waited.

"This will be your office." Mrs. White touched the light switch in passing, and the chandelier sprang to life. "Now, there is no better time to clarify your position. All rules must be understood and followed. Failure to do so will result in your termination." She paused as if she expected me to say something.

Rules. Growing up at the monastery, I was accustomed to rules, though not inclined to follow them. I nodded in acknowledgment.

Evidently pleased with my silence, she said, "Have a seat," pointing to the uncomfortable-looking chair behind the desk. "First, you'll refer to me for everything. Mr. Sterling suffers from an unknown disease. At times, he becomes violently ill and needs rest and isolation. He mustn't be disturbed."

A mysterious disease? Could this be why he didn't socialize and why he wanted his affairs in order? So much for being a bloodthirsty murderer. He hadn't looked sick to me, but why should I doubt the housekeeper?

"Second, you are not to discuss Oak's Place matters beyond these walls. Third, do not wander the premises. I'll show you the areas you are welcome to, and I strongly suggest you stay within those boundaries. Understood?"

"Yes, of course."

She handed me a notebook and pen. "Now, you may wish to write this down." She opened the doors of a large armoire, revealing a host of books from which she carefully extracted several leather-bound volumes. "The family's solicitor was in charge of this, but he retired when we moved to America." With a loud thump, she dropped the load in front of me. "Mr. Sterling owns quite a few properties. You'll find deeds, tax information, rents, and so on in these books. Like the ad explained, your job is to organize, update, and maintain." She slipped onto the armchair and launched into a lengthy harangue about my duties and her expectations as to how I should accomplish them. "I'll meet with you in the mornings to help you get started, but I hope you'll catch on quickly."

So do I.

With everything Mrs. White said, at least one thing was clear—she was both the lawmaker and enforcer at Oak's Place.

CHAPTER 2
~ NO REAL EXPLANATIONS ~

The rain abated, faint rays of sunlight penetrating the lingering clouds, as I drove the Buick home. Along the way, I passed boarded-up shops and a few active stores before arriving at the movie theater near the edge of town. The small affair had recently begun screening a new film entitled *Snow White and the Seven Dwarves*. Even when it seemed profligate to spend a few coins on a ticket, or downright *foolish*, as Granny would say when we observed the people waiting to get in on a Friday night, it gave me hope that the economy might turn around, with no more lines of folks looking for work or charitable provisions.

I rounded a corner and saw a few young men moving down the pavement. A good-looking blond-haired man smiled and waved at me. I waved back, wondering if he was searching town for work. Work. My mind jumped to the strong, commanding presence of Mr. Sterling, his eyes at once frightening and beautiful, inviting and guarded. *"Have we met?"* he had asked. Then his gaze found mine as if expecting me to say something—something lost in a distant memory. While the entire encounter went round and round in my head as I searched for something I might have missed, the rest of the drive was a blur.

The Buick made a sound of protest as it crossed into the monastery grounds. Somewhat imposing from the outside but marvelous from within, my home—a two-story, ancient gothic structure with corner towers and stained-glass windows—soared over me. The car growled as I brought it to the rear courtyard and jumped out. With short, quick steps, I crossed the cobblestone path to see a storm brewing just inside the kitchen window, where Granny sat at the table.

"I was afraid you had forgotten your way home," came the first arrow as I walked through the door. Granny pulled off her glasses and placed them on the table. Dressed in her black habit, she looked more like a county judge than a nun. Her eyes pierced mine, notching a second arrow. "You could have told me where you were going. I was worried sick about you."

"I'm sorry. I should have." I crossed my fingers at the white lie. I had deliberately sneaked out, fearing that had she known, she would have sent a flaming cherub to detain me, not to mention every saint she'd ever prayed to. I knew she meant well, but so did I. I grabbed the newspaper from the countertop and sat down to show her the ad. "I applied for the job. Granny, listen—" Taking her hands in mine, I told her about my visit to Oak's Place, omitting any details that might alarm her. Unconvinced, she bombarded me with questions, forcing me to carefully consider each answer twice in order to maintain my story.

"I don't know, Florence." She drummed her fingers on the table. "I hate to judge Mr. Sterling, but we can't ignore the unpleasant rumors."

"That's true, but you taught me not to judge. Besides, Mr. Sterling and his staff seemed quite normal." I was alarmed at how easily I lied, but desperate times called for desperate measures.

"Hmm . . ." Granny moved to the stove, where she set the kettle down.

"His health is frail. I suppose that's why he wants his affairs in order. And I suspect that's also why he doesn't show up in town," I added to ease her concerns.

"If that's the case, why leave his homeland? Wouldn't it be better to remain close to his interests while healing?"

"Be that as it may, we need the income, and I don't foresee another job opening anytime soon."

"So you got the job?"

"I did."

Granny pulled two cups and a new box of chamomile tea from the cupboard. "And you say this Mrs. White is a refined lady?"

"Yes, and judging from the rosary around her neck, she's quite religious." I omitted that Mrs. White's gaze left me unsettled.

"I wouldn't take that at face value. Some adeptly hide their twisted ways behind masks of religion. I'm not judging, just being careful." Granny returned to the table, teacups in hand. "Who else is there?"

"Mr. Vines, the chauffeur." I took a few sips of the tea, its sweet, flowery taste helping me unwind. "Mrs. White also mentioned a gardener and a cook. I'll meet them tomorrow."

"I guess there is no harm in giving it a try, but Florence"—Granny seized my free hand—"under no circumstance will you stay there if you feel unsafe. Money will come some way or another. It always does. Promise me you won't hesitate to quit if need be."

"I promise." I hoped time would justify my words, for I honestly had no idea who Mr. Sterling or his employees were or why they resided in Geneva.

"I guess we'll both be busy, then." Granny grinned impishly.

"What did you get into this time?"

"Well . . ." Granny gulped down the rest of her tea. "Sister Callahan is bringing a few sisters from Cambridge to tour the United States. They'll stay with us for a time. Isn't that good news?"

"What can possibly be good about that?" Sister Callahan's stout figure and dominant personality forced their way into my mind.

"Oh, child, no need to be so excited about it. Things are different now."

"That's right. There are no girls to torture except for me." The last time she visited, she'd displayed the most exquisite talent for minding everybody else's business. She'd ensured the girls were flawlessly presentable, attended their classes on the hour, and went to bed ten minutes before the appointed time. In other words, we had to behave like canonized saints.

"Besides," Granny interrupted my unpleasant memories, "it's not our choice."

"When are they arriving?"

"I'm not sure. They are still working out the details."

"How long are they staying?"

"A few weeks, I suppose."

"Does Friar Thompson know?" Sister Callahan had taken an unusual liking to the local priest, who was terrified by her relentless eagerness to befriend him.

"I haven't found the courage to tell him." With a smile, Granny collected the cups and brought them to the sink. "But you must remember that, often, people like Sister Callahan, though a bit rough around the edges, can teach us a great deal."

"Like perfecting the virtue of long-suffering," I said under my breath.

The night thickens, and I can't find my way out of the woods. Terror grips me, and I run like a hunted creature. Someone or something chases me.

"Florence, my lady, I'm here. I'm here," comes a voice, tantalizingly familiar, and then blue eyes gaze into my soul. I know those eyes, but the face is young and vivacious, not the face of the man I met yesterday. His arms encircle me, replacing the anguish with a sense that I am finally home.

"Florence, whatever you do, don't trust—"

The remnants of last night's odd dream accompanied me to Oak's Place, the drive there swift, like the young Mr. Sterling who had comforted, then warned me. Of what, exactly, did he warn me?

I went to remove my coat when Mrs. White entered my office. "Good morning, Miss Contini."

"Good morning."

She checked her wristwatch. "Thank you for being on time. I appreciate punctuality."

I smiled, pleased that she seemed in a better mood today.

"Keep your coat on and come with me. I'll introduce you to the staff."

We took the main hallway to the kitchen. Opposite a wall of cupboards and an oversized stove stood a giant fireplace, certainly one of many and a winter necessity in a house this large. For now, the weather was pleasant and the French doors that led to the back gardens stood open, a gentle breeze blowing through the space.

"Where has she gone now?" Mrs. White said with exasperation. "One of these days, I'm going to have enough."

As if summoned by the housekeeper's threat, a woman in her thirties with flaming red hair and hazel eyes surfaced from outside. Upon seeing us, her fair skin grew more pale.

"About time you showed up," Mrs. White fired. I had the impression that were I not present, a severe reprimand would follow.

"I'm sorry. I got a bit distracted and lost track of time," the woman responded. "I'm Zaira." She held out her hand.

I shook it. "Florence Contini."

Mrs. White filled a glass with tap water, glancing at Zaira with disappointment.

"Oh yes, yes. We spoke on the phone yesterday."

"That's right." I smiled, recalling her subtle British accent and politeness when I'd called about the ad.

"I'm glad you got the job. Mr. Sterling overheard our conversation and asked me what your name was three times—to make sure he got it right, I suppose." Zaira giggled. "I figured he would hire you. Besides you were the only one to come."

Mrs. White choked on her drink, gasping for air.

"Are you all right?" Zaira patted her back.

"Yes. Yes," she wheezed, tapping her chest repeatedly. "Give me a second."

Zaira turned back to me. "So you live in town?"

"I do."

"I've been dying to explore the area but haven't had time. Maybe you could show me around sometime." It sounded like a plea for help.

I couldn't imagine being tethered to the house with the brooding Mrs. White and the intriguing Mr. Vines always about. Just this morning, he was sitting in the courtyard. With arms folded, his dark gaze fixed on me as I descended from the car and climbed the front steps. When I greeted him, he responded with an almost imperceptible nod. And I had the strange feeling he had been awaiting my arrival. "Most definitely."

"Well then." Mrs. White intervened, all recovered from the drink incident. "Let's find Mr. Snider. Come along." With quick, short steps, she hurried outside.

"Nice meeting you, Zaira," I said over my shoulder as I hustled to keep up with the housekeeper.

"Zaira's passion for communication, I'm afraid, knows no bounds. But you must remember you aren't here to fraternize with the staff. You must do your job and not distract others from doing theirs."

I didn't respond since I could picture Zaira and me becoming friends. Besides, if we fulfilled our responsibilities, I saw no harm in socializing.

The housekeeper continued toward a battered stable and a black-roofed cottage. She pointed to the latter. "The staff sleeps in here, except for me. I have a room in the house."

I wondered if that was due to Mr. Sterling needing assistance.

"Where has the man gone?" Her sharp eyes scanned the trees. "Oh, I know. Come on, keep up."

We traveled along a path south into the woods, where the vegetation became dense, blocking out most of the light. My hearing intensified, picking up the faintest of sounds: our steps against the carpet of fallen leaves and twigs, birds hopping from branch to branch, the scurrying of creatures in the underbrush.

"Ah, there he is," Mrs. White said.

Across the barricade of greenery, I spied a figure moving with great urgency. Mrs. White lengthened her strides in front of me, shifting just enough to obstruct my view. As we finally approached Mr. Snider, he sat peacefully on a stump, an axe and a pile of firewood nearby. He wore blue overalls and a beige shirt with rolled-up sleeves. And despite his weather-beaten face and the unkempt brown hair beneath his straw hat, his countenance was pleasant.

"You've been at it again," Mrs. White said, scanning the brush, "haven't you?"

"As you can see." He nodded at the freshly chopped wood.

Mrs. White frowned.

I had no idea what she alluded to, but I felt sure it wasn't about the firewood.

"This is Florence Contini. Just making you aware that she'll be working at the house." Though she spoke softly, the creases of discontent in her forehead deepened.

"Mr. Snider, it's a pleasure to meet you." I shook his gloved hand.

"The pleasure is mine. Having someone agreeable around—in addition to Zaira, of course—will be a nice change."

Mrs. White's lips tightened.

"That's a lot of wood," I noted to soften the sting of his remark.

He grunted. "It's barely enough for a week or two."

"Right, then. We'll leave you to your chopping. At least that's something you can do all right," Mrs. White growled, effectively ending the conversation and quickly retreating through the trees.

With a chuckle, Mr. Snider seized the axe and, with incredible force, split a log in two.

"Until later," I said.

"Miss." He swung the axe again.

I rushed after Mrs. White, and soon, we came to a part of the path where it narrowed considerably, the surrounding shrubs and low branches threatening to smother it. Off to the right, a sudden movement caught my eye. Before I could make it out, the dark silhouette vanished amid the foliage, unsettling my heart.

"Mrs. White," I leveled my steps with hers, "who else works in the house?"

"You've met everyone. Mr. Vines, Snider, Zaira, and I."

"Is that all?"

"Do you think I'm lying?" She looked at me sideways, clearly still annoyed by the encounter with Mr. Snider.

"Of course not. It's just that I thought I saw someone in the trees back there."

"Probably an adolescent. They cut through the woods now and then on their way to town." She spoke matter-of-factly, but the way she scrutinized the spot to which I pointed told me she had someone or something specific in mind.

I forced my lips into a tight smile. I sensed something unusual about the figure, something unnerving. I glanced over my shoulder again. Everything was still.

As I passed Mr. Sterling's office, I wondered if he sat behind the closed door and, more to the point, whether I would see him today. I reached my office and turned to the armoire that housed the business books and documents. I would have to organize them—no easy feat, considering I had to study and categorize them individually before filing them.

Thankfully, time passed quickly, and the sorting became almost mechanical. Flipping open a folder, I saw it contained the deed to a parcel of farmland. I placed it on the stack labeled "Farms," then reached for the next folder and placed it in the pile labeled "Assets." I'd almost finished my work when I dislodged a tiny book that fell from the armoire onto the floor. Curious, I retrieved it and turned to the first page as the scent of old ink and paper filled my nostrils. My eyes danced across the spidery inscription: "Family Tombs, Dates, Names." I shivered. I disliked cemeteries, funerals, and death. Nevertheless, I looked more closely at the handwriting. Did it belong to Mr. Sterling? I felt compelled to turn the page and read more.

I started when Mrs. White suddenly exclaimed, "Ah, I have been looking for that. Where did you find it?"

"In here." I signaled to the armoire.

"I see. It was misplaced."

"Would you like me to file it?" I offered, aware that creating a category for the deceased hadn't crossed my mind.

"No. I'll take care of it." She took it from me, a dark emotion crossing her face as she fingered the pages. Then she snapped it shut and, in one swift motion, buried it in her dress pocket.

"Where are the others?" I asked.

"Mr. Vines and Mrs. White usually eat in their quarters or the garden," Zaira informed. "Same with Mr. Sterling. I brought his food to his office earlier."

"As for the first two," Mr. Snider rumbled, "thank heaven that's the case. I rather enjoy eating in peace."

"Oh, Mr. Snider," Zaira said. "Do you ever tire of quarreling?"

He swallowed another mouthful of crab pie. "Nope."

I knew what Mrs. White had said—that Mr. Sterling needed rest and isolation. Still, I hadn't envisioned him being a shadow in his own house, moving about as if he didn't exist. His nickname started to make sense. While those unsettling thoughts swirled inside my head, I failed to notice Mr. Vines until he stood beside me.

"I hope you are finding Oak's Place to your liking," he said.

"I am, thank you."

"If nothing else, you'll love the British food. It's the best in the world, as you know."

As I know? Apart from today's lunch, I did not know much about British food. I smiled but didn't respond.

Mr. Vines placed the dirty dishes he brought with him in the sink, and, to everyone's surprise, pulled up a chair as if ready to carry on a thorough discussion.

"Well, Miss Contini, I'm glad you are here. Time goes by fast, doesn't it? Or at least that's what we'd like to think when in reality it's just an illusion. In the end, the past always comes back to haunt us."

My eyes turned to him, feeling like he said something pertinent in his riddles.

"I see we are having a meeting," Mrs. White exclaimed, entering from the hall.

"I ought to get back to work." Like a cat on a hot tin roof, Mr. Snider sprang up, cleared his place at the table, and walked out.

"Deborah, come sit by me. We were just talking about you," Mr. Vines lied.

"Good thing I came, then. What are you divulging now?"

"There is nothing to worry about." He reached for her hand. "Loosen up a little, would you?"

Mrs. White brushed him away. "I'm fifty years old. I have no time for games, Vines."

"Ah, there it is again, the subject of time." He smiled in a strange way. "It flies for some, while it seems to stop for others."

Mrs. White threw a nasty glance at him before her gaze settled on me. "Miss Contini, have you ever been to Europe?"

"I have not."

"Shame. It's such a beautiful place," she said.

"Indeed it is," Zaira agreed. "You'll have to visit England someday."

I nodded, but I doubted it would ever happen. "It must be difficult for you to be away from home and family," I noted.

"I miss them terribly." Zaira shifted on her seat. "But I'm enjoying my freedom. My parents, I'm afraid, refuse to let go of their Victorian ways, and I felt caged at home. Needless to say, when Mrs. White recruited me to come to America, I jumped at the opportunity."

An ocean apart, I thought, was quite a bit of freedom.

"Ah, freedom to do as we please—a natural desire," Mr. Vines agreed.

"One that must be kept within proper boundaries." Mrs. White's gaze darted from Mr. Vines to Zaira.

"And you, Mr. Vines? Do you miss your folks?" I ventured.

"I would if they were alive, but Deborah and I don't have living relatives. I'm single, and her husband passed away years ago. Other than unwanted memories, nothing exists for us in England."

"You can say that again." Mrs. White sighed. "We moved here hoping to leave them behind, but some recollections simply refuse to leave us alone. You might be too young to understand, Miss Contini, but when you love someone from the depths of your heart, you can neither move on nor forget. You are stuck in time."

"I'm sorry. I can't imagine losing someone you love."

"Hmm . . ." Mr. Vines shifted in his chair, and I noticed an anxiousness in his eyes, as if one of those unwanted memories plagued him.

"I must say, death can be your worst enemy while, at times, your best friend," Mrs. White said.

"A friend? How is that possible?" Zaira's tone was one of disbelief.

"Sometimes, the suffering is too much—such as when facing a terminal illness. Then, death comes as a relief. So, those left behind, though grieving, understand its merciful arrival." In disturbing contrast to the vulnerability of her words, Mrs. White's voice sounded calculating and detached. But it wasn't my place to judge. Her detachment might be how she coped with loss. And despite that loss, here she was, far from her land and people, soldiering on.

"Grief manifests in many forms," Mr. Vines assured. "The worst kind comes when the one you love doesn't love you back." He glanced at Mrs. White. "Isn't that right, Deborah?"

"We all have shadows to chase us and to chase after," Mrs. White answered.

My gaze traveled through the French door's glass into the outside world. Mr. Snider crossed the grounds, pushing a wheelbarrow.

"Ah, the old fellow." Mr. Vines followed the direction of my eyes. "Never stops moving, does he? You know, he is a military veteran from the Great War. Mr. Sterling met him in one of those postwar houses and kept in touch with him."

"Mr. Sterling used to travel the region visiting with soldiers, helping with their recovery." Mrs. White sounded positively proud of her employer.

"When the time to move to America came, Mr. Sterling reached out, and Snider accepted the job," Zaira further explained. "At that point, Mr. Snider had been separated from his wife for years. She took their two sons and left him. He never saw them again."

"That's terribly sad." My heart went out to him. Even when I didn't know my family, I still yearned for them. I couldn't imagine how he felt when he had a past filled with his family's memories. "Why did she leave?"

Zaira opened her mouth to answer but shut it again.

"If we were busybodies, Miss Contini, who view boundaries as mere suggestions and privacy as a concept not meant for others, we might sit here long past the lunch hour to discuss the lives of those not present," Mrs. White scolded, glancing at her wristwatch. "I think you know all you need to know about Snider."

"I'm sorry. I didn't mean to pry." The question had been innocent enough, a natural course of the conversation. Her rebuke, though, was a reminder that I was here to do my job and not to meddle in their personal affairs. Even though I got the message, I still thought her strictness was a bit too much.

"I think coming here was a good change for Mr. Snider," Zaira added, smoothing the tense moment.

"That remains to be seen," Mrs. White muttered as she left the table.

Needing a breath of fresh air, I took the path bordering the house, the discussion still circling in my head. The shade of the trees on one side of the path and the massive walls on the other accentuated the chill I felt as I thought of Mr. Vines and Mrs. White and the oddness about them—an oddness I couldn't place. Perhaps it was just unfamiliarity. With time, I might gain their trust and friendship.

A crackling sound followed by a quick motion in my peripheral vision stopped me. I glanced into the woods. There. The noise of leaves as if carried by the wind came again, but there was no wind. *Someone is watching me.* The hair at the back of my neck stood as my gaze darted from tree to tree, shrub to shrub, and the forest floor in between. While I saw nothing to justify the disturbance, I couldn't shake the eerie feeling that I wasn't alone.

I lengthened my steps, hurrying to the opposite, less gloomy side of the house. Rounding the corner, I collided with Mr. Sterling, the impact sending me into the thorn-covered rose vines that climbed the wall. Reflexively, my arm went out to protect me.

"Flor—" He stopped midsentence. "Miss Contini, are you all right?" He took hold of my arms, stabilizing me.

"Mr. Sterling, I'm sorry."

"Are you all right?"

I surveyed the damage. "It's nothing. Just a few scratches."

"Let me see." He rolled up the sleeve of my dress.

As he examined my arm, I couldn't help but notice how stunning he looked in the light of day.

"Have Zaira clean it just in case." He ran his fingers over the undamaged skin of my arm, and my cheeks grew warm.

"Thank you. I will." I pulled away.

"Maybe I should have Mr. Snider cut down the vines," he said as if gauging my reaction.

"I wouldn't be so drastic," I said promptly. "I'm sure the roses are beautiful when in bloom."

"Beautiful indeed. But tell me, where were you going in such haste? You would think something chased you."

"I suppose the chilly day might have chased me to the sun." No way would I confess that my discombobulation came from whatever lurked in the woods. "Unless, of course, there is something I am unaware of."

His face contorted with an emotion I couldn't decipher. Grief, fear, or maybe anger? "No, Miss Contini. There is nothing to worry about." His gaze dropped to the path, and he resumed his walk, leaving me baffled.

CHAPTER 3
~ UNAVOIDABLE ~

A gray mist hovered about the streets the next morning as I steered the Buick onto the quiet main street. The newspaper boy waved at me as he pedaled past the car, his bicycle loaded with a stack of papers. A black-and-brown shaggy cat jumped off a store awning and ran up the pavement. Other than the boy and the feline, the day was too young for the usual buzzing of town.

I glanced at my wristwatch and slowed down, not wanting to show up to work too early. However, I couldn't deny that my heart throbbed with anticipation at the idea of another chance encounter with Mr. Sterling. Considering that I hardly knew the man, the desire was unnerving so I brushed it off. When I again looked at the road, I noticed a woman come onto the sidewalk from an alley. The ends of her red hair escaped the scarf wrapped around her head. I pulled to the curb and rolled down the window.

"Zaira. Good morning."

"Oh, good morning." She smiled, but I noticed a nervous twitch in her lips.

"Where are you headed?"

"Uh." She averted her eyes. "I came to . . . buy some lavender tea. See, I can't go a day without it."

"Did you find some?"

"No, the stores are closed."

I checked the time again. "They won't open for another half hour," I noted, but surely, she knew that. So why was she in town at this hour and on foot? "Are you going to wait?"

"Oh no. I ought to get back."

"Would you like a ride?"

"That would be lovely." As Zaira got in, I noticed that the slight tremor in her lips had now extended to her hands. "Please, don't mention this to Mrs. White. The only day I'm supposed to leave the house is my day off."

"Don't worry. I won't." I smiled reassuringly. "Listen, I can come back during lunch and get the tea if you'd like."

"Oh no. It's all right. Chamomile will do until Saturday."

As I pulled away from the curb, I had the distinct impression she wasn't being truthful with me. This wasn't an isolated event. "*People in this house have a tendency to vanish when one needs them*," Mrs. White had said.

"Unless, of course, Mrs. White does the shopping before that," Zaira further said.

"What about Mr. Sterling? Does he ever come to town?" I couldn't miss this chance to satisfy my curiosity, especially when Mrs. White wasn't within earshot.

"Not if he can help it."

"I know his health is delicate, but leaving the house once in a while might do him some good," I said casually.

"After all he's been through, I reckon socializing is the last thing on his mind."

"What do you mean?" I lingered at a stop sign to stretch our time together.

"Well, from what I know, he once had it all—a happy marriage, a remarkable career, and, of course, money." Zaira might have felt indebted for the ride, for me not reporting her escape, or perhaps just happy to divert the topic from her outing, but she spoke freely. "That changed when his wife passed away in childbirth."

Though I had carefully analyzed his documents, I found no

information to confirm his marriage, as if it had been meticulously removed. "Wait, Mr. Sterling has a child?"

"No, the baby died too."

"Oh, that's terrible. Poor Mr. Sterling. I can't imagine what he must have gone through." My heart hurt for him. I understood the yearning to have a family, to feel the security of belonging.

"I know. Mrs. White is convinced his sickness is psychological, a result of his losses. That's why, after his parents' demise, she convinced him to move to America. She hoped his health would improve in a different environment. And it did for a while, but not for long. He saw a handful of physicians, including one here in Geneva, but no one could help him."

"She might be right."

"She might. Death wreaks havoc on one. I lost my brother and three of my cousins to the Great War. It took our family a long while to overcome the gloom and move on with our lives. And we mustn't forget that Mr. Sterling fought in the war too. The poor fellow has had more than his fair share of suffering."

Another idea surfaced. "On the other hand, his body might be terribly ill and damaging his mental and emotional self."

"Hmm, I suppose it could go either way." Zaira removed her scarf and weaved her fingers through her hair as the Buick turned onto Oak's Place property. "Please, Florence, don't repeat our conversation. You know how much Mrs. White disapproves of gossip and speculation. And, truth be told, all I said might be just that. I heard it through the grapevine and years after it happened. I became acquainted with Mr. Sterling just before we came to the States."

I sat at my desk, a mass of inquietudes vying for my attention. Front and center lay Mr. Sterling's tragic story and my growing desire to learn more about him—a desire that continued to baffle me.

My hand trembled as I extracted a folder from the drawer. It contained his release papers from the British Army. I flipped through the papers until I found the image I had already studied several times, the eyes staring into my soul from the depths of the past. Someone had attached a picture of General Alexander Sterling in a uniform decorated with ribbons and medals, his eyes radiating a happiness that had since been lost. I assumed it was taken before the loss of his family. For surely they were the source of his joy.

Resisting the temptation to steal the photograph, I trapped it within the folder and returned it to its place. More times than I cared to admit, I wished I could take it to the monastery, where I could ponder upon it in the solitude of night. Thankfully, I had enough sense to remind myself I was here to do a job. Nothing else.

Raised voices from outside drew me to the slightly open window. Up the path, Mrs. White and Mr. Snider engaged in a heated argument. Mrs. White passionately flung her hands into the air, reinforcing whatever it was she was so upset about. Mr. Snider growled something and walked away. Not ready to end the fight, she took after him.

What in the world caused such enmity between them? I didn't have time to explore the answer, for as soon as they disappeared, my gaze darted to the obscure figure of a man amid the trees. With a gasp, I jerked back and pressed my hand to my heart. The man retreated into the woods and disappeared before I could get a closer look. Did he watch the house? Unlikely. Mrs. White mentioned the adolescents cutting through the woods. Maybe she was right, after all.

I continued to scan the area until my stomach grumbled, yearning for a cup of tea—the perfect fuel to keep me going until supper. Before turning from the window, I looked at the grounds once again. It was eerily still. Just in case, I pulled the window closed, the latch clicking. I then made my way to the kitchen, still bothered by the trespasser's presence.

There, I turned on the faucet, filled the kettle, and placed it on the stove. *Where can the tea be*? I found two lavender boxes on the shelf in the first cupboard I searched. *How is this possible*? As far as I knew, Zaira hadn't returned to town, and neither had Mrs. White.

In short order, the kettle hissed. I placed a teabag in a cup and filled the cup with hot water. I moved to the table, watching the steam rise like a ghost leaving its host. The clock near the fireplace ticked a steady rhythm as I savored the drink. Time—keeper of the past, builder of the future, master of our lives. Mr. Vines described it as an illusion, but it felt real to me. Why did I feel I was wasting it and as if something more pressing should be done with my life? If only I knew what that might be.

Zaira emerged from the corridor, raking her hand through her hair.

"Look what I found." I lifted the teabag by the tag and smiled.

She looked at me as if I had said the stupidest thing she'd ever heard.

"It's lavender tea." I raised my eyebrows in question. "You said we were out."

"Oh. Yes . . . yes," she exclaimed. "There were two boxes hidden in the pantry behind the coffee tins. I'm afraid I missed them."

Did the tone in her voice or the improbability that she had indeed missed them tell me she lied? And if so, what had she been doing in town?

"Hmm." My eyes narrowed.

"It's a nice day, isn't it?" She swiftly brushed aside the tea dilemma.

Nice? "I wouldn't mind a little sunshine. It's a bit too gloomy for me."

"True, very true," she said as she moved about picking up things and putting them back down absentmindedly.

I got up to add more water to my cup. "Would you like some tea?"

"No, thank you."

I turned from the stove. "What's the matter, Zaira? Why are you moving about like a fire burns unattended somewhere?"

"It's just so strange," she muttered.

"What is?"

"I . . . shouldn't tell you."

"Tell me what?"

"The thing is . . . I was in the courtyard, and . . . ." She rubbed her forehead, revealing exasperation.

"Did you see the trespasser?"

"What trespasser?"

"I saw someone in the woods, but if not that, then you must have heard Mrs. White and Mr. Snider quarreling."

"What?" Her face contorted in confusion. "No, none of that, though you'll have to tell me about it later."

"What, then? Tell me."

"When I came back inside, I walked past your office. The door stood slightly ajar. I thought it strange since you've been keeping it open." Zaira lowered her voice to a whisper. "I peeked through the gap, and there he stood, hovering over your desk, going through your purse."

"Who?" I assumed she spoke of Mr. Vines. With his incomprehensible riddles and slinking steps, I wouldn't be surprised if he'd sneaked into my office. "Mr. Vines?"

"No, for heaven's sake! Not Vines."

"Who, then?"

"Mr. Sterling, He was in your office."

"Mr. Sterling? I thought he lay sick in bed."

Zaira shrugged. "I'm just telling you what I saw."

"I hoped he liked my face powder and lipstick," I joked.

Zaira's eyebrows knitted. She did not find it funny. Neither did I, but it seemed unlikely that Mr. Sterling would do such a thing.

"Did he see you?"

"I don't think so. I retreated as fast as I could, mortified by his actions."

I mulled over the information in my head. No matter how I looked at it, it just didn't add up. Maybe Zaira was just confused, but it didn't seem very likely. Still, I had to double check, "Are you sure it wasn't Mr. Vines? He is tall and lean too, and I left the lights off in my office."

"Be that as it may, I'm not blind. Besides, I saw Mr. Vines changing the car oil on the side of the house before I came inside." Zaira hurried to the kettle. "I suppose I need some tea after all—and an aspirin. I have worked myself into a fit of emotion."

My better judgment begged me to let it be, but I couldn't. I rapped on his door, the sound echoing through the hallway. Where I got the courage to do so I didn't know, but I'd acted impulsively, and now that his voice invited me in, it hit me.

Mrs. White had been clear. "*Under no circumstances is he to be disturbed.*" Too late, it occurred that maybe "the rules" weren't hers but

Mr. Sterling's. What would he say when he saw me? What would I say? I couldn't accuse him of rummaging through my handbag. Maybe I should move on and pretend I hadn't knocked. I'd spun on my heels to do just that when the door opened to reveal Mr. Sterling.

"Miss Contini." His forehead creased with curiosity.

"I didn't mean to bother you." I had to tread lightly.

"Come in, please."

I stepped inside and instantly felt the warmth of the bright fire in the hearth.

"How may I help you?" He gestured for me to sit at his desk while he took his place on the opposite side.

"I'm sorry I wasn't in my office when you came looking for me earlier. I thought you might need my assistance."

Before responding, he beheld me for an uncomfortable minute, his eyes burning into mine. "You are mistaken. I have not been to your office."

I took no comfort in knowing I wasn't the only one telling tales, for either Zaira or Mr. Sterling prevaricated. And I couldn't very well argue with him, for I'd only hoped he would realize I'd seen him and tell me the truth or at least make up an excuse for being there. "I must be seeing things," I blurted, instantly regretting it, for I openly questioned his truthfulness. This was his house, and I couldn't prove he had violated my privacy.

"You wouldn't be the only one," he answered disconcertingly.

"Mr. Sterling, I shouldn't have bothered you." I stood. I had to end the discussion before I lost my job. "I'm sorry."

"Are you sorry you're lying or that I wasn't in your office?"

"Excuse me?"

"Considering I didn't visit your office, are you apologizing for lying? Is it an excuse to see me?" His bluntness startled me. A whipping would have been less humiliating.

Even when an excuse to see him hadn't occurred to me, now that he mentioned it, I realized I had jumped at the chance. Yes. I had wanted to see him, speak to him—but now I regretted it. But he would never know. Worse yet, I couldn't implicate Zaira to defend myself.

"So, Miss Contini? Your answer?" he pressed in a soft tone.

"I might be mistaken. Perhaps Mr. Vines visited my office. But I assure you, I'm not lying." I hoped heaven and the host of saints Granny prays to would forgive my lies. My dishonesty since arriving at Oak's Place, I feared, just about matched my honesty for the past twenty years.

"Right, then."

Right, then? Did he believe me? Or was he now sure I lied? I wasn't about to ask. I moved to the door.

"How is your arm?" he asked. "Did it heal all right?"

My arm? That was the last thing on my mind. "It did. Thanks for asking."

He produced a disarming smile, and I felt frustrated to be drawn to him.

At five o'clock that evening, I left Oak's Place, still struggling to shake off thoughts of my encounter with Mr. Sterling. Had Zaira lied? If her trip to town hadn't been related to lavender tea, I suspected she had been deceitful not just this once. On the other hand, if Mr. Sterling rummaged through my purse, he wouldn't simply admit to it. It would be too humiliating, especially when nothing justified the behavior. But then, of course, Zaira could be mistaken, and he had been looking at something other than my handbag.

I tightened my grip on the steering wheel, certain I missed something important. The chilliness in the air brought my inner discussion to an end. I looked at my white knuckles. I was freezing. I pulled over to retrieve my gloves from my purse only to realize I had left them at work. Going back was the last thing I wanted to do, but the bitter cold felt unbearable, and I would need them tomorrow. I turned around, the wheels of the Buick squealing against the pavement.

I arrived at the house at dusk, planning to retrieve my gloves and leave unnoticed. But upon entering the foyer, I heard raised voices coming from Mr. Sterling's office. Pressed against the wall, I inched down the corridor.

"You don't understand," Mr. Sterling argued.

"Oh yes, I do. You are fooling yourself. Today was close. Way too close," Mrs. White refuted. "You need to move on. Look at you. You're killing yourself."

"I was trying to move on, but it hurts so much. Why does she have to haunt me?" he exclaimed in a broken voice.

"Let her go. It's the rational thing to do."

"After all these years of suffering and regret, how can I?"

"You play a dangerous game. But if that's what you want, you'll have to tell her the truth."

"I can't do that. She won't understand. I don't understand it myself." Mr. Sterling sounded almost helpless.

The noise of a chair scraping the floor escaped the room, as if someone stood abruptly. My heart hammered against my ribs, warning me that I couldn't be caught eavesdropping. I backed away and tiptoed to my office. I found my gloves and left the house with a sick feeling in the pit of my stomach. Whatever Mr. Sterling and Mrs. White discussed might remain a mystery, but they could never know I'd heard them.

My confrontation with Mr. Sterling now seemed remote, replaced by this latest incident. What truth did they speak of? Most importantly, who haunted him?

CHAPTER 4
~ FEAR AND EXCITEMENT ~

Like a malfunctioning phonograph record, I kept telling myself to do my job, collect my salary, and forget about Oak's Place anomalies and Mr. Sterling's personal life. It was easier said than done—even more so when I sat here in my office, the silence stretching too long, too deep. What secrets lingered in the stillness of the house? The conversation I'd overheard between Mr. Sterling and Mrs. White replayed relentlessly in my mind. Who did she want him to get away from, and why? Try as I might, I couldn't shake the feeling they referred to me. But we had nothing besides a job between us. And after I'd insinuated that he lied about being in my office, I'd surely ruined the possibility of friendship.

Then I couldn't dismiss the idea that there might be some truth to the gossip about him. And if so, did he worry I might stumble upon his secrets and make them public? Possibly. But he should have thought about that before hiring me. And as if that wasn't enough to keep me awake at night, the image of the trespasser in the woods refused to leave my thoughts.

Reaching a tipping point, and perhaps as an act of rebellion against Mrs. White, I unburied the books at the bottom of the piles in the armoire—the books she told me were of no significance. Though it was a tedious job, I carefully went through them only to learn she was right. I found nothing to satisfy my curiosity.

Mrs. White's rule to not wander about the house echoed in my head. If they had nothing to hide, why all the restrictions? Glancing at my watch, I made a decision. If there was anything that explained what Mr. Sterling and the housekeeper were talking about the other night, I would find it in his bedroom or office.

I crept down the corridor with furtive glances, my breath catching at each unexpected noise. What I was about to do, if not criminal, qualified as dishonest. Finding his office door closed, I pressed my ear to the wood, trying to hear over the pounding of my heart. Seconds passed before I heard someone clear their throat. He was inside. I moved on, sliding through the halls like a prolific thief, until I entered the one leading to his bedroom. *Almost there. Almost there.*

When Mrs. White's voice hit my ears, I froze and my stomach knotted. I forgot her quarters were two doors before his.

"O merciful God, take pity on those souls who have no particular friends and intercessors to recommend them to Thee."

I exhaled in relief. Her words came from inside her bedroom, the door ajar.

"Who, either through the negligence of those who are alive or through the length of time, are forgotten by their friends and by all," she continued.

I knew of the prayer for the forgotten dead. Did she pray for her deceased husband or someone else?

"Spare them, O Lord. Spare them, O Lord. Spare them, O Lord," she chanted, and the knot in my stomach tightened. A brief silence preceded a few sniffles, then footsteps.

Before I knew it, I'd retreated, almost running back to my office. What possessed me to be so intrusive? If Mrs. White had caught so much as a glimpse of me scurrying away like a rat on fire, it wouldn't be long until she came after me. And I had no excuse, at least not a truthful one. What was it with this house that turned its inhabitants, including me, into untrustworthy people?

I sank into the chair behind the safety of the desk, feeling my heartbeat in my ears—a steady beat of guilt. I picked up a pen and forced myself to continue my work, though my hand was too shaky to write.

And just then, a disturbance from the hallway convinced me Mrs. White had come to reprimand me. Playing innocent, I kept my gaze down.

"Good morning." Mr. Sterling's voice caught me completely off guard.

"Mr. Sterling . . . I . . ." I was speechless. He was the last person I would have expected to see.

"Miss Contini, are you happy here?" He moved into the room. "Let me rephrase that. Are you comfortable working here?"

At that moment, I felt certain I would never understand him. Was he a potential friend or an enemy? Whatever the answer, at least he seemed unaware of my trespassing in prohibited areas. Still, I responded cautiously. "Yes, as comfortable as one can be at work."

"I know, it's just work, isn't it? However, this house can be depressing for a young lady. It's far from town, intimidatingly spacious, and sometimes as cold as an iceberg."

"It does get chilly, especially in the mornings."

"You could work in the dining room and take advantage of the fireplace." A hint of kindness shone in his eyes.

"Thank you. I'll consider it." I felt awkward, not knowing what to make of his presence or apparent concern for my well-being.

"I hope the thirty-minute drive from town twice a day isn't too tiresome." He sat at the edge of the desk.

"Not at all. Besides, Mrs. White gave me two weeks off for Christmas, so I'll have a long break." I pushed the chair away from the desk, away from him.

"Christmas. It always comes with all the noise and busyness."

"You speak as if you don't like Christmas."

"It's bittersweet for me. I embrace the anticipation and hope of the season, but it leaves me feeling empty when it's gone. Enough of that. I came here to ask something of you."

"Certainly."

"Could you make a list of suggestions to improve this old place?"

It took me a moment to process his words. A renovation meant opening the door to a host of workers—not exactly something a hermit or fugitive welcomed.

"You don't think it's a good idea?" He glanced at me questioningly, and I realized I hadn't responded. Still, he continued. "When I bought this house, I didn't care about its condition. The last thing I needed was people invading my privacy, disrupting the peace," he explained as if reading my mind. "But I'm ready for a few updates."

"I'm glad to hear that." I tried to hold my tongue but failed. "I must ask, why the change of heart?"

"Change of heart . . . hmm." His gaze shifted away from mine. "Let's just say this is a good time for change."

"I'm happy to put together some ideas. Do you have anything specific in mind?" I leaned forward to reach for my notebook, and the silver bracelet around my wrist slipped out from under my sleeve.

Mr. Sterling's eyes snapped to it. "Where did you get that?"

"The wristlet?"

"Yes. Where did you get it?" His tone demanded an answer.

"It was left with me when I was abandoned at the monastery."

"May I see it?"

I handed it to him.

"Florence Contini," he read the engraving.

The way he observed the piece of jewelry and turned it in his fingers with such tenderness gave me the strange impression this wasn't the first time he had seen it. The thought sent chills through my body.

"Excuse me if I'm interrupting something important." Mrs. White's voice boomed from the threshold.

Mr. Sterling shot to his feet.

"What's the matter?" she asked.

I then noticed how pale he had gone.

"Nothing at all." He curled his hand, concealing the bracelet.

"I'd like to discuss a pressing matter with you," she told him, her lips twitching. Had she seen me stalking about? Would she tell him?

Mr. Sterling moved away from me. Would he take the wristlet? "In response to your earlier query, I trust your judgment, Miss Contini. No specific instructions. Let me know what you come up with."

"I shall."

When Mrs. White withdrew into the corridor, he returned to my desk and handed me the bracelet, avoiding my eyes. I watched him leave, wondering about his interest in the seemingly insignificant jewelry.

Moving the cup back and forth beneath the faucet until no soap remained, I grabbed a kitchen towel to dry it, and returned it to the cupboard.

"You better tell me the truth right now," I heard Mrs. White command.

I moved from the sink to the French doors, but instead of stepping outside, I hovered near the glass, listening.

"I don't know what you are talking about," Mr. Snider retorted.

"Fiddlesticks! You know exactly what is going on, and you better tell me. It might favor you when your day of reckoning comes."

"Are you blackmailing me?" he growled.

"Call it whatever you want, but don't forget I am in charge."

"I didn't survive the Great War and moved across the ocean to be intimidated by you. Do whatever you want. See if I care." Mr. Snider's boots thumped furiously against the ground. I pictured him walking away, arms flung angrily into the air.

I slipped out of the kitchen and down the corridor, ashamed to have eavesdropped yet again. My thoughts turned to the other day and to my foolishness in sneaking to Mr. Sterling's room. My guilt over my actions only intensified when he'd spoken cordially about the renovations. My impertinence had to stop before I found myself in a regrettable situation —or worse, lose my income. Still, what had Mrs. White pressed Mr. Snider about? What did she have on him?

I entered my office and looked out the window to see snowflakes falling. Even though snowy weather tended to bring things to a halt, I loved watching it. The cessation of winter amazed me, for it was an illusion. Life hid among the dreary months, invisible to the natural eye yet ready to flourish in the spring.

An unexpected yearning to see Mr. Sterling seized me. I hoped to share an idea for the renovation before I left on holiday break. However, my plans were shattered when Mrs. White informed me that he had suffered a relapse and was confined to his bed.

Sighing heavily, I immersed myself in work. Minutes, then hours slipped by. When I looked at the time again, it was almost five o'clock, and I felt the strain of a long day. I flipped through the last file on my desk, thick with complex documents. I stared at a line with ornamental handwriting. A piece of art, but for goodness' sake, how many years of practice did this person endure to master it? Just to read it took dedication. My head spun, my vision blurred, the letters jumping around on the page. I was drifting into sleep.

Fighting the urge to give in, I left the chair to move around. My eyes needed a brief rest—they felt heavy as if they were sealed together. Just then, the spirit of disobedience came upon me full force, and my weariness vanished. I would not see Mr. Sterling for two weeks and worried about his health. I resisted the idea for a while, reminding myself I had already decided to mind the rules. Yet, as if the devil had entered my body, I failed again. I left the chair, appeasing my guilty conscience with the notion that Mrs. White was bound to be in the kitchen, discussing the dinner menu with Zaira.

The click-clack of my heels on the stone floor echoed through the corridor, exacerbating my anxiety. I could almost see Mrs. White bursting from the shadows like a hawk snatching a field mouse. *Any second now*, I told myself, but just then, I found myself next to Mr. Sterling's bedroom.

The sound of groaning came from within. Turning the doorknob, I stepped into the darkness of the room, focusing on a sliver of light filtering through the curtains until my vision adjusted. I could now make out the bed and his outline. He let out a few quiet whimpers, and I froze, shocked by my lack of decorum. I had to retreat. I took a step back.

"Florence?" The weight of illness tinged his voice. "Is that you?"

"I heard you from the corridor. I just wanted to help."

"Come closer."

With my heart pounding in my ears, I neared him. His face shocked me. It was dreadfully white. "Mr. Sterling . . ." He stretched out his hand, and I took it. He was cold, so cold.

"Why did you take so long?" he asked.

"I . . ." What should I say? "Mr. Sterling, what can I do for you?"

"You took so long." He was delirious. "I waited for so long . . . so long."

"I'm sorry. I'm here now."

"You care."

"Of course I do. Should I call the doctor?"

"Why the doctor? I have never felt better. You are here."

My heart went out to this lonely, helpless man. I had to help him. Perhaps I'd come to Oak's Place for this very reason—to help him survive what not only haunted him but threatened to kill him. I insisted, "I will go find help."

"No. Stay with me." Before I knew it, he had pulled me down beside him, wrapping his arms around me tightly. Resting my head on his chest, tears welled up in my eyes. It was the first time I had ever felt complete, at total peace with myself and the world around me. In that moment, I knew I belonged in his arms.

"Promise me you won't leave," he whispered.

"I promise." I looked up. His mouth was close, so close. My lips brushed his . . .

"Florence! Florence, wake up!" A voice came first, then a hand shaking my shoulder.

I blinked, pushing away the drowsiness of sleep, and found myself back in my office, resting my head on the desk. The dream ended, and Zaira stood there, hovering over me. "Zaira?" I straightened on the chair.

"Are you all right? I couldn't wake you."

"I . . . was exhausted." I yearned to return to the dream, to his embrace. Nonetheless, I felt relieved it had been a dream and I had averted a possible disaster with Mrs. White and maybe even Mr. Sterling.

"Go home and get some rest. It's almost six o'clock."

"That late?" I hurried to clear my desk, then gathered my coat and handbag.

"I envy you. You must be excited about your vacation, but I'll miss having you around." Zaira accompanied me to the courtyard. "This house is as dull as ditchwater."

"It'll go fast." I really hoped it would. "Have a merry Christmas. And call me if you get bored."

"Don't mind if I do. And a happy Christmas to you! That's how we say it in England."

"Wish Mr. Sterling a happy Christmas for me."

"I shall, whenever I can," she assured.

"I wish I could've seen him today."

"Trust me, it's better you don't. When he is sick, his appearance is frightening. His eyes stare at you lifelessly. It's a terrible sight to behold."

"I can imagine." In my dream, I had seen Mr. Sterling exactly as she described him. I drove away with a heavy heart.

The culmination of another excruciating financial year had arrived. The hope and eagerness to restore our country to a healthy economy would carry us into the upcoming year, but the statistics remained bleak.

For now, Christmas came as a reminder to slow down and appreciate the good things. Though deeply grateful for Granny, who was everything to me, more and more often, I found myself aching to know of my origin. Who were my parents? Did I have siblings? Would I ever know? Because the unanswered questions pained me, I quickly boxed them back up and stored them away.

On Christmas morning, Granny handed me a package tied with red ribbon. I was thrilled to find a navy dress inside. I clutched it to my shoulders, measuring it against my body. It was perfectly designed in the latest fashion—a V-neck, three-quarter sleeves, and tight at the waist, where it bowed slightly outward. I couldn't wait to wear it.

"It's gorgeous!" I now knew what she had been working on when I heard the sewing machine whirring late at night. "Thank you, Granny, thank you."

"You're welcome, child." Her embrace held the same tender, loving affection as always.

"I hope you like my gift as much as I like yours." I handed her an envelope containing the tickets to *Snow White*—a luxury owed to my employment at Oak's Place. "And please, just this time, don't worry about the *unnecessary* expense."

Granny adjusted her spectacles and unsealed the envelope. "Goodness gracious. This is exub—" She edited her sentence. "Exciting."

"It'll be fun. We both need a breather from real life." I smiled.

"You are right, dear. Let's celebrate with some coffee." Granny turned to the stove. After months of tea, we could afford coffee again.

"I'll get the cups." I turned to the cupboard and spotted a crow with lustrous black plumage through the window. He launched from the pine tree and flew in front of the glass, his mournful caw ringing across the grounds like the cry of a lost soul. Perhaps it was the bad omen attached to these birds, but my skin prickled with goosebumps, and the sensation sent my mind back to my childhood. On occasion, my friend MaryLu and I would see the ghost of a monk in his black tunic and cowl scurrying down the monastery corridors, passing through walls, and moving about the courtyard. My thoughts jumped to the trespasser at Oak's Place. His presence unnerved me. Just then, a new idea sprang up. What if he wasn't mortal? What if he was a ghost?

My uneasiness rose naturally, and I let it out. "Granny, why do some ghosts linger in this world?"

"That's a random question." She placed the kettle on the burner. "Have you seen one recently?"

"No, I just thought about the monk who used to wander the monastery," I replied with only half of the truth. She didn't need more worries. "Do you remember him?"

"Oh yes. I do. Thank heaven he hasn't shown up in years."

"You haven't answered my question."

"The common belief is that they have unfinished business."

"Hmm." I looked out the window again. The crow had flown away. "How do you think they go about it?"

Granny glanced at me over her spectacles. "It's better to leave those things alone."

"I know, I know." I pushed the idea to the back of my head. It was a silly idea, after all. I handed her the cups and picked up the almanac from the counter. I opened it on the table, my fingers tracing the days of vacation I had left. Eight.

"You seem excited about going back to work." Granny poured the coffee for us and settled beside me.

I grinned. "I'm ready to do something other than clean." With no penchant for idleness, Granny kept me busy scrubbing every inch of the monastery in preparation for the European sisters' arrival.

"Is that the only reason?"

"Well, yes."

"Child, I know you better than you want to believe. I have noticed the way you speak of Mr. Sterling."

I opened my mouth to argue, but then closed it without saying a word. True. I spoke of him compulsively. Worse yet, the dream I had had on the last day before the break replayed in my head mercilessly—his anguish, his pleading for me to stay, the contentment I felt in his embrace.

She went on. "I'm aware that you are an adult, but you haven't lived as long as I have. And I recognize the face of love when I see it."

"Who said anything about love?" I hadn't thought about love and Mr. Sterling at the same time.

"I just want you to keep in mind that there are two kinds of love. One is real, and if reciprocated, worth fighting for. The other is a passing emotion—one that must be kept within proper boundaries, so it doesn't turn into an obsession that destroys your life. You must distinguish between the two. Start by analyzing the facts. Let's go over a few things." She pushed her coffee aside, serious about this. "What do you know about him? Not much. How did he obtain his vast fortune? You don't know. Could he be hiding from something or someone? Is that why he is here? You don't know. Will you ever find out? You can't answer that either." Her clarity sobered me.

"There is nothing to worry about, Granny." I gathered the package from the table, struggling to untangle my feelings for Mr. Sterling while dissecting her assessment. "Thank you for the dress."

"One more thing." She removed her glasses, her eyes intent on me. "He is older than you."

She was right, but the soul was ageless, and I didn't care as much about the years in life as I did the life in the years. A multitude of other things were more alarming than age—if it ever came to love.

CHAPTER 5
~ UNEXPECTED ~

"Mr. Sterling has gone back to England," Zaira informed. "He left the day after Christmas."

"England?" I choked out. Somehow, I'd thought he would always be here, close to me. "Why?" I fisted my hand, crumpling the list of ideas for the renovation.

"I don't know." A mischievous light in her eyes indicated she did know.

"What is it? Tell me."

She sighed. "You are going to think I spend my life circulating gossip."

"Don't be silly. Tell me."

Zaira brought a pot of potatoes to the table to peel them, and like water through a broken dam, her words spilled out. "I happened to be dusting the paintings in the corridor when I heard them conversing in his office. Mrs. White huffed and puffed about the trip. Mr. Sterling's exact words were, 'I can't die without knowing. I must find out for myself.'"

"What was he talking about?"

"That, I don't know. However, Mrs. White argued that he couldn't handle the trip in his current state and implored him to reconsider. But he said he'd made up his mind and ended the discussion."

"I'm afraid she's right about the trip. It'll be rough on him."

"Indeed. Although, if it's any consolation, Dr. Petersen dropped off some nausea medicine. That's his worst symptom, I think."

"Hopefully it helps." I picked up a potato and a knife, my anxiety rising. I pressed the knife against the brown skin with some urgency, the peel falling away in a curl. Soon, I finished the first potato and reached for another.

I can't die without knowing. I must find out for myself. Know what? Find out what? For the rest of the day, his words pressed into my mind like a sliver under my skin, causing a festering uneasiness.

―――――――

Mrs. White left with Mr. Vines for New York City. The unusual trip took Zaira and me aback, but we welcomed the reprieve.

"Florence, will you stay with me for the weekend?" Zaira asked at the end of the day. She said nothing more, but I understood the prospect of being alone with the gruff Mr. Snider.

"Why don't you come to the monastery?"

"You know how much I'd like that, but I can't. Mrs. White left me in charge here." Zaira reached for my hand. "Say yes. We can sleep in the guest room."

"I'll call Granny and let her know. With one condition: tomorrow, we go downtown. There are a few shops I think you'll like."

"Oh, Florence, that sounds marvelous!"

―――――――

The spacious guest room had tall ceilings and two windows facing northwest. Breathing deeply, Zaira lay sound asleep in the bed across from mine. Only a miracle would bring her back before morning. I wasn't so lucky. Staying overnight at Oak's Place didn't seem so dreadful —until the lights were out and an ominous silence settled in. Two women sleeping alone in a mansion in the middle of nowhere, with Mr.

Snider in the cottage far from earshot and a stranger roaming the grounds would make anyone restless.

The harder I tried to fall asleep, the more alert I became. Perhaps instigated by Granny's analysis of my situation during the holiday, the whirlwind of questions I'd tried so hard to avoid came back with a vengeance. Who roamed the woods and why? What secrets did the staff conceal? What or who haunted Mr. Sterling? And, worst of all, why was I so resolved upon finding out?

Granny spoke of obsession. Was that my problem? I rubbed at my temples and the headache threatening to surface. I dealt with a complicated puzzle; no matter how hard I tried, I couldn't piece it together. Driven by my need for answers, I surrendered to my old friend, the spirit of disobedience.

Guided by the faint moonlight coming through the windows, I slipped out of bed and down the corridor. A chance such as this, with Mr. Sterling and Mrs. White out of the house, wouldn't come again.

The first stop was his bedroom. Locked. With a sigh of disappointment, I crept to the next location of interest. My sweaty hand turned the doorknob, and I slipped inside his office. I flipped on the light and moved to his desk. This was wrong, so wrong. I wavered momentarily but then, like a thief, tried every drawer. All locked. I checked the documents sitting on top. Nothing relevant. In a way, I felt relieved. It lessened the seriousness of my intrusion.

As I neared the lifeless fireplace, I felt a longing for him. I turned to the sofa. The frayed upholstery and decorative pillows told me he spent countless hours here. I wondered what memories occupied his mind as he lay in front of the fire, battling his illness.

My gaze fell to the floor, where a newspaper peeked out from under the front of the couch. I pulled it out and sat down, soon engrossed in the 1916 London edition, twenty-one years ago—a time and place that had been Mr. Sterling's world, a world I hardly understood.

Thinking of the books I'd read, I imagined a land dotted with ancient castles, marvelous architecture, and extensive estates with breathtaking manors, all of which sharply contrasted the young, bare America. I envisioned Britain's high society setting the tone for behavior and fashion as they enjoyed luxurious social gatherings, oblivious to the work the domestic engaged in to make it happen. I saw their elegant clothing and structured manner of courting and marrying.

Then came the middle class, striving for improvement and progress while filling their free time with gossip and unrealistic expectations. Regardless of their social status, they all faced a common challenge—the Great War. Little did they know in 1916 how many hundreds of thousands of their children, poor and rich alike, would die defending their country. Their time had been so different from ours, and now, two decades later, America stood apart from the Old World in just about every possible way.

But why had Mr. Sterling kept this paper? I turned a coffee-stained page, scanning the articles. Nothing seemed unusual until the name Sterling jumped out at me. As luck would have it, the page had been damaged, the coffee stain blending smoothly with the ink, blurring some lines.

> *. . . made it clear on several occasions that . . . and Lieutenant Alexander Sterling are deeply in love, and their affection is the foundation for their engagement and upcoming marriage . . .*
>
> *The recent scandal and the allegations the lieutenant is pursuing the well-recognized lady to advance his rank have been dismissed by her prominent fa . . .*

The article matched what Zaira said about him. He had been married. But here was a new proposition. Had he married for power and ambition, or had he loved her? How would it have been to be the wife of the young Alexander Sterling?

The sun had barely risen when I rolled off the bed only to discover Zaira had already left hers. I searched the house to no avail. After waiting in the kitchen for an hour, I couldn't wait any longer. This was out of character for her. I slipped into my coat, buttoned it, raised its collar against the cold, and crossed the yard toward the cottage.

I let myself into the sitting area Zaira had shown me last night. From there, a short hallway led to the dormitories and washroom. I was about to tap on Zaira's door when a loud noise came from Mr. Snider's room, then another, as if he was tossing furniture about. The pricking of my skin and the quickening of my heartbeat told me I shouldn't be here. But where in the world was Zaira? Ignoring my gut feelings that I should leave, I tried the doorknob and found it unlocked. I stepped inside her quarters to find them empty.

With stealthy steps, I returned to the corridor. There was a creak. My gaze flung to Mr. Snider's door. It swung inward with the sound of splintering wood, and he stood on the threshold. In a sleeveless top, pajama bottoms, and a mane of unkempt hair, he appeared menacing—and judging by his muscular arms, a man of great strength, which I hadn't considered. Beyond him, I spotted an overturned chair and a few other things scattered across the floor. Finding the direction of my eyes, he moved as if to block my view. Now that he stood inches away, I saw a dark gleam in his eyes.

"I'm sorry, Mr. Snider. I didn't mean to bother you. I'm looking for Zaira." Almost imperceptibly, I sidestepped toward the exit. "Have you seen her?"

He grunted and shook his head—the veins in his neck bulged, pulsating with an emotion that I couldn't place. Was he surprised to see me here and annoyed that I had disrupted his morning? Or was it something else entirely?

No matter. Without thinking or breathing, I simply shuffled out of the cottage and across the yard, overwhelmed by the awkwardness of the encounter. Once inside the house, I sunk into a chair, wondering what had just happened. Mr. Snider was in a dreadful mood.

Midmorning, Zaira walked into my office grinning, evidently unsuspecting of my worries over her absence.

"Where have you been?" I rose from the chair glad to see her.

"For a morning hike."

"You should have told me. I was worried about you." I sounded like

Granny. "A whole lot of nonsense went through my head." I had contemplated the awful scenario of Zaira being attacked in the woods by a wild animal to being assaulted in the cottage by Mr. Snider—yes, I was now ashamed to have gone that far—to other similar, but not likely misfortunes.

"I'm sorry. I decided last minute, and I didn't want to wake

you so early," she explained. "Once I started walking, I lost track of time."

Since I wasn't the epitome of honesty, I had no right to question her. Nevertheless, my encounter with Mr. Snider and her lengthy disappearance overrode my conscience. "Do you expect me to believe that?"

Zaira appeared taken aback. "I do."

"Well, I don't."

"Well, you should because it's the truth."

Unwilling to drop the subject, I further said, "I was so worked up about you that I even went to the cottage."

Her eyes widened. "You did?"

"Mr. Snider wasn't happy about it."

"You saw him?" She seemed taken aback. "You shouldn't have gone there."

"Why not? What's wrong with Mr. Snider—and don't tell me nothing. There is something odd about him. Tell me."

"Florence, seriously, I don't know what has gotten into you, but I assure you there is nothing wrong with me or Mr. Snider." She sounded almost convincing. "His bedroom is off-limits because it's his sanctuary, that's all."

Sanctuary? The state in which I had seen his room resembled a battlefield, not a refuge.

"Besides, you might have misunderstood his mood. You know, he might be a bit lonely, and seeing a gorgeous woman at his door might have excited him," Zaira joked with a sparkle in her eyes.

I frowned, but perhaps she was right, and I had overreacted. After all, if someone barged into my quarters at will, especially so early in the day, I wouldn't exactly be happy about it.

"Now, it's a nice day. Shall we go to town?" she proposed, dismissing the edginess of the previous topic.

"Let's go." I reached for my handbag. An outing to town would benefit us both.

Outside of her disappearance on Saturday morning, the weekend turned out to be a riot. Zaira's bright eyes and charming accent left few heads unturned in town. And she had been favored by Granny, who enjoyed her visit. "She's such a beautiful, intelligent young lady," Granny said. "Make sure to invite her again."

I was about to leave Oak's Place when Mr. Vines and Mrs. White returned from their outing.

"I think they had a good time," Zaira observed as the couple stepped out of the car. Mrs. White, so unlike her, giggled at something Mr. Vines said. He had a noticeably pleased look in his eyes.

After a brief greeting, I drove away, eager to get home. Zaira's boundless energy and vivacity wore me out. I parked the Buick near the kitchen and flung open the door, stopping short at the sight of Sister Callahan, who launched from her seat when she saw me. She looked just as I remembered her—stocky, chubby face, and black habit.

"Fannie, dear, you've grown so much!"

I disliked the nickname tremendously. I must have been seven or eight years old when she first assigned it to me. Over the years, I repeatedly told her that I preferred to be called Florence. But it was no use. I would always be Fannie to her.

Sister Callahan launched in my direction. I scanned the room for Granny. She stood by the stove, smiling. Two other sisters, also in black habits, waved from the table. Before I could react, Sister Callahan hugged me with the strength of a bear.

"Hello, it's nice to see you," I managed to say.

"Come, now. Don't just stand there. You're letting in a terrible draft." She pulled me in by the arm and slammed the door shut, nearly hitting me with it.

"Florence, this is Sister Miller and Sister Sullivan. Like Sister Callahan, they originate from the Church of Saint Mary in Cambridge. They oversee the young sisters currently settling in upstairs," Granny introduced, and a brief greeting followed.

Sister Miller, a woman about Granny's age, had a round face filled with shyness. Sister Sullivan was older, with a frail frame, thin face, and long fingers. Her bright gaze revealed a great wisdom accumulated over a lifetime.

"Enough about us. Tell us, Fannie, what have you been doing since last I saw you?" Sister Callahan inquired.

"My name is not Fannie." I couldn't resist telling her. Not that it would do any good. "It's Florence."

"I know it's Florence," Sister Callahan replied as if I had said the dumbest thing. "But why tell it to the whole world when Fannie is a prettier name?"

I rolled my eyes in defeat.

"Biscuits are ready." Granny pulled a batch from the oven.

I helped serve tea, and after discussing the sisters' exhausting journey to America—which only intensified my angst for Mr. Sterling's trip—and their plans for the upcoming weeks, I escaped to my bedroom. My determination to avoid Sister Callahan cemented itself. I knew she meant well, but she wore my patience thin.

On the way, I encountered some of the younger sisters, their youth startling. Some looked barely out of childhood. Why had they decided to become nuns? I admired them, for it was a noble calling, but it involved giving up so much. I couldn't renounce my freedom and personal desires that easily. I suppose I lacked not only patience but also selflessness.

With a sigh, I lay on my bed and drifted into sleep.

The sun rises, casting golden hues over the meadow. Against its sphere, a young Mr. Sterling appears, filled with resplendent light. He holds my hand, and I feel a profound connection transcending time and space, a connection that makes my heart burn with deep affection for him.

CHAPTER 6
~ A NEW BEGINNING ~

Winter's grip loosened as February ended. I watched the woods through my office window, the east sun melting the last traces of snow. However, no signs of new life appeared. The tree branches remained bare, the gardens colorless. A shadow rose behind me, and shivers crawled up my spine. I swiveled, afraid to find a ghost there, but instead, I saw the eyes that haunted my dreams.

"I didn't mean to frighten you," Mr. Sterling said promptly.

"I . . . didn't know you were back." I couldn't help but notice he looked younger, healthier.

"Late last night." There ensued a moment of silence in which our eyes didn't meet. "Did you have a good Christmas?"

"Yes, thank you. How was your trip?"

"Interesting."

He inched closer, and our gazes locked. His eyes showed a deep tenderness, and I suddenly felt as if I had slipped into one of my dreams. Escaping the moment's intensity, I said the first thing that came to mind. "I have the list you wanted."

"The list?"

"For the renovation."

"Oh yes."

I moved to the desk and handed it to him. "These are, in my opinion, basic but much-needed improvements."

Mr. Sterling dropped the paper onto the desk without looking at it. He then took my hand and pulled back my sleeve to reveal my bracelet. His finger traced the engravings on it. "Florence Contini . . ." He drew closer and whispered, "If I told you this bracelet was why I went to England, what would you say?"

His closeness, his touch, made my head spin. Who was this man who made me forget I had a brain?

"I would ask you why."

He lifted my hand and pressed it to his heart. "All I can tell you is that my heart is beating again, thanks to your bracelet."

"What do you know about it? Please tell me." My words broke the spell. He released my hand and stepped back.

"Forgive me. I don't know what I was thinking." He retrieved the list. "I'll look over this." He walked out, leaving me happy at his return yet confused by his interest in my bracelet. Nothing had changed. I was slowly getting accustomed to the mysteries at Oak's Place.

I sat on one of the benches scattered throughout the garden, contemplating some of the things I had written on the list I gave Mr. Sterling.

Reface the exterior of the house.
Repaint the interior in light colors.
Replace windows.
Resurface fireplaces.

He hadn't gotten back to me, and I feared he might not like the suggestions. Were they too drastic? Too much change? I lifted my face to the weak sunshine. Before me rose the statue of the lady and child. I marveled at the details. Since my conversation with Zaira, I suspected the statue reminded Mr. Sterling of his late wife and child. Were they the specters who haunted his life? The newspaper in his office suggested that greed might have been the reason for his wedding. Was there something more significant than grief behind their loss?

Like a flash of lightning in the night, Mrs. White's prayer shot through my head. "*O merciful God, take pity on those souls who have no friends and intercessors to recommend them to Thee, who, either through the negligence of those who are alive or through the length of time, are forgotten by their friends and by all. Spare them, O Lord.*" Could she have been praying for the late Mrs. Sterling? And if so, why would Mrs. Sterling have had no friends?

Footsteps approached me from behind on the garden path. I straightened on the bench and waited.

"Of course, I'd find you here with the lady." Mr. Vines gestured to the statue.

"It's an impressive piece."

"Remarkable indeed. The lady who traveled all the way from England. She neither slumbers nor lets others rest." His cunning gaze descended on me.

"Does the lady have a name?" I ventured.

"If I told you, you wouldn't believe it." A self-satisfied smile filled his face.

"Try me. You might be surprised."

"Some names, Miss Contini, are buried deep in another time from whence they can't escape, yet now and then, they are heard and felt, loud and clear."

"Hmm . . . a mystery, then?"

"One developing right in front of our eyes."

Surely, he mocked me. "If what you say is true, I'm bound to solve the mystery, right?"

Like the flip of a switch, his countenance changed, and his scornful mood passed. "Let me ask you something."

"Certainly." I got to my feet.

"Are you afraid of snakes?"

"Snakes?" *What an odd question.*

"Yes, snakes."

I'd occasionally encountered them in the monastery gardens but never cared for them. "No, I don't think so. Why do you ask?"

"No reason at all. Have you seen one around here?"

"No."

"If you come out often, you will. They like to bask in the sun on the pavers."

"I will remember that," I responded with confidence. His disturbing riddles upset me, but I wouldn't give him the pleasure of knowing that.

Mrs. White hurried in our direction.

"I leave you in good hands." Mr. Vines started back toward the house, whistling softly.

"There you are. Only you would be out in the cold," she hissed.

"It's not bad."

She extended the list of renovations to me. "Mr. Sterling approved the project. He added a few things and would like to start right away."

"I'll see to it." I kept my excitement hidden beneath a mask of calm. "Thank you."

With the current economy, finding people to work on the renovations proved a swift process. Mr. Sterling approved a construction company from Yates County, and the transformation of Oak's Place began. As one perk of the workers' presence, the house staff's quarreling diminished considerably. And curiously, even the trespasser seemed to have taken a break from the woods.

I came to the house earlier than usual to clear my office for the painters. My arms heavy with books, I made my way to the dining room, from whence came the most mesmerizing music I'd ever heard.

Mrs. White hovered near the fireplace, observing Mr. Sterling at the piano. He played a soulful melody that made my heart ache. I placed the books on the table and joined the housekeeper. Her countenance was unstable. I thought she would cry, but instead of tears, I saw anger in her eyes.

"It's been almost twenty years since he played," she muttered and left the room.

Mr. Sterling stopped playing, and without turning to look at me, asked, "Did you recognize the melody?"

"I didn't."

"Hmm. I thought you would."

"Should I have?"

"Most people do. It's Beethoven." He left the piano. "What do you think of the paint?"

"It's perfect." The cream color highlighted by the sunshine coming through the new window conveyed a peaceful, welcoming feeling.

"I hope these changes help you feel more comfortable."

"I think everyone will enjoy them." I was flattered that he cared.

"It's difficult to believe it's the same house. It looks so different."

"It feels different." I hesitated for a moment. "Do you agree?"

"Indeed. It feels like a blank page full of possibility." His fingers brushed my cheek, and my heart hammered against my rib cage. Did he have more than the renovation in mind? "You had a bit of paint there."

"Oh, thank you. It's from the front door. I didn't realize it was wet."

He grew closer and touched my face again.

"I ought to finish clearing my office." I turned and hurried away, my sense of exhilaration mirroring the butterflies in my stomach.

CHAPTER 7
~ THE STORM ~

Sunday arrived as the warmest day of the year thus far. Granny and the sisters were at the local parish helping Friar Thompson organize a charity project he had worked on for months. I felt for the priest—Sister Callahan presented a real test of his long-suffering. Before they left, she prepared an extensive list of the things she'd found wrong with the project and how to improve them. Surely, she had some remarkable ideas. I just hoped she would present them kindly.

I spent the day weeding the garden borders, amazed at how invasive the weeds were. In contrast, the perennials' tender green shoots hadn't fully broken through the thawed ground. At twilight, I went inside, and after eating a bit of broccoli soup, turned in for the night.

The trees clump together. The air is dense and hard to breathe. Soldiers in black clothing surround me. Their leader aims his rifle at a man kneeling on the ground. I can't see his face, but I plead for his life.

A blast rings in my ears. The soldiers vanish, and the man collapses. I turned him over to find his shirt covered in blood. I rip it open to stop the bleeding, but the deadly bullet has hit its mark. The young Mr. Sterling lies dead in my arms. I wail in pain.

I bolted upright, fear clutching my heart. The wretched nightmare had felt too real, and so had my anguish at seeing Mr. Sterling dead. In the semidarkness, the walls seemed to close in, suffocating me. I threw on my robe, grabbed some paper and pencils, and headed up the narrow stairway tucked in the corner of my room to the east tower.

Dawn sent faint shafts of light across fields, buildings, and small pockets of forest. I drew a breath of fresh air, trying to make sense of my dream. But I doubted another explanation existed beyond my confusion about my employer and his past.

I sat at a metal table near the short wall that encompassed the terrace, and sketched Mr. Sterling's face as I remembered it from the picture in my office. The rising sun vanquished the last of the shadows as I outlined his dark eyelashes. What secrets lay behind those captivating eyes?

"Mr. Vines is driving me to town," Mrs. White announced after lunch. "Miss Contini, if you'd like, you can go home now." It was more a command than a suggestion.

"Thank you. I might."

"Here is the grocery list." Zaira handed her a piece of paper.

She folded the paper and marched out of the kitchen.

"Is something wrong with Mrs. White?" I asked. "She looked quite unsettled."

"You can say that again. To tell you the truth, the pantry is well-stocked, but she insisted that I make a list, so I did. But then, of course," Zaira said pensively, "it might have something to do with—"

Zaira and I turned at once when Mr. Sterling unexpectedly entered the room.

"Miss Contini," he said. "Come with me, please."

Zaira's eyes widened with curiosity at his request, reflecting my reaction. I gave her half a smile and followed him through the French doors. We crossed the yard to the stables, where he opened the door to let us in. Two horses, one white and one jet-black, watched us from the stalls, their eyes glimmering in the semidarkness.

"Oh my. They are beautiful!"

"They are. I bought them from a farm in Knoxville. They arrived just yesterday." He swallowed hard. "I thought you might like to go for a ride. You like horses, don't you?"

My fingers gently slid down the black one's neck. He was soft, velvety. "I was terrified of them when I was little. It took Granny, the nun who raised me, a little work to get me to trust them. It was worth it, though. I love riding."

A look of sadness etched his features. "Maybe this isn't a good idea? You aren't appropriately dressed anyways." He glanced at my skirt. "You'll be safer riding astride."

"I'll be fine. Tell me their names."

"I have only named this one." He pointed to the white horse. "Her name is Lady."

Lady. The word from his lips rang in my ears like a piano key held indefinitely. And mingled with it came Mr. Vines's word about the garden statue, *The lady who traveled all the way from England. She neither slumbers nor lets others rest.* Had Mr. Sterling named the horse keeping his deceased wife in mind? If that was true, she still held a tight grip on his heart, perhaps hindering the possibility of a new love blossoming.

"As for this rascal, I couldn't come up with one. Would you like to give it a try?" Mr. Sterling informed, pulling me out of my thoughts.

"I'm not very good with names."

"I have a hard time believing that when you bear the perfect one." His strong British accent revealed a trace of nervousness.

"Thank you." I was flattered by the compliment but wondered what he meant by "the perfect one."

"Come on, you must think of a name."

"All right." I contemplated the animal's intimidating presence, and I had it. "General." The word came naturally, as if I had said it a million times before.

"Why General?"

I suddenly remembered he'd been a general, so I wasn't about to say strong and beautiful. "He just looks like one, that's all."

"Right, then. General it is."

I watched Mr. Sterling as he fastened the saddles on the horses. Evidently, he had done this innumerable times. He led them out of the stable while reciting the safety rules as if I were a child.

But I responded with, "Yes, I will remember that," or "Yes, I know," or "Sure, I'll do that."

Before I could react, he lifted me by the waist and set me sideways on Lady. "Don't worry. She is docile." He checked the reins one final time.

"I'm not worried."

He then mounted General, his long legs making it look effortless. Without delay, he took point. As we rode farther into the woods, the gray day turned dark. Occasionally, he gestured to a tree or some wildflower and told me its name. But there wasn't much opportunity to carry on a conversation. We rode for quite some time before reaching a meadow.

He dismounted at the edge of the trees and extended his arms to me. I reached for his shoulders, and his hands went around my waist as I slid off Lady. I landed so close I didn't dare look up at him when he vacillated before letting go of me.

Gathering the reins, he secured the horses to a tree and then walked into the meadow. He lay on the grass, eyes closed. I sat beside him, wondering if he had intentionally brought us here or if the stop was just a coincidence.

When the silence stretched too long, I had to ask, "Mr. Sterling, have you been here before?"

"I know I'm a bit older than you, but when you call me Mr. Sterling, it makes me feel ancient. Please call me by my first name."

"Alexander?"

"No!" He laughed. "My mother called me Alexander when she was upset with me. Just Alex."

"All right. Alex."

"What shall I call you?" He rolled onto his side, propping himself on one elbow.

"Miss Contini," I joked, and he rewarded me with another laugh. For a moment, I could see the young Alex of my dreams, the Alex whose face wasn't etched with sorrow and whose eyes weren't shadowed and troubled. "Florence is fine. But you haven't answered my question."

"No, I have never been this far," he responded a bit too quickly.

"I wonder how large the area is."

"I have a map in my office. You are welcome to look at it if you'd like."

"I'll take you up on that. Truth be told, I had no idea this part of town existed until I started working for you."

"I'm glad you learned something new." He smiled. "And since we are speaking of learning new things, tell me more about you."

"Me? You'd be bored."

"Try me." He seemed to seriously want to know.

"Well," I started, "growing up in a religious school with a nun for a mother wasn't exciting, but I love the people I grew up with. And along the way, I gained a good education. Apart from that, there isn't much to tell."

"That can't be it."

Hoping that if I opened myself to him, he would do the same in return, I asked, "What would you like to know?"

He sat up. "Everything."

"Everything?" I considered what everything meant, and for the first time since meeting him, I realized how little of the world I knew. He'd had an army career, a family, and countless experiences I could only dream of. For goodness' sake, I didn't even have a family legacy. My contemplations took me aback, for I realized I wanted to impress him.

Finally, I was beginning to accept what was happening to me, yet I didn't know how to deal with it. I had never thought about men the way I thought about him. Was this the sudden fever of love that overpowered reason? I couldn't say, for I had never experienced it; I had only read about it in books.

"Start from the beginning. You were left at the monastery, but there must be something more, you know." His words came out as naturally as if he had rehearsed them.

If nothing else, I could carry on an intelligent conversation. I shifted from my emotional side to the rational one. "All I know is that it was summer twenty years ago. On her morning walk, Granny heard a cry from the garden. She followed the sound and found me wrapped in a blanket on the ground. She said I stopped crying as she cradled me in her arms, and she's loved me ever since."

"How old were you?"

"Days? Maybe a week? I don't know."

He pointed to my wrist. "You said your bracelet was left with you, right?"

"Yes. Granny thought it might have been my mother's and that Florence Contini might have been her name. To maintain that possible link with the past, she named me the same."

Alex rubbed his chin thoughtfully. "And did anybody ever come asking for you?"

"No."

"I'm sorry."

"Me too, but I'm lucky to have Granny. She is a great woman and mentor. She tried to be fair and not spoil me—"

"I think she failed in that."

His good humor surprised me. I laughed. "She did. I always got away with things."

"Like what?"

"Like escaping from the girls' dormitory to have my own space. The dormitories felt like a hospital with their rows of beds. Besides, it wasn't fun when the girls left for holidays, and I was left to stare at their empty beds."

"I can understand that."

"I moved to the room in the east tower. The sunrise is breathtaking from the top."

"The monastery sounds interesting."

"You should visit sometime. I'd love to show you around."

"I might." It sounded like a definite never. "What about your classes? Tell me about your teachers. Nuns, I suppose."

"Yes. We had a troop of wonderful sisters throughout the years. A monk taught a history class only once and not for long." A soft breeze caressed the meadow, and I noticed some clouds on the horizon, inching in our direction.

"A monk?"

"From a church in Montrose. A fascinating storyteller the girls were besotted with."

"And you?"

"He was all right." There was no need to disclose how unattractive I thought the monk was.

"Just all right?" Alex lay back and folded his arms behind his neck.

"Yes, just all right." From the corner of my eye, I admired his physique—lean, sculpted strength and grace.

"History lessons. Nice," he mumbled. "Tell me, Florence, have you dated much?"

Such an intimate question. No matter. I seized the chance to turn the tables on him. "Not much, just a couple of men in town, but enough of me. Tell me about you."

The breeze suddenly changed to a gale, the tree branches bending accordingly.

"Wow—amazing how fast the weather turned." Alex rose and extended his hand. "We should head back."

"Almost as fast as you changed the conversation." I smiled.

He seemed a bit startled by my remark, but was quick to respond, "You know enough about me from the documents you handle."

"Maybe about your finances, but you have a history besides your investments, don't you?" I couldn't explain where I found the audacity to speak to him like that. Perhaps it was my growing frustration over the past few weeks and coming to terms with my feelings for him.

"We need to go, or we'll be caught in the storm." He headed to the horses, the subject of his past having raised an almost tangible wall between us.

"I would like to know," I insisted.

"If you knew, you would run. My past would haunt you like it haunts me. I would lose y—" He let out a sigh of frustration. "I don't want to talk about it. Let's go."

Lady snorted and swung her head back and forth, seemingly more desperate than Alex to flee the situation.

"All right, don't fuss." He soothed while trying to untie her as she continued to grow impatient. "We are going."

Branches creaked in the increasing wind, and a fleet of rooks catapulted from the treetops, cawing with a nerve-racking pitch. My gaze darted from the black cloud of birds to Alex, then to a spot past him in the trees. The trespasser stood there, barely visible through the vegetation, watching us. Shivers coursed through my veins, reminding me of the encounters with the monk's ghost at the monastery. Backed by the familiar feelings, again, I wondered if this man was a ghost. My eyes fixed upon him, yet, I was unable to distinguish his nature. "*The common belief is that they have unfinished business*," Granny had said. If a ghost, could he possibly have unfinished business with Alex from the war or his personal life? The thought unsettled me; he could be very human and have even more reason to stalk the house if he pursued Alex. I just couldn't tell for sure if the trespasser was alive or dead.

"Are you ready?" Alex asked, waiting for me to mount.

I contemplated drawing his attention to the stranger, if for no other reason than to gauge his reaction. But when I looked back, the figure had vanished. "Yes. I'm sorry." Once on Lady, I ordered myself to rein in my imagination. The trespasser might be just that, a trespasser—a recurring one.

The first raindrops fell, and lightning flashed. Alex's hair flopped across his forehead as he turned to General, momentarily transforming him into the young man in my dreams. His previous words tumbled through my head. "*If you knew, you would run. My past would haunt you like it haunts me.*" What could be so terrible?

He mounted General, and we headed back just as the heavens unleashed their fury, the rain now coming in sheets. The trees bowed and arched over our path, spooking the horses. The animals flared their nostrils and neighed as they took two steps backward for each step forward.

"It's too dangerous to ride." Alex jumped off General and nodded for me to do the same. "Hold her reins tight and stay close to me."

I slid off Lady and pressed into the wind while she pulled against me. "It's okay, girl, you're fine," I sputtered through the rain on my face.

Twilight closed in as Oak's Place finally came into view.

CHAPTER 8
~ SURRENDERED ~

The sky crackled with jagged bolts of lightning, painting arcs across the darkened expanse, while thunder reverberated through the forest, shaking the trees with its powerful resonance.

Mr. Snider spotted us from the porch and hustled to our aid. "Allow me, sir." Dressed in full rain gear, he took the horses.

"Make sure they are fully dried," Alex said.

"Yes, of course, sir." Mr. Snider led the soaked and frightened animals to the stable.

Alex grabbed my hand, and we half walked, half trotted through the pelting rain toward the beckoning light of the kitchen. In my haste, I tripped on an uneven paver and lost my footing, my hand slipping from his as I fell into the mud beside the path.

"Florence! For heaven's sake. Are you all right?" He pulled me into him, then lowered his face to mine, where he said close to my ear, "Please tell me you aren't hurt." His lips brushed my cheek as he spoke, and I trembled, not because I was wet and cold but because I had never felt so warm inside.

"I'm fine."

"Let's get inside before we drown."

Zaira waited in the kitchen, prepared. She handed us a couple of towels.

I moved to the sink to wash off the mud. From the corner of my eye, I saw Alex kneel to unlace his shoes near the hearth. I opened the tap, rinsed my hands and face, and squeezed the water from my hair. Before another fit of shivering gripped me, I quickly dried off.

"Trade me." Zaira exchanged my towel for a dry one and hurried out of the kitchen.

I wrapped it around my shoulders and looked over at Alex.

He unbuttoned his cardigan and pulled it off, along with his shirt. His back and shoulders were broad and strong, his waist and hips slim. When he turned to pick up the towel and dry himself, I saw the scar on his chest, near his heart—the exact spot where the bullet had entered his body in my dream.

I was dumbfounded. I'd seen the wound. I'd tried to stop the bleeding. It felt so real. Where had the dream come from? How could it have mirrored reality so closely? I was losing my mind.

Zaira hurried back in with two blankets—one for Alex and one for me.

"Thank you." Alex wrapped it around himself, then huddled by the fire. "Zaira, could you lend Florence some clothing before she catches a cold?"

"I was going to suggest as much. I'll run to my quarters as soon as Mr. Snider returns with the umbrella."

"Thank you, Zaira." I sat near Alex and searched for his gaze, but he watched the dancing flames in front of us.

"Oh, I almost forgot. Sister Dolores called. I told her you were busy but would call her as soon as possible." Zaira handed us some broccoli soup. The steam rising from the bowl made me feel warmer already.

"I should've been back home by now. She might need me. I should go."

"Go? You aren't going anywhere," Alex exclaimed. "Driving in this weather would be suicidal. You'll have to stay here tonight."

As if to reinforce his words, a clap of thunder shook the house.

"I have never seen a storm like this!" Mr. Snider growled, emerging through the French doors. "It's going to destroy everything in its path."

"How are the horses?" Alex inquired.

"A bit scared, but they'll be fine. I'll check on them later." Despite his assurance, Mr. Snider looked quite unnerved. The responsibility of caring for the grounds, the horses, and maintaining wood for the fireplaces seemed overwhelming.

"Where are Mrs. White and Vines?" Alex asked Zaira.

"I'm afraid they might be stranded in town."

"The workers?" he asked again.

"They left at the first raindrop," she answered.

I gulped down the rest of my soup and attempted to rise, but Zaira quickly took the bowl from me.

"Stay by the fire. I'll fetch you some clothes." She dropped the bowls in the sink and threw on her raincoat.

"The umbrella is just outside the door," Mr. Snider said. "I'll come with you."

"Thank you both," Alex said to them and turned to me. "Call Sister Dolores. She'll agree that you should stay."

"I'll call from my office." I tightened the blanket around me and left the kitchen, unable to dismiss the image of the scar on his chest from my mind. How could I have seen it in my dream before seeing it in real life?

Confirming Alex's words, Granny concurred, and other than being a little shaken by the thunder, she was all right. "This building is a fortress. I'm safe here," she said. "Besides, with Sister Callahan and the others' help, we can manage any eventuality just fine." Her only concern was for my safety, and soon after we hung up, the telephone and power lines went dead. Keeping in mind that Granny had the European sisters' company gave me a sense of reassurance. They would be safe in the fortress. Armed with Zaira's dry clothes and a candle, I retired to the guest room. With no fireplace to warm the area, the stone floor felt like ice against my bare feet as I struggled to strip off the damp layers, desperate to get into Zaira's nightgown. As I slipped into it, the cozy flannel fabric conveyed instant warmth.

After extinguishing the candle, I slipped into the soft sheets, pulling the covers up to my neck. I closed my eyes and listened to the gusts of wind and torrents of rain hurtling against the windowpane. Safe from the storm, I pulled my thoughts to the inside world, and a sense of guilt pricked at me. I had forgotten something I ought to have done.

"Hang your clothes by the fireplace." Zaira's earlier advice jolted me from the bed. A second jolt came at the realization that I had also neglected to bring some matches with me. With a groan, I retrieved my wet clothing and felt my way through the corridors.

The fire burnt low, casting a soft glow over the now-deserted kitchen. I spread my skirt and blouse on the hearth and extended my hands toward the heat. Another lightning bolt struck nearby, shaking the walls. In that moment, I felt a hand on my shoulder and shrieked.

"It's just me," Alex whispered.

"Oh my." My hand flew to my heart. "You frightened me."

"I'm sorry." He briefly touched my hand. "You're freezing."

"This house is as cold as a tomb."

"Have you been in a tomb?" He smiled but sounded serious.

What an odd question. "No, of course not. It's a figure of speech."

"Come sit by the fireplace in my office. I just added firewood, and it's going strong." Before I could answer, he placed his hand on my back and guided me out.

In the office, the fire burned brightly, eliminating the need for a candle. We settled on the sofa, leaving space between us. I noticed a blanket and pillow on the floor near his feet. Did he sleep here often?

"Are you afraid?" he asked, his gaze lost in the dancing flames.

"The ferocity of the storm makes me a little uneasy, but I'm not scared."

"I'm not talking about the weather."

"What, then?"

"Me. Are you afraid to be with me?"

"No, of course not." Even when I wasn't sure where my feelings for him would lead, I trusted him to be honorable. Nevertheless, I knew where the fire poker was.

"Well then, I must say that you are beautiful—so beautiful it hurts to look at you."

The words thrilled me, but I didn't dare believe he'd said them. A log caught, sparks leaping into the air and a wave of heat washing over us. But I hardly felt it in the face of the feelings raging inside me.

Alex stretched his arms out, pulling me into his embrace. The strength with which he held me assured me he wouldn't let go. The same contentment I experienced during some of my dreams now filled me—I felt safe, as if, after a long journey, I was finally home. Afraid to say something to break the enchantment, I rested my head against his chest and fell asleep.

When daylight streamed through the window, I wondered if I'd dreamed it all—the meadow, the horses, the storm, his closeness. No. I could feel the warmth of his body melding with mine.

Sometime during the night, we'd shifted to a lying position on the sofa. The blanket from the floor now covered us. My head still rested on his chest, his heart beating softly underneath my ear. His arms tightened around me, letting me know he was awake.

"Good morning," he whispered.

"Good morning."

"Rhetorically speaking," he said. "If the not-so-pleasant gossip about me were true, would you still be here?"

"Oh...you know about that."

"From the moment the invitations to social events rained on me, and I turned them down one by one—so, would you still be here?"

"I suppose it depends on what truth we are speaking about."

"That's a safe answer."

"So . . . what parts might be true?"

"Like I told you in the meadow, there are things that haunt me— things I can't understand," he said evasively. "All I know is that my past is eating me alive and there is nothing I can do to change it or fix it."

A pause. I didn't know what to think or say, for it was evident he wouldn't go into the details.

"I'm a bitter man with much baggage. I'm not sure this is the right place for you. You should be out there enjoying life with people like you —people who are enthusiastic about life, who don't shy away from new opportunities." The guarded statement revealed that a possible relationship between us troubled him.

"I'm where I want to be." I could hardly believe my candidness, but it was true. I looked up at him, wondering if at last, this was the moment we had avoided, the moment of surrender.

Alex rolled off the sofa. "Zaira will be here with breakfast any moment now."

Zaira. The staff. I feared my closeness to Alex would cause a definite rift with Mrs. White, but hopefully, not with the others. Nonetheless, I shrunk at the thought of Zaira seeing me with Alex in my—hers— nightgown. "I'll eat in the kitchen. I better change first." Feeling foolish at his evasion, I quickly left before my coworkers saw me.

CHAPTER 9
~ DREAMING ~

The storm abated, but the aftermath was catastrophic. The telephone line had been restored but not the electricity. From Mrs. White's call this morning, we learned she and Mr. Vines were stranded in town as much as we were at Oak's Place. The wind knocked down several trees and electrical lines on High Banks, the only access road to the house. Complicating matters, parts of the pavement lay underwater. It would take a while to clear it.

"Would you like to play Monopoly?" Alex entered his office with a board game. "I bought it on my way back from England."

I left the window and joined him at the desk. "You like board games?"

"They're all right. Help pass the time." He moved to the hearth and fed it a few logs from the pile beside it.

"I'm not sure." I thought of the games I played with the girls at the monastery. I always lost.

"Ah, Miss Contini." A playful light danced in his eyes. "Do I detect a trace of cowardice?"

He could not have struck my ego harder. I could be many things, but not a coward. "Seriously, Mr. Sterling." I matched his playfulness. "You could benefit from some humbling."

He chuckled. "Perhaps, but it won't be today."

"We shall see."

While he set up the game, I inspected his features more closely. He looked healthier today, his skin radiant.

He looked up from the cards in his hands. "Why are you looking at me like that?"

"Like what?"

"Like you are thoroughly analyzing me."

"I'm not. I was thinking about the storm," I lied, embarrassed to be caught.

"That's funny. I was also thinking about the storm," he murmured, and I knew he'd seen right through my lie. "I'm sorry you are stuck here with me." He quickly distributed the cards on the desk.

"I'm not. I'm glad to spend time together."

"I'm forty-four years old, Florence. Don't you think I'm a bit old for you?"

"A hundred years old is old. You aren't even halfway there."

"I feel like it sometimes." He rolled the dice and moved a few spaces, then handed it to me.

"The age difference has its advantages, you know." In part, I attributed my growing audacity to Mrs. White's absence. I hadn't realized how much she intimidated me.

A shadow of amusement crossed his face. "Tell me."

"I feel safe with you."

"Roll the dice." Alex reminded me, and I did.

"And I must confess." I jumped two spaces on the board. "You aren't unpleasant to look at, but you already know that."

"That's another way of saying I'm not good-looking." He said this with such sincerity I couldn't help but laugh. "Well, it's a good thing that what I lack, you possess in abundance—enough for us both."

"Thank you." My gaze dropped to the game board, my cheeks burning.

"Before you overthink what I said, let me clarify. I meant beauty, not intelligence, for I'll win this game." He chuckled.

"You are a very arrogant man, Mr. Sterling."

"I've been told that before. I'm still not convinced."

I rolled my eyes.

The game went on, our pieces moving around the board as we bought properties, paid dues, and tried to get ahead of each other.

Alex pointed to a card. "I'd like to buy the railroad, and you owe 10 percent income tax to the bank. Oh, and I'll also buy two more houses."

"Seriously?" I was about to lose.

"What's the matter?" He smiled. "I can let you win if you'd like."

I frowned.

"You said it yourself. I have more experience buying and selling things. It's definitely the age difference."

"Sure it is," I mocked. "You just happen to know and have it all."

"Having it all is dangerous. You've got more to lose." He made a move that sealed his win.

"Where there is no risk, there is no gain." Through the windowpane, my eyes found the majestic statue of the lady and child. His gaze followed mine, and it felt as if a cloud of darkness descended upon the room.

"Risk can be an unforgiving enemy. The things that matter most shouldn't be risked or bought with money. I'm a wealthy man, but I'm also the poorest."

Though I yearned to ask a few questions, I knew it was a sensitive topic, one he'd avoided in the meadow. I'd wait until he was ready to talk about it.

***

The afternoon brought another downpour. At Alex's request, Zaira set up dinner in the dining room. She also spared me from wearing the same clothes I had for the past two days by lending me a long-sleeved purple dress with a golden belt.

Alex sat at the head of the table, highlighted by the flames dancing in the fireplace. He wore dark trousers and a white button-up shirt with rolled-up sleeves. As I entered, he rose and pulled back a chair for me.

"Thank you."

Zaira had set out large cream-colored plates with flowers carved at the edges and heavy silverware adorned similarly.

"These belonged to my parents." Alex touched the carved crystal goblet.

"They are beautiful."

Zaira entered the room carrying a tray as if she served royalty. No doubt she loved to show off her culinary skills. When it came to preparing, cooking, and presenting exquisite dishes, she proved a master of deception. Just when I thought I had seen her best, she surprised me with something even more delicious. And so it was tonight. Al dente, Fusilli pasta and vegetables seasoned with delicate spices formed an unforgettable dish.

"Zaira, I have to admit the presentation of your meals is no less spectacular than the flavors," Alex praised as she placed the food on the table.

She blushed. "Thank you, sir."

"I should take cooking lessons from you," I told her.

"I doubt you need them," Alex said convincingly.

"You say that because you haven't encountered my cooking," I refuted.

"I agree with Mr. Sterling," Zaira said. "However, I'd love to teach you a few of my tricks if you'd like. Nothing too complicated." She underestimated reality, for I had seen how she worked to create such perfection.

"Done. Thank you."

"I'll take care of this," Alex said to Zaira, grabbing the serving spoon. "Please don't worry about the dishes. You've done enough. Thank you."

"Very well, sir, but know I made chocolate cake for dessert."

"Wonderful. I'll get it when we are ready," he assured.

Zaira left, looking pleased. She had gone above and beyond, and I was now confident she approved of Alex and me dating.

Alex served the food and refilled our drinks. "I hope she never retires. I love her cooking."

"I know. It's heavenly." I forked some noodles.

"Florence, you have no idea how you have changed my life." He placed his hand on top of mine.

"I don't. Why don't you tell me?"

"Perhaps one day I'll be able to tell you everything." He let go of my hand. "Let's enjoy the food before it gets cold."

I took a bite, racking my brain for a way to broach the subject without pushing him. Then it came. "At least tell me this. Earlier today when you fell asleep as we read—"

He shook his head slightly. "Sorry. I can't believe I did."

"Don't be. I wasn't bored."

"That's what I'm worried about."

"You said some interesting things." I twirled the fork in the pasta. "Would you tell me about them?"

"If I only remembered them."

"You said, "Heavy fire, hold your post, Marne."" I carefully selected the words, leaving out those that might cause him to shut down.

"I see. I dreamed about the Great War. Marne, named after the river, was a crucial battle when the British and French stopped the German advance into Paris, saving the city from being taken." He looked into the fire, his eyes saddening. "It was brutal, and it dragged on for a long time. You know, when the British entered the conflict, I drove by White Hall in London and saw young men lined up in the street, waiting to volunteer."

"Brave men."

"They were, but they had no idea what they were headed for. They didn't realize their chances of survival were close to zero. But I can't blame them. I knew the statistics and was still anxious to go."

"You didn't want to return?"

"By then, I had nothing to return to. Ironic. Me, who didn't care to survive, did."

Did he not care because of the loss of his wife and child? Afraid to ask, I said, "I'm glad you did. I'm glad we know each other."

"Forgive me. I haven't dreamed of the war for a while. I got a little carried away. What else did I say?"

"You said, 'Florence, please forgive me. It was my fault. I didn't come back from London in time.'"

"That's interesting. My trip was on schedule. Anything else?"

"You insisted that if you'd have come back in time, I would not have been hurt."

His body stiffened, and the words spilled from his mouth. "I'll say. Sounds like I carried on a full discussion in my sleep. Isn't it amazing how dreams can be so nonsensical?"

"You can say that again." Unlike my incomprehensible dreams, at least he had the war and its trauma to justify his.

He pushed the chair back and stood. "Would you like some dessert?"

"Later, perhaps." I glanced at the piano in the corner of the room. "Will you play for me?"

He hesitated.

"Please."

"All right."

Almost in slow motion, he placed his fingers on the keys and began to play. I leaned against the wall and closed my eyes. The intensity with which he played belied his stoic façade. All the emotions behind those conversations when he'd changed the subject or didn't answer my questions now seemed to flow through the music. Only after the music stopped did I realize tears dampened my cheeks.

"Do I play that poorly?" He walked over and brushed my tears with his thumb.

"Terrible," I joked.

"What's the matter?"

"I have never heard someone play like that. It felt like you poured your soul into it. It was beautiful."

"You are beautiful. You deserve better than me."

"It's not what I deserve that I care about but what I want."

"And what do you want?" His eyes searched mine as if trying to read my soul.

"I want to be a part of your life." Saying it aloud felt liberating.

"You will never know how much that means to me." He pressed a soft kiss to my forehead, then trailed kisses down my cheek, and, at last, his lips found mine. I trembled, both from the sweet wildness that coursed through my veins and the fear that his secret past might conspire to keep us apart.

The Buick veered down High Banks Road. The pavement was strewn with fallen branches, uprooted trees, and standing water. Despite the chaos sprawling in every direction, there was a peculiar tranquility—a feeling of peace in the storm, as though everything were right for the first time in twenty years. As I drove the final stretch to the monastery, my mind caught between the intimate moments I spent with Alex and the allure of the unknown—the horse ride, the games, sleeping in his embrace. I couldn't wait to be back to him, to his world—even when I knew little about that world.

With a sigh, I turned my attention back to home. The storm had affected it too, but thankfully, it wasn't as bad as Oak's Place.

I let myself into the kitchen and found Granny, Sister Callahan, and a few others gathered around the table, captivated by whatever it was they were examining. In their black and white attire, they looked like oversized magpies circling their prey.

Granny turned at the creak of the door. "Child, it's so wonderful to have you home!"

"Fannie, Fannie is back!" Sister Callahan exclaimed.

"It's good to be home." I embraced Granny warmly.

Sister Callahan came straight at me, and before I knew it, she crushed me in her arms.

"Hello, Sister Callahan," I wheezed, struggling for air.

There was a collective greeting from the rest of the sisters as Sister Callahan released her grip. Catching my breath, I noticed several drawings on the table, *my* drawings, and a few others I didn't recognize.

Granny quickly explained: "Florence, forgive me for bringing out your drawings. Sister Cox here," she signaled to a thin woman with a pointy nose beside Sister Sullivan, "loves drawing herself, and I thought to show her your work."

"No, it's okay," I said. "My only concern is how ordinary they must seem." I picked up someone else's drawing. "This on the other hand—this is excellent." The scene depicted a garden populated by a colony of hummingbirds hovering over rose bushes. Their wings looked surprisingly real.

"You are kind," Sister Cox said. "I drew it after one of Saint Mary's gardens. And if I may say so, you are quite gifted. I love your drawings."

"Thank you." I attempted to sit down when Sister Callahan barked something and my knees locked, keeping me on my feet.

"Now—now! Who is this?" she asked, her eyes sparkling with excitement.

I did not know how to respond. The paper she advertised in total bliss was the sketch of the young Alex.

"He is so handsome!" Sister Callahan went on, "and around your age —isn't he? Who is he?"

"No one, really, just a product of my imagination," I lied. There was no need to disclose the truth, for if I did, it would open a flood of questions and assumptions I didn't want to talk about.

"Well, that's just too bad. If you ask me, I think he would be the perfect match for you." Sister Callahan laughed, and admiring the drawing one last time, she returned it to the pile.

I settled into a chair, grateful she had dropped the subject. However, once or twice, I caught her staring at the young Alex before looking at me. I feigned my best at ignorance while I studied the rest of Sister Cox's work, taking mental notes of her clever techniques.

CHAPTER 10
~ FOLLOWING THE HEART ~

My happiness lay in coming to work, being with Alex, and feeling his closeness. No matter how often we were together, my stomach always twisted with anticipation. As the Buick rumbled down High Banks Road, sweet images of the past days and our time together—reading in his office, horseback riding, strolling through the gardens, playing games—ran through my head. While grateful for his affection, desire, and respect for me, I remained frustrated by his continued reserve.

Would the love I saw in his eyes ever be enough for him to break free of the past and explore a life with me? I dreaded the answer. He hesitated to visit the monastery and meet Granny. And he pulled away from me every time Mrs. White reminded him of how "out of place" and "inappropriate" our relationship was, which she did in subtle ways. Now and then, the conversation I heard between them not long after I came to Oak's Place made me think.

"*I was trying to move on, but it hurts so much. Why does she have to haunt me?*" he had said.

"*Let her go. It's the rational thing to do.*"

"*After all these years of suffering and regret, how can I?*"

"*You are playing a dangerous game. But if that's what you want, you'll have to tell her the truth,*" Mrs. White had told him.

What truth had Mrs. White so concerned? Should I know about it?

Alex's health complicated matters. He had been ill five out of the last twelve days. Again, I wondered if his physical ailments played a part in his emotional and intellectual suffering or the other way around. Whichever, I feared I would lose him to a faceless enemy, one I could neither fight nor defeat. Especially when Alex wouldn't allow me near him when he was sick. He'd retreat behind closed doors, battling his demons alone.

As I parked the car in the courtyard, I said a silent prayer that he would feel well today. However, each time I let myself hope, a feeling that my dream would turn into a nightmare pricked my heart.

I got out of the Buick and started toward the house but stopped in my tracks. With quick, short steps, Zaira disappeared into the trees. Considering her schedule, it seemed odd she'd be out for a walk at this hour. Interestingly, her mysterious outings had stopped during the renovation. And now that I thought about it, I hadn't seen the trespasser for a while. Of course, as I had invested most of my time in my relationship with Alex, I might have failed to notice a few things. However, with the renovations completed, the old routine might make a full return.

My curiosity getting the better of me, I followed her at a distance, careful not to attract her attention. My heartbeat thumped in my ears, my conscience reminding me I shouldn't be spying. When she suddenly stopped, I hid behind a large white oak. For once, the verdant forest sided with me, concealing my presence amid the low branches as I peeked at Zaira.

Highlighted by the sunlight filtering through the canopy above, a man about Zaira's age came into view, and she let out an exclamation of joy. They clasped each other in a passionate display of affection. Zaira's disappearances and questionable explanations fell into place. She sneaked out of the house to meet this man.

I backstepped, hoping to leave undetected, when a rustling in branches overhead caught my attention. An old crow with dusty gray feathers jumped from one branch to another, moving toward me.

Please don't give me away. A few more steps. Almost out of view—almost there.

The bird shifted above, his eyes intense on me with surreal intelligence.

Please don't.

He emitted the most mournful sound, making my skin crawl.

Zaira spun toward the noise, her gaze landing on me. "Florence!"

Oh, please, Earth, swallow me. My cheeks burned hot as the couple neared. "Zaira, I'm so sorry," I offered. "I didn't mean to . . ." I couldn't finish.

"It's all right. Someone was bound to see us sooner or later." Zaira sighed. "This is Oliver, a friend from town."

"Nice to meet you." A well-built man, Oliver's brown hair and bright smile nearly put me at ease.

"Likewise. Please forgive my intrusion." I turned to leave.

"Florence, don't tell Mrs. White about this," Zaira pleaded. "See, Oliver used to deliver the milk, and when she realized we'd grown fond of each other, she discontinued the service—you know, her no-visitor policy. She won't tolerate this indiscretion, as she'll call it. She made it clear that I can do whatever I like on my day off, but even then, not at the house."

"Don't worry. I won't say anything." Though I disagreed with Mrs. White's obsessive control and Victorian ways, I somewhat sympathized with her. She did her best to run a tight ship, and the staff breaking the rules must make her feel like her boat would sink.

"Thank you, miss." Oliver smiled. "Just so you know, Zaira tried to stop me from coming, but I refuse to see her just once a week. Even when I try hard not to come, I can't help myself."

The man in the woods. Oliver watched the house. It was creepy, but love had a way of producing irrational and sometimes risky behavior. This I knew from sad experience. My thoughts skipped to my previous assumptions. I laughed at the idea that the man could have been someone hunting Alex from his past. Or worse, a ghost roaming the woods. I sighed inwardly, relieved to have fewer mysteries to worry about.

The other man who knew the woods like the palm of his hand now crossed my thoughts. "Does Mr. Snider know about this?"

"Yes. I couldn't keep it from him. He caught me slipping out at night and spotted us together a few times," Zaira replied.

Then it dawned on me. "That morning in town, the lavender tea was an excuse. You spent the night there."

Zaira pursed her lips and nodded.

"I'll see you at the house." I retreated, wondering whether Mrs. White might already suspect Zaira's "indiscretion" and Mr. Snider's cover-up. Could it be the cause of her hostility with the groundskeeper? At least the conversation I had overheard between them suggested that much. However, I sensed something more.

Zaira. I smiled. She was in love and shouldn't have to meet Oliver in secret. Could Alex change the rules? Should I bring it up? No, I should stay out of it. Despite having allowed the workers on the grounds for the renovations, he still seemed to need seclusion. I walked past the Buick, climbed the front steps, and entered the house.

I found Alex in his office, standing before the window. His eyes darted from the statue of the lady and child to me, traces of guilt and resentment in them.

"Good morning. How are you feeling?" I started toward him, anticipating his embrace.

"Not well." He raised his hand, stopping me. "I don't want you to see me like this."

I froze. "It wouldn't hurt to get another opinion."

"They'll provide the same diagnosis. It is what it is."

"I'm not convinced." I desperately wanted to help him, but it seemed he had given in to his fate.

He squared his shoulders and beheld me with alarming seriousness. "You should walk away before you get hurt."

"Walking away is the only thing that will hurt me."

"There is nothing I can offer you—nothing besides money."

A wall of fear and despair stood between us.

"That's not true, and you know it," I said defensively.

His gaze returned to the statue. It was evident. His heart belonged to the woman represented by the sculpture. I wondered if she had loved him the same as he loved her. "You should find someone your age, someone who can fully be yours."

His obstinacy angered me. "Is that what you want me to do? Leave so you can feel sorry for yourself, hoping the dead will come back to life?"

"You could never understand. When you love the way we—" He shook his head angrily.

I tried to hold my tongue, but the hurt compelled me. "I could never compare with her. Is that it? She was just too wonderful, wasn't she?"

"The problem is the opposite. You remind me too much of her. Too much!"

In a good or bad way? It didn't matter. I could not change the past or his disposition. "Very well. Tell me to never return, and I won't." Tears burned behind my eyes, but I contained them.

After a moment, he turned away from the window, his gaze lost in time, trapped in the memories. He opened his mouth as if to speak, but instead, he left the office without looking at me.

Interpreting his silence as a signal for me to go and consumed by insecurity, I left the house. As I fumbled through my pocket for the car key, out of the corner of my eye, I saw movement in the brush. I shifted to get a better look, and a scream caught in my throat.

The trespasser stood there, closer than ever, and it was not Oliver. Though I couldn't see him clearly in the shadows, I couldn't deny it. He looked and moved about with the translucence of glass.

A ghost. I stood transfixed while the boundaries of reality blurred. Mrs. White said we all had shadows to chase us and to chase after. I supposed my childhood gift, or curse, for seeing the dead remained present. However, unlike the monk, this specter seemed aware of the mortal realm and of me. Yes, it was clear now—he haunted *me*, and I had to know why.

It might have had something to do with the accumulated frustration and hurt from my encounter with Alex, but I needed answers. Chills ran through me as I plunged into the vegetation, never losing sight of him. The closer I got, however, the farther it seemed he slipped away. *Oh no, you won't escape me.* I had no idea what I would say to him or what would happen if I even had the chance, but I had to try. I increased my speed to almost a trot. As if playing hide-and-seek, he moved behind a tree. I reached the spot, out of breath, my eyes darting about the area. He was nowhere in sight.

"Show yourself! Who are you? What do you want?"

The ensuing silence challenged my courage more than if the ghost had struck me. Not seeing or hearing him, I didn't know what to expect. I shrieked in anger. Had I chased a mirage? Had I lost my mind?

Before anyone spotted me, especially Sister Callahan, I headed straight to my bedroom. I couldn't deal with her just now. Zaira's relationship with Oliver, the argument with Alex, and the ghost had my emotions swinging from sanity to lunacy, and my head spanned from trying to place fact and fiction in their proper places. Whenever I believed I had taken a step forward in uncovering Oak's Place's mysteries, something pushed me backward.

I dropped onto the bed, rubbing my temples. Alex's rejection stung me most. He hadn't told me to leave and never return, but he hadn't asked me to stay. The tears that had threatened me all afternoon, at last, streamed down my cheeks. I loved him but feared he didn't feel the same way. *You could never understand. When you love the way we—*" he had said. I buried my face in my pillow to muffle my sobs as I released the tension and pain. Thoughts came and went until I drifted asleep.

"Child, may I come in?" Granny called.

When I hesitated, the door creaked open. "Florence, what's wrong?"

"Nothing, Granny. Nothing."

"You can't fool me. I saw you running across the courtyard hours before you were supposed to be home—which, if I may say so, is quite rare these days."

I hadn't told Granny much about my relationship with my employer. But there was no need. She knew.

Granny sat on the edge of the bed. "Oh my, you've been crying."

"I'm so confused." I sat up and faced this woman who loved me unconditionally—this woman I trusted.

"Oh, child, you are in over your head, aren't you?"

"I feel so foolish and so lost. How did this happen to me?"

"You are not foolish. It happens to almost everyone at some point."

I broke down in tears, and she pulled me into her arms. Granny listened patiently as a torrent of emotions spilled out. "He will never love me as I love him. His heart dwells in the past, and I can do nothing about it. Why can I not accept that and move on?"

"Let me tell you a story." Granny let go and sat up a little. "I was a novice at Cambridge when I fell in love with a dazzling man. I was ashamed and felt extremely guilty for it. I was betraying my beliefs, my morals, and the church—"

"*You* were in love?" I felt terrible not to have ever considered the possibility. True, she was a nun, but she was also a woman.

"Madly."

"Wait, if you hadn't taken the vows, you could have changed your mind, right?"

"Yes. I could have, but he couldn't."

My eyebrows shot up. "He was a priest?"

She nodded. "That's one reason why I moved back to the States. I couldn't bear to be close to him. He went on to have a successful career in the church, becoming a cardinal at a fairly young age."

"I can't imagine how hard that must've been." For the first time that day, I managed to stop feeling sorry for myself.

"That was the easy part." Her eyes were misty, but she contained the tears. "Years later, I returned to England and found him on his deathbed. What he told me still hurts, Florence." She averted her eyes. "He said he always loved me."

"Oh, Granny!"

"And he couldn't die without telling me. He said he'd have left everything for me, but he didn't dare interfere because I was a novice. He convinced himself to ignore his feelings and stay on his religious path.

That day, child, was the saddest day of my existence." Her tears spilled over.

I had never seen her cry, and it broke my heart. "Did you tell him how you felt?"

"I did. He died with a smile on his face, holding fast to my hand." Granny placed her glasses in her pocket, retrieving a handkerchief to dry her eyes. "We both lived not knowing the truth and suffered greatly because of it. Don't get me wrong—I love serving in the church, but there is something greater than that, something I didn't understand until it was too late: the love between a man and woman." She twisted the handkerchief in her hands. "I'm telling you in hopes that you'll avoid the mistake I made—once time is lost, you can't get it back. Mr. Sterling may have heart wounds, but you might be able to help him heal. This is, of course, if he loves you and wants you in his life. You must find out if that's the case, and if it is, you must fight for him. Florence, do you truly love him?"

"I do."

"Well then, speak to him. He is waiting downstairs in the kitchen."

CHAPTER 11

~ MOONLIGHT ~

Sister Callahan had Alex cornered near the door. "Fannie, what took you so long? This poor fellow must have thought you weren't here and we were trying to keep him around longer."

Alex looked amused, but his face was pale, and shadows encircled his eyes. He looked more ill than this morning.

Sisters Sullivan, Miller, Cox, and Granny hovered near the table, their eyes fixed on Alex. I wondered if he had refused the invitation to sit, opting to stay close to the exit for a quick getaway.

"Good evening, Mr. Sterling," I greeted.

"Miss Contini." He bowed slightly.

"Have you come to finish your portrait?" Sister Callahan asked him.

Realizing she recognized his face from my drawing, I felt as if I'd been punched in the stomach.

Looking intrigued, Alex answered, "I'm here to speak to Miss Contini. But what drawing are you referring to?"

"Well, yours, of course. Fannie is doing a good job. You do know about it, don't you?"

"Oh, that drawing." Alex feigned understanding. "No, I'm not here for that. I need to speak to Fannie about work."

Fannie? My skin burned with embarrassment.

"Work, eh?" Sister Callahan sounded skeptical.

Alex turned to me. "Can we speak outside?"

"Certainly."

"Make sure to come again soon!" Sister Callahan cried.

"Most definitely." Alex smiled.

Bright moonlight illuminated our path as we strolled to the evergreen garden where Granny found me as an infant, the unresolved emotions from our encounter at Oak's Place accompanying us. Alex's heart might be trapped in the past, but mine was willing to bridge the gap. I glanced at him sideways, hoping to discern his mood.

I sat on the base of the water fountain. Alex remained on his feet, hands in his pockets.

"Fannie? I didn't know you had another name."

I laughed, but Sister Callahan would get a payback. "I'm not sure where she got the nickname. And so you know, I dislike it very much."

"She's quite a character." Alex smiled, but I saw the tension in his eyes. "I'd like to see my drawing, though. There is one, right?"

A payback wouldn't do. I'd ship her back to England in a tiny, uncomfortable box. "Maybe, but you haven't told me why you came."

"I wanted to see you."

"You could've waited until Monday." I twisted my fingers nervously.

"No, I couldn't. I feared you wouldn't come back."

"And I feared you came to tell me to stay away."

"None of that."

I breathed a little easier.

"Since the day you set foot at Oak's Place, everything I believed and accepted as true has been uprooted." His countenance revealed a depth of feeling I hadn't seen in him. "There are things I don't understand, things that hurt so deeply I almost convinced myself I was insane." He extended a hand to bring me to my feet. "I wanted to stay away from you, but I couldn't. I didn't want to hurt you, but I did. Today, when you said you'd leave and never return, I realized I could never ask that of you. Even when it would be better for you, I'd die if I did.

"Florence, I'm not ready to tell you about my past, about the things that haunt me. Maybe with time I'll be able to accept them and put them behind me. But I assure you I've always done my best to be honorable. If you can't believe anything else, at least believe that much. And if you do, I'll ask if you can wait until I'm ready to tell the whole story."

In the glow of the moon, once again, I saw the shadow of the man he'd once been. A sense of déjà vu filled me, overturning reason—somehow, somewhere, I had known him. But that was impossible. "I can."

"Right, then." He reached into his pocket, looking as if he had not expected that answer. "If you can take me as I am and forgive me for the grief I have caused you . . ."

My heart pounded in my chest as I anticipated his next words.

He pulled his hand from his pocket and opened it to reveal the most astonishing ring. Sparkling diamonds glistened in the moonlight, surrounding a dark stone in the center. "Florence, will you marry me?"

Were his words or my emotions the cause of my paralysis? I couldn't tell, but my thoughts danced joyfully with my heart. Even though marriage hadn't crossed my mind, and truthfully, I hardly knew the man, it felt right. I stood in wordless bliss until I could no longer contain my answer.

"I will."

Alex placed the ring on my finger, relief washing over his face. He encircled me in his warmth, pressed a gentle kiss on my lips, then deepened it with a passion that swept me off my feet.

On Saturday, Alex returned early enough that we watched the sun rise over Geneva from the east tower. His visit, along with the ring on my finger, solidified last night's proposal even when the magnitude of the commitment hadn't set in. And the part that had, though I fought it, was overshadowed by my lingering doubts about the unnerving events of the past months. Still, I didn't regret the engagement.

"You didn't exaggerate when you described the view from here. It's awe-inspiring," he observed.

"It really is."

We watched the sun climb higher and higher in the sky, chasing away the vestiges of the night and casting sunbeams over the horizon. And I couldn't help but notice the sparkles of vitality in his eyes, the glow of his skin. He looked younger and healthier than I had ever seen him.

He reached for my hand. "How did Sister Dolores take the news?"

"She's happy for me. On the other hand, Sister Callahan said she'll keep a close watch on you." I smiled.

"I'm sure she will." Alex chuckled. "Speaking of Sister Callahan, may I see my portrait?"

"Your portrait?"

"The one you drew of me."

"Oh." My face grew hot. "It's not very good."

"May I be the one to determine that?"

"Promise you won't laugh at it."

"I promise."

"Come with me." We descended the spiral staircase to my bedroom. From my desk, I pulled out a few drawings. He reached around me, taking the papers.

"These are very good." He flipped through the first drawings enthusiastically, studying the last ones carefully. "You said you've never been to England." He sounded doubtful.

"I haven't."

"But these drawings are of the New Forest," he stated in disbelief.

"Perhaps you've seen it in a book?"

"Maybe." I dug deeper into the drawer and found his portrait.

"Here." I handed it to him.

He contemplated it for a moment. "This is a shadow of what I used to be."

I smiled at the word *shadow* and wondered if he knew of the nickname he'd been given in town. If he didn't, someday I might tell him.

Alex dropped the papers onto the bed. "Let's go downstairs."

"Would you like to see the chapel?"

"Sure. I haven't visited a chapel in ages. It might do me some good."

. . .

We entered the arched wooden door into the chapel only to be ambushed by Sister Callahan.

"There's the happy couple!" she exclaimed. "When is the date?"

"What date?" Alex asked.

"For the wedding, of course."

"Sister Callahan, it's too soon for that," I objected.

"Nonsense. You should tie the knot before you get in trouble," she responded with a knowing look.

"I hope to marry Florence in the next couple of months," Alex said.

My eyes darted to him. Surely, he joked.

"What's the meeting about?" Granny stepped in through the side door.

"We were talking about their wedding, but I'm afraid they don't know what they want." Sister Callahan briefed Granny.

"That's understandable." Granny placed a box of cleaning supplies on a pew and adjusted her spectacles on the bridge of her nose. "They barely got engaged."

"I better speak to the sisters. We might be able to extend our trip." Sister Callahan moved through the exit, her habit slapping against her legs. "I can't miss the wedding."

"If you're serious about this, you better decide on a date, and the sooner, the better. It will save us a lot of grief," Granny suggested. "Oh my, I forgot the feather duster." She crossed herself in front of the Virgin's statue and withdrew.

Alex pulled me into his embrace. "I wouldn't mind it if we married in a week."

"Don't ask me again or I'll do it," I teased.

"Marry me next week," he whispered, dead serious.

His closeness almost convinced me to say yes, but practicality and my lingering uncertainty about his past stopped me. "No, Mr. Sterling. It's too soon."

"Two weeks, then."

"Still too soon."

"It's better than one."

"I'll think about it." A more troublesome thought than timing occurred to me. "I worry about her reaction. She doesn't necessarily adore me."

"Who?"

"Mrs. White. Does she know?" She was an integral part of his life, and I couldn't help but feel I would be overstepping her boundaries, and the retribution might be swift.

"She does, but don't worry about her. She wants the best for me, and you are the best for me."

I hoped she felt the same way.

Sunday was almost over, and Alex hadn't come. I paced my room, wondering why he hadn't even called. Did he regret his hasty proposal? Maybe he didn't have the heart to break the engagement. I couldn't wait any longer. I had to know. I headed to the kitchen to ring Oak's Place.

"Good evening," Mrs. White answered.

"Good evening, this is Florence. May I speak with Mr. Sterling?"

"I'm sorry, but Mr. Sterling has relapsed and cannot answer calls." Mrs. White tried too hard to sound casual.

A relapse? How could that be possible when just yesterday he had radiated with health?

"I'll let him know you called." She was ready to hang up.

"Wait, I must insist on speaking to him. Please, just for a moment." Begging wasn't my preferred method of negotiating, but I couldn't give up so easily.

"I don't think waking him to answer a call is wise when it took him hours to finally find rest. Do you?"

She was right. Still, not talking to Alex bothered me tremendously.

"Please call me if anything changes," I said in wishful thinking.

"Good night, Miss Contini." The line went dead, leaving me sick to my stomach.

I checked my watch, debating between logic and emotion. Logic dictated I waited. It was past 10 o'clock, and he might not wake up until morning. Rest, at the moment, might be his best friend, so I shouldn't disrupt him or the household. After all, I had no pressing matter to do so, and this wasn't the first time he had been this ill. I just missed him.

Conversely, emotion compelled me to drive to Oak's Place right away. There was something about his sudden relapse that didn't sit well with me—something I couldn't explain, but the more I thought about it, the more bewildered I felt.

I wrestled with the decision, considering different scenarios and their possible outcomes. Finally, I grabbed my handbag, fetched the Buick key, and pulled on my coat. No. I shouldn't show up at Oak's Place this late at night. After all, Mrs. White would let me know if he took a turn for the worse. There was no reason to think otherwise. True, she wasn't fond of me, but she did Alex's bidding, and he would want me to know.

Logic won. I peeled my coat and headed to my room, praying I wouldn't regret my decision.

CHAPTER 12
~ LIES AND BITTERNESS ~

The day dawned in a misty veil. The air hung heavy with moisture, lending an otherworldly quality to the foggy roads. With only a few yards of visibility, I wondered what awaited me at the property. As I exited the car, I found Zaira and Mr. Snider in the courtyard, discussing the fate of some terracotta pots.

"I'm glad you are here. I'm afraid Mr. Sterling's health has taken a turn for the worse. He hasn't been this sick since we left England—I mean, as to need assistance during the night. Mrs. White hasn't left his side except to get him a cup of tea last night, and then again, this morning," Zaira said with urgency.

"Of course she hasn't," Mr. Snider echoed my thoughts. "She wouldn't waste an opportunity to be needed. Now, Miss Contini, I'm not one to meddle in others' affairs, but there are things amiss at Oak's Place. Strange things in motion. If you have any idea what they might be, I encourage you not to waste time. For Mr. Sterling's sake, you must act before it's too late."

"What do you mean?" How could I fix whatever haunted Oak's Place?

"That's the thing." Mr. Snider groaned. "I know something lurks in the dark, but I don't know what." Before I could question him further, he picked up the shovel from the ground and took the path skirting the house.

"He gives me the chills," Zaira said. "But he is wise and observant."

Funny, I thought, that he had spoken about things being amiss when I almost certainly knew he had plenty of secrets of his own. However, I couldn't help but agree with him. If I only knew what I could do. "Has the doctor been called?"

"Yes, Dr. Petersen stopped by on his way out of town yesterday. If you ask me, I don't think he was here long enough to be of any help—as usual. I doubt he takes Mr. Sterling's sickness seriously. He prescribed rest and medicine to reduce the discomfort."

"Thanks, Zaira." I hurried up the front steps and entered the foyer.

Mrs. White stood there, enshrouded in the gloom of the corridor, a solid barrier between me and Alex's bedroom. "May I have a word with you?"

"Perhaps after I see Mr. Sterling." I tried to get past her, to no avail.

"He's finally fallen asleep. Let him rest." Her gaze brooked no argument.

I wanted to push her out of the way, but she might be right. Besides, it was best to avoid an ugly confrontation. "Very well."

"Let's speak in your office." Mrs. White signaled for me to go first.

What did she want to say? Why now? I came into the room and glanced outside the window. I was about to round the desk when I saw the ghost amid the trees, enveloped in the fog, watching me. My heartbeat quickened, and suddenly, I felt vulnerable. It was apparent he was determined to stick around. And thus far, I hadn't considered what this specter might be capable of, especially when he could evade me at will as he'd done the other day. However, I had a ghastlier matter at hand.

Mrs. White cleared her throat, and I resumed the march to my seat. The ghost's quandary would have to wait.

"I know you have unanswered questions, things that puzzle you about Mr. Sterling." With those words, she'd ensnared me in the conversation.

"That's true, but this might not be the time to discuss it." I didn't want to sound desperate.

"On the contrary, this is the perfect time. You see, first, you can't marry a man you don't know. Second, I worry about my eternal salvation."

"Your eternal salvation? What does that have to do with anything?"

"I have made many mistakes in the name of love—mistakes that destroyed my life. I can't change the past, but I can appease my conscience by telling you the truth. Whatever you decide to do with it is up to you. As for me, I'll be free of the torment in my soul." She pulled an envelope from her pocket. "At first, I hoped you would stay away, and then I hoped your relationship would fail, but things got out of control, and I can't watch this madness any longer."

Could her fervent prayers have been on behalf of her own soul?

"Let me tell you a story that will answer your questions." She dropped onto the flowery armchair, her fingers tapping the envelope on her lap. "All I ask is that you listen and spare me some sympathy if you can."

"Go on."

"Once, there was a young, ambitious lieutenant who was accustomed to having anything he wanted," she started as if she were telling a child's fairy tale. "After years in the British Army, he wasn't advancing as expected. He was cunning and handsome. To his luck or condemnation —I don't know which—he pursued the ward of his superior officer, a general—for the sake of clarity, let's call him General Marcus. Like others before her, she fell helplessly in love with the lieutenant. They married, and he was almost instantly promoted. His advancement brought him contentment, but his unwanted marriage only misery. His wife had served her purpose in helping him to the top, and now she was useless to him."

Could this possibly be true? The newspaper article in his office had cast suspicions on the sincerity of the groom's love. I suddenly felt ill. Like when I read Shakespeare's play about Juliet waking to find Romeo's corpse beside her, I knew something life-altering was afoot.

"Remember, we are speaking of days during the Great War. England fought many traitors and internal battles. It was a time of confusion but also opportunity. So, the solution to his problem came unexpectedly." Mrs. White fingered the rosary around her neck, and her voice shook as if horrified by the images that entered her thoughts. "News reached General Marcus of unmarked ships sailing from the North Sea toward the English Channel. The army did not know how to proceed. The vessels were not authorized to be on British waters, and communications were down.

"General Marcus sent the lieutenant to contain the situation while he stayed in the New Forest to guard his only child, a baby girl—his wife died giving birth to her. His ward—the lieutenant's wife—who was now expecting, also stayed with the general.

"The lieutenant sailed to intercept the enemy. To everyone's relief, the vessels turned around without any conflict. Then he got news of another ship slipping through their defenses the previous night, reaching land farther south. He discovered they planned to attack the general's home. Instead of messaging London for help, he formed a terrible plan.

"General Marcus was one of the country's wealthiest, most powerful men. The lieutenant was next in line to take his place in the army and his estate—if only the general's baby daughter and his ward weren't in the way. However, the obstacles might be removed if the enemy reached the New Forest." Mrs. White clutched her rosary so hard I feared the beads would come off the string. "It wasn't difficult to delay the message long enough to accomplish his purpose without anyone ever suspecting him. Greed and power took control, and everything went according to plan. No one survived the attack at the manor."

This is ridiculous. Alex would have never killed his superior and his daughter, let alone his own wife and unborn child. Never. She's fabricating a story to keep us apart. Still, I would listen, intrigued at how far she would go.

Mrs. White strode to the window, her countenance heavy with sorrow. "The lieutenant was pleased until he discovered the nanny and the baby were missing. He searched far and wide, but it was as if the earth had swallowed them. It intrigued him. How could the nanny have fled so quickly? The answer came when the soldiers discovered a tunnel beneath the house leading into the forest. Worried that the nanny might know something, he hunted them, determined to end their lives.

"The only person who knew the truth was the lieutenant's lover—the one who would never betray him, the one who would do anything to be with him one more time . . . to feel his hands . . . his lips . . . his passion.

"But let's name the actors in the story. Alexander Sterling became the general in command after the passing of his superior, General Marcus Contini." She emphasized the last name. "The faithful one who knew and protected his secret was I."

A wave of revulsion swept over me at the thought of Alex and her being lovers. No. It had never happened. Mr. Vine's words echoed from the past, *"Grief comes in many forms. To me, the worst kind is when the one you love doesn't love you back. Isn't that right, Deborah?"* The double meaning was only too evident. Not only did Mr. Vine love Mrs. White, he knew of her love for Alex. But I was convinced Alex had never reciprocated her love. And that might be the reason why she tried to poison me against him.

"And let us not forget about the baby," she fired again. "Her name is Florence Contini. Yes, you are that baby."

I rose from the chair, my temper flaring. Out of all the absurdities she had said, this topped them all. "You are lying! I don't believe any of it!"

"You're blinded by love, so here." She handed me the envelope. "See for yourself."

I retrieved the contents. The first paper documented Alexander Sterling's acquiring Marcus Contini's inheritance. The second detailed military dates and ranks. "This doesn't prove anything. Marcus Contini could be anybody."

For the first time in our discussion, Mrs. White vacillated, momentarily contemplating me. "Perhaps this will help you see clearly." She extracted two photographs from her pocket.

The first photo showed a young Alex standing next to an older man with a thick mustache, both dressed in military uniform. I read "General Marcus Contini and Lieutenant Alexander Sterling" on the back of the image. The second picture showed a lady from the waist up. Except for the long hair arranged on her head like a crown, the resemblance was undeniable. Her hands were proudly placed on top of her rounded middle. She was an expectant mother—*my mother.*

"Notice her wrist," Mrs. White urged.

There, I saw a bracelet. I held the picture close. It matched the one on my wrist.

"Yes, that's your mother, the brave woman who died giving birth to you."

An overwhelming tide of emotions paralyzed me while I struggled to grasp logic. I couldn't move. I couldn't speak. I couldn't deny the truth any longer. Heavy tears welled up in my eyes and then flowed down my cheeks. All the years of searching, wondering who I was, and resenting the fact that my parents abandoned me came to an end—and so did my belief in Alex's goodness.

Now, I understood his astonishment when he heard my name for the first time, why my being an orphan disturbed him, and why he'd wanted to know more about my roots. I now understood his shock and curiosity upon seeing my bracelet and why he snooped in my purse. Even the mysterious conversations between him and Mrs. White now made sense.

"Old sins cast long shadows," Mrs. White said. "Not in a million years could he have anticipated that the nanny would bring you to America. She must have left you at the monastery. And so you know, he went to England to dig up immigration records. I'm not sure he found anything. Anyhow, his biggest punishment is to have fallen in love with the person he wanted to kill. Believe me, he hates himself for it. At first, he wanted to know if you knew the truth. He hired you to keep you close. '*A contained enemy is no enemy at all*,' he said. But perhaps he hadn't overcome his old addiction to the attentions of the fairer sex and you became a game that backfired. And you know his sickness? I suspect a product of his troubled conscience."

My heart constricted. I wiped my eyes with my sleeve, forcing myself into composure. "Please stop. I've heard enough."

She ignored me. "I also wanted to give you the cemetery book, thinking you might want to visit your parents someday, but he took it from me. I should have let you see it that day, but sadly, I was still too loyal to betray him."

I had forgotten about the little book in the armoire. Mrs. White had snatched it before I read the names in it. The more I remembered, the clearer things became, deepening my despair.

"I've thought nonstop about that wicked day since you got here. Your father must have learned the truth right before the attack and sent you away in the nick of time. And that ring on your finger belonged to his wife. She wore it the day she was murdered."

The door opened, and Alex's frail figure appeared in the doorway. I looked into his beautiful eyes and wished I were dead.

CHAPTER 13
~ AWAKENED ~

As Alex neared the desk and saw the pictures I held, I could see the severity of his illness. His frame quivered. His skin was impossibly white.

"What have you done?" he snapped at Mrs. White.

"It was time she knew the truth," Mrs. White snapped back.

"How could you?" I cried.

"I told you, you wouldn't understand. I'm sorry." Alex's face showed a deep, almost convincing remorse, but the distance between us had become infinite. "Please listen—"

"Listen to what? More lies?" I loathed myself for falling into his trap and into his arms. The ring on my finger that felt so magical hours ago now burned like fire. I couldn't take it off fast enough. "I don't want to see you ever again!" I dropped the ring onto the desk, and with it my heart. "I wish your wife still wore it! I wish she wasn't dead!" I stormed past him out of the office, my footsteps echoing in the hollow corridors.

Tears blinded me as I drove away. I had left my happiness at Oak's Place—a fleeting illusion. Alex had eliminated his pregnant wife—my father's ward—for financial gain. He also stole my family from me. Had my father indeed suspected Alex's betrayal? Or had he died trusting Alex? I would never know.

Why had life dealt so unfairly with me? Why fall in love only to be used and deceived? How could Alex be this cruel? The questions went round and round in my head with no answers, at least not ones I could understand or accept.

I couldn't face Granny, not yet. I drove around town for hours before I parked the Buick and wandered the streets like a soul in limbo, suspended in a transition between heaven and hell. And I found no consolation in Mrs. White's assurance that Alex's punishment was to have fallen for me, for I doubted he knew what love was.

Before long, the air turned from stiflingly warm to chilly as the sky darkened with menacing clouds, and thunder rumbled in the distance. At that moment, I stopped crying for Alex, my sadness and anger replaced by a desire to learn more about my roots. I had enough knowledge about the area where Alex came from to send out some inquiries. If heaven smiled upon me, I might connect with distant family and learn more about my parents. This new determination allowed me to breathe without the walls of my chest squeezing against my heart.

I returned to the car and went home, where a group of sisters chatted with some locals near the entrance. In preparation for tonight's fundraiser, the sisters wore red habits, a drastic change from the usual black. They radiated joy. I envied them. They didn't have to deal with the deceit of love.

I entered the kitchen and found Granny waiting at the table. I had to make up an excuse to escape her presence. She would see right through me, and the wound felt too fresh to discuss it just now.

"Where have you been?" she asked, removing her spectacles to wipe them with a cloth. "Mr. Sterling called earlier looking for you, so I know you weren't at his house."

I couldn't believe his nerve. Hadn't he done enough damage? Did he worry about what I might do with the truth? Coward.

"I went shopping."

"Am I supposed to believe that? You look like something the cat brought in."

"It must be the price of clothing. I looked and looked but couldn't bring myself to buy anything. What I did get was an awful migraine." I rubbed my temples to back my lie.

"All right. We'll continue the discussion later." Her tone told me she wasn't fooled.

"I need to lie down." I was already on my way out of the kitchen.

"Make sure to take some aspirin. The sisters and I will be at Friar Thompson's parish. Call me if you need me."

"Thanks, Granny."

Minutes later, a bus picked up the sisters. And as if in punishment for my lie, pain throbbed behind my forehead. I needed aspirin, after all. I returned to the kitchen, found the bottle in the cupboard, and swallowed three.

The telephone rang, shrill and determined. Fearing it was Alex, I ignored it. But when it persisted, I reluctantly lifted the receiver, hoping to prevent my head from shattering.

"Hello."

"Florence?"

"Zaira?"

"Oh, I'm so glad to reach you. Mrs. White said you resigned. Is that true?"

"I'm sorry, Zaira, but I have a splitting headache. Let's talk tomorrow?"

"Wait, I called to tell you that Mr. Sterling might not survive the night. As I told you this morning, the doctor is out of town, and we can't bring down his fever or stop his vomiting." Zaira waited for me to say something. I couldn't. The endless wave of emotions had left me numb. "I don't know what happened this morning, but he needs you."

"Mrs. White can take care of him." She had been his lover. Something I could never have anticipated. But in retrospect, it explained her obsessive behavior. She would give anything "*just to be with him one more time . . . to feel his hands . . . his lips . . . his passion.*" Well, she could shine now.

"For goodness' sake, Florence! He wants you by his side. He loves you."

He doesn't know what love is. "Try calling the neighboring towns for a doctor," I suggested icily. "Good night, Zaira."

Tracing my steps back to my room, I wondered how I would feel if

Alex died tonight. Could I forgive the man who caused my father's death? Could I ever love someone else?

It might have been the aspirin, but as soon as my head hit the pillow, sleep transported me to oblivion, where I hoped to escape my nightmare.

"Florence, Florence," a distant voice called. I tossed and turned, and somewhere between rest and restlessness, I heard it again. "Wake up! Wake up!"

"I don't want to wake up," I protested deliriously.

"Wake up! You have been given an opportunity to wake up!" the voice persisted.

I blinked awake. The lamp on the nightstand cast a faint light through the space, and in the penumbras in the corner, I saw the ghost. He had always been at the edge of my vision, hiding in the woods, never too far but never too close. And now here he was, in my bedroom. I bolted upright, struggling to slow my frantic breathing as my mind snatched at shreds of logic. An apparition couldn't hurt me, could it?

"You . . . have been watching me," I stuttered. "Who are you? What do you want?"

He came out of the shadows, his looks somewhat settling my uneasiness. He was far from the eyes gleaming with otherworldly malice and the vicious energy I had unconsciously conjectured. In front of me stood a young man dressed in military attire with an angelic face and a childlike innocence about him. He had brown hair neatly arranged to one side, and his chocolate eyes reflected an inner circle of golden flecks, as if a fire burned within. As his attire led me to believe, he must have been involved in Alex's past.

"I'm a guide." He smiled—one of the sweetest expressions I had ever seen—and peace swept through me, washing away the grief of the past hours and the fear of his presence. "Come." He held out his hand, and I took it. "Look." He pointed to the bed as I stood beside him.

I gasped, struggling to find words. "I'm dead." My inert physical body lay under the blanket. "I'm dead." In utter confusion, I raised my hands to look at them. I couldn't understand how I still had a body. It was lighter and deprived of tangibility, but it was a body. It was still me. I even wore a blue dress like the corpse on the bed. I was a reflection in a mirror—a reflection filled with intelligence. In other words, a ghost.

"You're not dead. But we have a short window of time to accomplish our purpose."

"What do you mean? What is happening?"

"I'm here to take you back in time. You are caught in a web of lies, but if you come with me, you'll know things as they are and as they were. Your mortal body is subject to time and space, making it impossible to leave its sphere. But your spirit body is not. We can see and hear anything that exists and has ever existed. We are in the presence of truth. But we must hurry because your physical body can only briefly withstand the separation from its spirit form before it shuts down, preventing its unification. And then you'll truly be dead. But it's your choice. You can go back to your life and stay in darkness, or you can awaken to the truth."

His eyes held wisdom that contrasted sharply with my limited understanding. Life was short and complex, and this temporal separation —inconceivable as it seemed—bore a great weight. I feared walking away from my mortal body into the unknown. But the immediate return to mortality to face Alex's evil deeds appealed far less. If I returned to reality, I knew that even with my focus on researching my roots, I would be on the verge of madness. For, try as I might, I couldn't deny or forget that I still loved the man. After all, I didn't think that truth could get any worse than it already was. "I want to know. I'll come with you."

"You have chosen the right path."

I followed him up the staircase leading to the tower, but instead of the terrace, we emerged in a green field, the sun shining brightly above us. The surreal scenery reminded me of a museum painting or, more so, my drawings.

"Where are we?"

"The New Forest."

Then, in the blink of an eye, our surroundings changed, and we stood at the edge of an impressive manor surrounded by ancient trees. Several gardens sprawled across the grounds, housing all kinds of shrubs, water fountains, and statues carved to represent angelic beings, humans, and animals. We neared the door, and at eye level, I saw the words *Forti Radici* inscribed on the stone wall.

"I'll leave you here until it's time to go back," my guide said.

"Wait, you can't!" I panicked. "I don't know how to function in this form."

"Don't fret. You'll know what to do. Besides, nobody can see or hear you."

"That's not necessarily good, is it?"

"Listen, all you have to do is find yourself." He signaled to the entrance.

"Find myself?" I sputtered. "What does that mean?"

"Trust your instincts. Don't waste time. I'll come back for you."

"Wait, you haven't told me your name."

He vanished with a reassuring smile. Who was he? Why did I feel I somehow knew him?

I turned to the door, a more imminent problem pressing upon me: I would be stuck in this space until I fulfilled my purpose, trapped with the daunting warning that I must hurry if I wished to return safely to my mortal body.

I reached for the brass doorknob, marveling at its beauty. When my hand went right through it and into the house, I smiled. My spirit wasn't bound by mortal limitations. It all made sense now. I passed through the wooden door into the foyer.

Sunlight spilled through the high windows, sending a golden glow across the marble floors. Straight ahead, the staircase, its thick banister defined by rich tones, led up to a second-story landing that split in two directions. No less impressive was the artwork displayed on the walls and stunning hand-painted images on the ceiling. When had I seen all this?

"Don't waste time," the warning echoed in my head.

I floated down a lengthy corridor, then passed through a set of double doors with intricately carved flowers. A spacious kitchen with a massive table at its center welcomed me. My gaze jumped from the fireplace to the range cooker to the window, where, outside the glass, a young woman in a long red dress moved briskly toward the back door. Her waist-length honey-blonde hair complemented her delicate facial features. Forgetting I was invisible, I momentarily panicked as she entered.

Oblivious to my presence, she moved to a chair, and my mouth dropped. She looked exactly like me. Except for the longer length and style of her hair, we were identical—just like the picture Mrs. White had shown me of my supposed mother.

While I grappled with this reality, my curiosity drew me close as she extracted a letter from her pocket. Her face lit up as she unfolded it.

April 2, 1915
My dearest Florence,

I'm happy to inform you that an opportunity to come home sooner than expected has presented itself. I hope to see you in a matter of days.

I'm the luckiest man alive to be your father, and I can't wait to see your beautiful smile again. I trust that Mrs. Allerton is taking excellent care of you as always.

Love,
Your father, General Marcus Contini

PS. Lieutenant General Alexander Sterling will accompany me. Please have Mrs. Allerton fix one of the upper rooms for him.

Was I dreaming? No. I had never felt more alive—my senses never more sharp, clear, or alert. The daughter of General Marcus Contini wasn't separated from him at birth, and, more so, he'd lived to raise her. A slight shimmer at her wrist caught my eye. I glanced at my intangible bracelet. The same. Only hers wasn't worn with time.

"*All you have to do is find yourself.*" The guide's instructions hit me like light piercing through darkness.

Piece by piece, the puzzle of our forgotten past came together. It didn't matter whether it was her past or mine; we were one and the same. It hadn't been my mother in the picture. It was me. How or why, I didn't know. But somehow, I'd lived before.

As she rose from the chair, a magnetic force pulled me to her, and my spirit flowed into her body. Suddenly, our minds became one and the veil clouding my memories fell away, allowing me to remember my life twenty-two years prior.

CHAPTER 14
~ BACK IN TIME ~

BREAMORE, THE NEW FOREST, ENGLAND, 1915

The news that Father would soon be home infused me with a vitality I almost forgot existed. Amid the suffering of the world, it was only natural to be on edge—especially when my father, General Marcus Contini, led the British army.

Britain entered the Great War in August of last year, honoring its treaty to protect Belgium after Germany marched into its territory. Soon after, my father insisted I come home from India, where I'd spent several months teaching children English and art. I adored and missed my students dearly. Their goodness and zeal for life brought light to a darkening world. And just now, Germany had launched a new, savage means of warfare directed at killing civilians. Two German zeppelins had dropped bombs on the eastern coast of England, spreading horror throughout the peaceful region. And with Britain's recent announcement of a blockade of the German ports, the chaos reached the point of no return.

Father spent most of his days away from home, leaving me under the care of the housekeeper, Mary Allerton, in the New Forest. For thousands of years, the forest had witnessed births, extinctions, invasions, wars, royalty, ghosts, witches, and snake catchers. But mostly, it remained a haven from the large-scale destruction going on in the world, and our family enjoyed it for generations.

In 1894, my mother passed away giving birth to me and my twin brother, Lucca. Lucca and I had been like two sides of a coin. More than a brother, he was my best friend, protector, and guiding light. Heart-wrenchingly, just two years ago, the enemy ambushed his troop and killed him. His premature departure left me feeling lost, like a kite without a string. I couldn't even look at myself in the mirror without seeing Lucca's reflection—thin face, brown eyes, and bright smile.

Mrs. Allerton had been my guardian angel during those dark days. Without her love, my despair would have consumed me. Yet life went on, and I learned to move on, too, never forgetting but always hoping for a better future.

I caught sight of Mrs. Allerton through the library window, her white hair, as always, pulled into a bun, her spectacles sparkling in the sunlight. She expressed herself with vigorous gestures as she instructed the gardener, Ames Leroy—a short French fellow who had worked for our family since I could remember. He had often threatened to leave Forti Radici because of Mrs. Allerton's obsessive ideas about how he should do his job, arguing that because the garden was his *chef d'oeuvre*, he should make the decisions regarding the grounds. "*Maybe they fight because they like each other*," Lucca once suggested.

Exiting through the side door, I felt the warmth of the spring day and a sense that my immediate future would be exhilarating.

"You should trim it back, thin it out," Mrs. Allerton insisted, referring to the hydrangea vines that climbed the side of the manor.

"They provide shade and beauty to the walls. I'm not going to cut them down. It took years to grow them!" Mr. Leroy snapped, his indignation making his accent heavier than usual.

"All they do is house spiders," she snapped back.

"Don't worry about that. I'll treat them for crawlers," he said.

"For goodness' sake, Mr. Leroy. Trim them back!" Mrs. Allerton demanded, placing her hands on her hips in irritation.

"*Femme folles!*" he muttered in French.

I cleared my throat to announce my presence. Mrs. Allerton waved her hand as if saying, "Not now," and their quarrel continued.

"My father is coming home!" I exclaimed over their voices.

Mr. Leroy turned, forcing Mrs. Allerton to do likewise. "Mademoiselle." He doffed his cap, briefly showing his gray hair. "That's good news."

"Indeed, it is. This letter came in the morning post."

Mrs. Allerton took it from me and scanned it hastily. "Oh my, it's true. General Contini is coming home." Her voice filled with delight. "We must prepare for his arrival."

Mr. Leroy sought the chance to get the pruners away from the vines. "I'll start working on the front gardens. Good day." He hurried away before Mrs. Allerton could object.

I retrieved the letter from Mrs. Allerton and retraced my steps.

She hustled to catch up. "Florence, wait! Did he say he's bringing company?"

"Some lieutenant or other." My father routinely traveled with groups of soldiers, and I often wished I could have him to myself for a bit. Instead, he was sure to spend his visit holed up, poring over maps and talking strategy with his men.

"Let me see the letter again," she asked breathlessly. "Yes, oh, yes. Lieutenant General Sterling. I've heard of him. Isn't he second in command?"

I shrugged. "Doesn't make any difference to me. One more dusty comrade coming our way."

"We must air out and dust the rooms," she started, then rehearsed a long list of unnecessary chores. She took pride in caring for the manor. The place would be cleaned from top to bottom, spotless in no time.

I couldn't help but say, "Don't you think you are exaggerating a little?"

"Nonsense! There is much to do." Her walk almost turned into a trot.

From the garden, I could see two military vehicles on the horizon. *Father is home.* I raced across the property, but the road seemed so far away. I couldn't wait to be in the security of his company, to hear his voice. I had missed him so much. I entered the field, and my father spotted me. The truck slowed, and he jumped out, a soldier following behind.

Then, suddenly, I was in his embrace, and it felt like *I* had come home. I closed my eyes and reveled in the scent of tobacco and fresh air that accompanied him; in the strong, steady beat of his heart beneath my ear; and in the happy rumble of his laughter.

"Father, I have missed you so much."

"My precious daughter. I'm so happy to see you." He squeezed me tightly against his chest.

"I can't believe you are home." I kissed his cheek, grateful he was the same—his limbs still attached. Even his brown mustache remained intact, making his face look as square and stern as always. In the army, men knew him for his strict leadership and discipline, but even more so for his distinct mustache.

"It's wonderful to be back." Longing laced his voice, his gaze going to the manor in the distance. "Hopefully, I can stay for a while."

The soldier who had trailed behind him reached us.

"Florence, this is Lieutenant General Alexander Sterling," Father introduced.

In the peacefulness of the green field under the day's diffused light, I saw Alexander Sterling for the first time. *This is Lieutenant General Sterling?* The shocking difference between what I had imagined and his appearance made me freeze. He was young, very young. Dressed in a navy uniform, pockets full of honorary decorations, General Sterling stood over six feet tall. His broad shoulders and thin hips accentuated his perfect posture. His blue eyes complemented his fair skin and dark hair.

Our gazes connected, and I found myself lost in a whirl of physical and emotional attraction. I had never seen a man so—I tried to avoid the word, but it came all the same—good-looking.

"Alexander, my daughter, Florence."

"My lady, it is a pleasure to meet you." The lieutenant held my hand longer than needed, his eyes sweeping over me as thoroughly as he might survey an enemy threshold. I pulled my hand away, hoping to conceal that my heartbeat struggled to slow down, and it had little to do with my run across the field.

"Welcome to Forti Radici, Lieutenant," I said.

As we headed to the manor, Father offered me his arm and spoke about his journey. Occasionally, I nodded to signal my attention, but Lieutenant Sterling had stolen my focus. I did my best not to look at him but failed miserably. And I soon realized he was aware of, and enjoyed, my scrutiny. My gaze fell to the wild grass, my cheeks flushed with embarrassment.

Being the child of General Marcus Contini had its implications. Men gravitated to me not because of my intelligence or looks but because of my father's rank. To protect my name and weed out the riffraff who chased money and prestige, I remained constantly alert. Would I ever find someone who loved me for who I was? Since my hopes were at their lowest point, I told myself to reign in the attraction and tread lightly with the new soldier.

"Mrs. Allerton, always so efficient," my father observed as we entered the garden. "Although this is totally unnecessary." Lowering his voice, he added, "I forget how many times I've told her as much."

The staff formed a line near the entrance. The military trucks were already parked, and the soldiers waited close by, stretching their legs after the long ride.

Father first greeted Mrs. Allerton, then Mr. Leroy, then Mr. Lewis, the chauffeur, followed by the rest of the staff, including Mr. Grant, the cook, and Lucy, his assistant. In turn, Father introduced the group of twenty soldiers.

"Oh, General Sterling," said Mrs. Allerton, sending a knowing look my way. "It's a pleasure to meet you."

"The pleasure is all mine, ma'am."

"You are awfully young to be a lieutenant general," she noted.

"I'll take that as a compliment." His face lit up with the most breathtaking smile I had ever seen.

I had no desire to be a fool, but something about him, something I hadn't encountered with other men, drew me to him. I had to take control. *Stop looking at him!*

"I'm sure your wife is quite proud of your career," Mrs. Allerton continued to obtain information—on my behalf, I feared. Knowing of my disappointment with the opposite sex, she had it taken upon herself to find me a suitable match. And if she decided the lieutenant met the requirements, she would do everything she could to get us together.

Did he have a wife? I didn't like the idea.

"My parents are happy for me. I'm not married . . . yet."

"Engaged, then?" Mrs. Allerton pressed.

"No, not engaged either." He glanced at me.

"How is that possible?" Mrs. Allerton sounded alarmed about his misfortune, but I knew she rejoiced inwardly.

"Mrs. Allerton," my father said, his interruption a relief. "My men could use a drink."

"Of course, General." Mrs. Allerton guided the company inside.

Tucking me under his arm, Father lingered outside to converse with Mr. Lewis about Silver—a 1910 Rolls-Royce Silver Ghost both men were in love with. Unlike other automobiles on the road, which looked like horseless carriages, the Silver Ghost represented breakthrough technology. Equipped with a six-cylinder engine, three-speed manual gearbox, and rear-wheel drum brakes, it could reach over twenty miles per hour on a good road, making it the most luxurious car ever.

"We'll have to take it for a ride tomorrow," Father told Mr. Lewis.

"Yes, sir, first thing in the morning."

Determined to forget about the lieutenant's magnetism before the call to dinner, I plopped onto my four-poster bed with my favorite novel, *Jane Eyre*. I soon lost myself in Thornfield Hall, a rather neglected place with a haunting, mysterious owner, but the distraction didn't last. I put the book down and listened to the chattering outside my door. Since only I stayed in this wing, it was odd. Then, Father's request to prepare an upper room for the lieutenant hit me like a splash of cold water in the face. Surely he'd stay on the opposite side, away from me.

I burst into the corridor and saw Mrs. Allerton near Lucca's bedroom, giving instructions to Sarah, a woman who knew how to get things done. They grew silent when they saw me. Mr. Lewis emerged from the top landing carrying a pair of military bags. Instead of turning right, he approached the housekeeper and placed the luggage near her feet. "Anything else?" he asked.

"That'll be all. Thank you, Mr. Lewis," Mrs. Allerton responded.

"What's going on?" I narrowed my eyes at her.

"Nothing, dear." The studied calm in her voice belied her.

"Why are these bags here?"

"What?" Mrs. Allerton rubbed her hands nervously.

I kicked one of the green sacks. "Whose are these?"

"They are mine." Of course, it had to be *him*. His voice came loud and clear as he passed Mr. Lewis.

I gave Mrs. Allerton a piercing stare. She was a traitor, and she knew it. Lucca's bedroom had become a shrine to his memory, a place I could remember him through his belongings and lingering smell. Someone invading his privacy in this manner shocked me. Neither could I have anticipated how wrong it felt.

"Why are they in this wing?" I turned to face the lieutenant general, feeling my temper rise.

"Your father said I should stay in this room," he responded, his tone serene but determined.

"That's General Contini to you, Lieutenant," I said sternly. "And there must be a mistake. My brother's bedroom is off-limits."

"I'll go speak to the general." Mrs. Allerton took the easiest way out. The whole thing was ridiculous. She was well aware that there were plenty of nice rooms available.

"Yes, you go do that!" I fumed.

Mrs. Allerton moved away with urgency. Sarah seized the chance to avoid the line of fire and followed her downstairs.

The lieutenant gave me a crooked smile. "Why the unnecessary fuss, miss? It's just a room."

"It's not just a room, and you can't stay in it!"

He inched closer and held my gaze. "Would you rather I stay in yours?"

His audacity rendered me speechless. Surely, plenty of girls would have answered yes, but not me. Regrouping, I mocked, "Wouldn't you like that?"

"I'll take that as a no." With a laugh, he picked up the bags. "Well, lady, orders are orders, and I wouldn't dare to disobey *General* Contini's. So, if you'll excuse me." He walked into Lucca's room. I was about to follow and throw him out, but he swiftly shut the door and secured the lock.

His arrogance unnerved me. He had to be removed from the quarters at once. I stormed down the stairs and stomped into my father's office.

"Why?"

"Sit down, Florence. Please." Father pointed to a chair. He had expected my reaction.

"Do you know how much this hurts? How could you?"

"Before you jump to conclusions, let me explain."

I sat down with a groan.

Father pulled up a chair next to mine. "When your brother passed away, part of me died with him. Besides losing your mother, losing Lucca was the hardest thing I ever endured. I see people die all the time, Florence. I see families grieving their dead almost daily. But it wasn't until I lost my son that I understood."

"Father, I know." His words painfully reminded me of my feelings.

"General Sterling came under my command soon after we lost Lucca. He is an amazing man. I can't tell you how much his support and help have comforted me."

"He can never replace Lucca."

"Of course not. No one could ever take your brother's place. But that doesn't mean others can't be as good as Lucca." Seeing the stubbornness in my countenance, he pleaded—something he wasn't accustomed to—but a great general knew which weapons to utilize. "Florence, listen to me."

I sighed and averted my eyes but listened.

"General Sterling has saved my life more than once during combat. He even took a bullet for me. When I saw him fall to the ground, bathed in blood, the first thing that crossed my mind was that he was someone's son, someone who would grieve his loss as much as I have grieved Lucca's. I still don't understand how he survived. The bullet barely missed his heart. But what I know with certainty is that without his loyalty, I would be buried next to your brother. I owe Lieutenant Sterling my life. He is not afraid to die for others. Do you know how few men are like that? How few are born fearless? That's one of the reasons he is the youngest soldier to have achieved the rank of lieutenant general in this country."

As my father spoke, my frustration turned into gratitude to have him here, alive. "I'm terrified you won't return one of these days. Why haven't you told me this before?"

Father ran his fingers through his mustache, something he did when nervous. "I couldn't. It would have only made you restless when I was gone."

"I'm already restless. I hardly sleep anymore. Will this nightmare ever end?"

"Sooner or later. But for now, we must enjoy the time we have together."

"I still don't understand why he has to stay in Lucca's room." I rested my head on his shoulder.

"Apart from yours, your brother's room is the nicest in the manor. You know that." He was ahead of the discussion again. The room was a hidden paradise, with luxurious furniture resting on thick Arabian rugs, a fireplace, a powder room, a sitting area, and the best view of the gardens.

"Yes, but the lieutenant probably won't know the difference." His arrogance was a fresh wound to my ego.

"I'm sure he would've been happy anywhere in the house, even in the stables, but I wouldn't be happy with that. He deserves the best."

I was smart enough to know I'd lost this battle. Still, listening to Father's feelings, and agreeing to the accommodations, didn't mean I'd abide the lieutenant's brashness. "Well then. I won't say another word about it."

"Thank you, Florence." My father helped me to my feet and enveloped me in his arms.

I pursed my lips, but the words still came out. "It doesn't mean I like it. I would gladly give him one of the stalls in the stable."

Father laughed.

CHAPTER 15
~ FALLING IN LOVE ~

I'd decided to avoid the undesirable company at all costs. I was in no mood to deal with the lieutenant. I'd spent the night tossing and turning, and Mrs. Allerton's insistence that I get out of bed at a "decent time," as she called it, didn't help matters. Hence, I planned to grab a bite and leave quickly.

I descended the staircase, and the lieutenant's comments from the previous night replayed in my mind. After dinner, referring to his actions to save my father, I'd said, "Surely, any soldier would've done the same," to bring him down from his pedestal. His disregard for my feelings about Lucca's bedroom continued to bother me, along with the determinedness to quell my attraction to someone whose manner didn't match his appearance. And as for my brother's room, I'd already made a list of what I would do to disinfect it once the lieutenant left, to restore it to its former sanctity.

"For your father, I'm sure they would have, but for you . . ." he'd taunted me.

"For me, I assure you, Lieutenant," I'd answered, "any soldier would give his life without a second thought."

I smiled thinking about my comeback, but that smile vanished as soon as I entered the breakfast room. The only person there was the one

I'd hoped to avoid. However, if I retreated, he would enjoy it too much. I'd bite the bullet.

Noticing the food hadn't arrived, I took the farthest seat from him.

"Good morning, Miss Contini."

"There is nothing good about it," I grumbled.

"Well, it's good to see me, isn't it?"

"Are you off your trolley, or is it a side effect of the war?" He turned a shade that almost made me laugh at my own words, but I kept a straight face.

"I won't take your rudeness personally. I understand you're upset because you had to rise early. I heard you whining about it to Mrs. Allerton this morning," he said matter-of-factly.

A wave of embarrassment washed over me. I could not believe he had heard. "I didn't whine, Lieutenant."

"It's Lieutenant General to you, miss. Or, if you prefer, General."

"I'll keep that in mind, *Lieutenant*." I smiled with false sweetness.

He smiled back and attacked again. "Well, if it wasn't whining, what do I call the irritating sounds I heard?"

"Excuse my tardiness. I'm afraid I got carried away chatting with the group in the dining room." Father entered with Sarah and another maid on his heels. "It's good to see you two conversing."

I bit my tongue. My reply to the lieutenant would have to wait.

"Your daughter is a delight." He stood as Father took his seat.

"We agree on that much." Father glanced at me, at the lieutenant, and then back at me. He knew my distance from his favorite soldier was not coincidental. "Alexander, come sit closer."

The lieutenant obliged, moving to sit across from me.

I wanted to leave, but hunger constrained me to stay.

Sarah spread platters of fruit, toast, and cold cuts across the table. I passed on the meat; it made me sick in the morning. The lieutenant took two pieces, some fruit, and a piece of toast slathered in peach marmalade. How could he eat so much?

"Mm, the marmalade is excellent," he commented.

I was flattered but kept it to myself. I helped Mr. Grant make two batches just last week.

"How did you two sleep last night?" Father asked. I didn't like the words "you two" and "sleep" in the same sentence.

"Excellent, thank you, sir."

"Just fine," I responded.

"How about you, sir?" the lieutenant asked.

"Better than I have in a long time. Nothing beats a comfortable bed."

"I agree, sir. The bed in my quarters is wonderful."

"Sure it is. Better than you've ever had," I said under my breath.

"I'm glad you find it to your liking." Father turned to Sarah. "Is there any porridge today?"

"Yes, sir."

Father moved swiftly to the serving table. "I must have some."

I reached for a piece of toast, and the lieutenant grabbed my hand.

"I heard what you said," he whispered.

"So you did." I tried to free my hand, but he gripped it firmly.

"And you are right."

Was he seriously saying I was correct on something?

"While the bed is the best I ever had, surely yours is better. I should try it sometime." He winked and let go of my hand.

I swallowed the lump that formed in my throat. "Of course, when I throw it out, you are welcome to have it, but I wouldn't hold my breath."

"Smells great," observed Father, sniffing the porridge as he returned to his seat.

"I'll have some myself." The lieutenant left and returned with a large portion.

"I'm glad you have a good appetite today, Alexander," Father noted. "I've never seen you eat so well."

"I know. I usually don't eat or sleep much. It must be the fresh air at Forti Radici." He threw a suggestive look at me. "Plus, I went for a long run early this morning."

"Oh yes, that would do it." Father nodded approvingly.

I was about to excuse myself when the conversation turned serious, as did the lieutenant. I hadn't seen this side of him, and without realizing it, I remained rooted to my chair. We discussed many topics, from politics to religion to warfare. His calm voice and clear mind took me aback, and time passed with unexpected swiftness. Nevertheless, when Father stood to leave, I beat him to it. I wouldn't be left alone with the unpredictable lieutenant.

The afternoon found me feeling restless. My emotional side urged me to stay in seclusion. My rational side urged me to get over it. "This is ridiculous," I told myself. "I'm hiding in my own house. Afraid of what? Myself?" I couldn't deny I liked the lieutenant I had seen at breakfast, but not enough to lower my guard. He might mean well, but not having dealt with a personality like his, I didn't know how to handle it. Logic eventually won out, and I changed into my riding clothes.

Stepping into the corridor, I gasped. The lieutenant stood outside Lucca's room, facing my direction, a shoulder against the wall. Retreat was not possible—not if I wanted to maintain my pride. He sported a white, long-sleeved shirt buttoned halfway up. Why did this insufferable man have to be so handsome? Now, more than ever, I could see why women swooned on a regular basis. And he certainly had the air of one accustomed to charming his way to anything he wanted. Too bad for him; I firmly believed that while charm struck the sight, merit won the soul. I put on my mask of indifference and braced for combat.

"Are you holding the wall in place, Lieutenant?" I mocked, doing my best not to look at his unbuttoned shirt.

"Actually, I was waiting for you."

"Seriously?" I scoffed.

"See this?" He extended his hand, palm open.

"A button?" I stared at it blankly.

"It fell off my shirt." He pointed to the empty spot. "Can you sew it on for me?"

His request seemed out of place when we were not even friends. Evidently, he just wanted to get under my skin. I rallied my forces. "Why don't you sew it on yourself? Surely, you are capable of that much."

"You don't know how to sew," he challenged with a chuckle.

"Of course, I do, but it doesn't mean I'll mend your clothes."

"Nah. If you knew how to sew, you would be happy to help me out."

"Definitely off the trolley . . ." I muttered, answering my question from this morning.

With surprising smoothness, he moved in front of me, forcing me into the wall. "No, I'm not off my trolley, Miss Contini, nor is it a result of the war. I assure you, I'm very intelligent."

"That's debatable, Lieutenant."

"Stop calling me lieutenant." He placed his hands on the wall on either side of me. I was trapped.

"Not a chance." I gave him a challenging smile.

He lowered his head to whisper in my ear. "I shall make you, then."

"I'd like to see you try, Lieutenant." I felt the warmth of his body against mine, my heart racing with new, unknown emotions.

When Sarah appeared at the top of the stairs, he stepped back, and I slipped out of his reach.

Shocked by his actions, I exited the house. A gentle breeze whispered across the grounds, refreshing my desire for an escape. I had to stop thinking about the man.

"Where are you going?" Mrs. Allerton called, emerging from the damask rose garden, carrying a basket overflowing with pink blooms.

"For a ride on Sunny." I bent to sniff the roses. "Oh, they smell heavenly, and they are so beautiful."

"You are going for a ride this late in the afternoon? And alone?" Mrs. Allerton's eyebrows rose.

"I won't be gone long."

"You should have invited General Sterling along."

"That's an idea." *As soon as pigs fly.*

"There is still time," she insisted. "I don't think he's doing much today."

Other than pestering me. "Perhaps another time."

"Don't go too far." Mrs. Allerton produced an expression of disapproval.

"I won't." I kissed her cheek and marched to the stable.

Sunny's glassy eyes looked at me from behind the stall, her brown coat glistening after her morning bath. Father called her a palfrey horse —lightweight and suitable for riding long distances.

"Are you ready for some exercise?" I saddled her, then rubbed her neck. She neighed in contentment. "Right, then. Let's go."

While Sunny wove through the trees with leisure, I relished the fresh air, the rustling of leaves in the trees, and the scurrying of animals in the underbrush. I glanced up as a large bird shrieked from above. "Would you look at that—a hen harrier," I said to Sunny as if she cared. Landing on a branch, the brown-and-white bird of prey watched me as if I trespassed on her territory. I kept Sunny moving steadily so as not to disturb the feathery creature. Another cry. She wasn't alone. A gray harrier with black wingtips perched two branches above her. "Oh, they must be a couple." If I recalled correctly, the gray one was the male, the brown the female.

Sunny pushed on, and the hen harriers were soon left behind to enjoy their tranquility. We passed a thicket of birch trees, and she made a few snorting sounds, then halted, her ears stiffening.

"What is it, girl?" I took in our surroundings but could see nothing amiss.

She snorted again and pawed at the forest floor as if alerting me to danger.

"It's all right." I patted her neck, but I knew the forest could be treacherous and concealing—a perfect ally to the unwanted. The thought filled me with chills, but I ignored them. I had to stay focused to exit the trees safely.

"Come on, girl. We mustn't linger."

Sunny moved on, and my awareness heightened, my eyes scanning farther than usual, my ears picking up the faintest of sounds. Up ahead, a clearing formed. I sighed in relief, my mind already mapping a different return route. I dismounted to give Sunny a break, and she headed straight to the flowing brook. I crouched beside her, watching her nostrils flare as she eagerly drank the cool water.

An earsplitting blast shook the quiet clearing, flocks of birds scattering from the treetops into the air. Sunny bolted, and I fell into the stream with a muffled cry. The icy water stole my breath, and I looked around, disconcerted, until I saw a figure emerge from the trees.

"I'm so sorry. I didn't realize you were here." Lieutenant Sterling extended a hand, but I ignored it, still stunned by the ringing in my ears and the frigid water. He came into the brook and lifted me into his arms. "Are you hurt?"

I shuddered. "No."

"You are freezing. We must get you back to the house."

The warmth of his body, and the softness of his voice invited me to stay in his embrace. But it dawned on me that he must be the reason Sunny fled and I was chilled to the bone, and the enchantment was broken.

"Put me down, please," I asked, and he did. "You fired that shot, didn't you?"

His look of guilt told all.

"What the devil were you doing?" I hugged myself, trying to contain the shivers.

"Hunting." I sensed a double meaning in his words.

I shook my head in disbelief, unsure whether to laugh or cry.

"Seriously, there was a feral boar in those trees." He lied shamelessly.

I glared at his pistol. "That's not a hunting rifle."

"I can hunt with any gun I want."

"You scared my horse away!" It would be a long walk back to the house, especially soaking wet.

"I can give you a ride." He whistled, and within seconds, his horse trotted into view.

"How convenient."

"Come on, let's go. I'll help you up."

"I'm not riding with you."

"Why not? What are you afraid of?" Amusement twinkled in his eyes. "You can ride in front. I promise I'll only hold on to your waist." His proposition galled me. A true gentleman would have offered me the privilege of riding alone.

"Listen, since I'm the daughter of your superior, I think I should ride your horse and you should walk." I smiled sweetly, fearing my manipulation might backfire.

"I'll tell you what," he started, and my hope that he might accept my proposal fled. "You can ride with me, or you can be the one who walks. It's your choice."

"Are you threatening me?"

"No, I'm giving you a choice."

"I'll walk."

"Well then, if that's what you want." He mounted his horse. "Goodbye, my lady."

He vanished into the thickness of the woods as if I mattered less than the feral boar he'd supposedly hunted. I stomped and cried out in rage. How dare he! The arrogant jackanapes! I didn't care if he was the apple of Father's eye. Someone had to put him in his place. Father would hear about this.

My sodden clothing and outrage at the lieutenant's cavalier treatment made for a miserable walk. By the time I finally cleared the forest, my eyes stung with tears of anger, but at the sight of home, I inhaled a calming breath and blinked my eyes dry.

"What happened to you?" a startled Mrs. Allerton asked as I stepped into the kitchen.

Lieutenant Sterling and a few soldiers sat at the table, chatting over their drinks. He grinned smugly at me. Right then and there, my plans changed. He would never know the satisfaction of my humiliation. Resisting the urge to retaliate became easier as a better tactic came to mind.

Mustering what benevolence I could, I answered Mrs. Allerton in a dignified tone. "Nothing. Why?"

"Your horse came back without you, and . . ." She touched my blouse. "You are wet. Your father was just about to send General Sterling to look for you."

I almost laughed. Almost.

The lieutenant stood. "We were worried about you, my lady." His charade was masterful.

"Thank you for your concern, *Lieutenant* Sterling. You are most polite. I just happened to encounter a wild pig in the woods. It scared my horse away. But luckily, I manage to get rid of it without any problems." I thoroughly enjoyed his look of consternation.

"A pig?" Mrs. Allerton repeated alarmingly. She hated the things.

"Well, now that I think about it, it wasn't a pig. It was an ugly, oversized wild boar," I stated with horror.

"Oh, Florence! A wild boar! They can be dangerous," Mrs. Allerton exclaimed. "You shouldn't have gone alone."

"Dangerous indeed, but I stayed at a safe distance." I glanced at the lieutenant. "Thankfully, there was only one of them, and I did enjoy the peaceful walk back to the house."

"You better change," Mrs. Allerton urged, "before you get sick."

"I think I'll be sick after seeing that horrible beast anyway. You should've seen it. It had gigantic, disgusting feet." I would have to offer a prayer of repentance later for speaking ill of the poor animals.

The lieutenant looked down at his feet.

My barb found its target, the taste of victory sweet. I wouldn't have traded a million pounds for the gratification I felt beholding his drowning self-confidence. Barely containing my glee, I continued. "Oh, Mrs. Allerton, its hideous head and big mouth will give me nightmares for years. My father would do well to rid the place of such horrid creatures." I felt Lieutenant Sterling's eyes pierce my back as I left the kitchen.

"You only need to avoid the man for one more night," I told myself. How difficult could it be? The soldiers would leave in the morning. I just had to endure a departing dinner, which, in truth, Father used as an excuse to invite acquaintances to dine with him. Though he did an excellent job hiding it from his comrades, this sentimental man dearly loved his family and friends.

I sat in front of the mirror while Mrs. Allerton parted my long hair into three sections and began pinning and twisting them into a complicated pompadour and psyche-knot style. She finished with an ornately beaded headband that matched my blue dress.

"Thank you." No matter how hard I tried, I couldn't get it right without her help.

"You are welcome." Mrs. Allerton smiled. "Won't you be turning heads tonight! Perhaps one in particular."

I ignored her. I most definitely didn't want to turn the lieutenant's head—unless it was on a platter.

"We must hurry now," she said. "Everyone has arrived already."

I descended the staircase, both hands pressed against my dress, lifting it a few inches above my feet. The last thing I needed was to make a grand entrance rolling down the steps. People stood in the foyer and adjacent rooms, conversing merrily. Among a group of soldiers, Lieutenant Sterling stood near the entrance in his navy uniform. Glad he faced away from me, I slipped through the crowd into the dining room.

A redheaded soldier headed in my direction. I remembered him arriving with Father's company but hadn't seen him since.

"It's a pleasure to meet you, Miss Contini. I am Thomas Frankfort."

"The pleasure is mine, Mr. Frankfort."

"Please, call me Thomas."

"Only if you call me Florence."

"Deal." He smiled. "I'd hoped to meet you earlier, but it's been one meeting or training exercise after another."

"My father keeps a tight schedule even during breaks, doesn't he?"

"Indeed, but I must confess I enjoy moving about the forest while we train with other troops."

"Oh yes. They come and go constantly. It's a great area for training."

"I must also say that you remind me a great deal of your brother." Thomas's sudden observation took me aback.

"You knew Lucca?"

"I spent a few weeks with him in military school. He talked a lot about you. I knew you were not identical twins, but the resemblance is remarkable."

"It's a sad reminder at times."

"I'm sorry. I didn't mean . . ."

"It's all right."

"Frankfort," a soldier called from the refreshment table, "get over here."

"Excuse our manners," Thomas said. "We have been on the road far too long."

"Please, don't worry. Go on."

Thomas bowed slightly and heeded the call.

I turned to see my father conversing with an older couple near the dining table, the lady's curvaceous figure and dark hair unmistakable. The husband's stunning slenderness and stern eyes were also hard to miss. Mr. and Mrs. Veils owned a banking firm in London. Their wealth, coupled with the many loans they extended throughout the region, made them quite famous and, at times, a bit insufferable. They weren't afraid to use their social status to expand their empire. However, Father had known them for some time, and despite their shortcomings, had grown fond of them. "*He who is without sin, let him first cast a stone,*" he reminded me whenever I was inclined to criticize.

"Remember my daughter, Florence?" Father said as I approached.

"Of course. The most beautiful girl in the New Forest," Mr. Veils complimented from under his thick black mustache.

"Apart from our Nelly, that is." Mrs. Veils chuckled.

"Nice to see you again," I said. "Regrettably, I don't think I've ever met Nelly."

"You haven't?" Mrs. Veils looked horrified at the idea.

"She is here tonight." Mr. Veils scanned the crowd. "There she is! That's our Nelly!" He pointed to a young woman across the room. She had inherited her mother's figure, and her blonde hair was cut short in the scandalous new style, though I rather liked the rapidly changing fashion. And it didn't appear to bother her partner. Nelly conversed intimately with none other than Lieutenant Sterling.

"We hoped General Sterling would be here tonight to meet our Nelly." Mrs. Veils was clearly pleased. "As we all know, he is the most coveted bachelor in England."

"He is a remarkable man," Father said. "Very fortunate will be the girl who wins his heart."

"Fortunate indeed." The Veils seemed oblivious to my not-so-subtle mocking tone. I slipped away to peek at the place cards on the table. Mrs. Allerton had thoughtfully assigned me a seat by the lieutenant. I would rectify that right now. As he was so besotted with Nelly, he deserved to sit next to her. While pretending to admire the setting, I delightedly switched a few of the cards. However, my delight faded when I thought of Mrs. Allerton. She would be dumbfounded by the new arrangement, and I would hear from her later. No matter. It was worth it.

As if summoned by my mischief, Mrs. Allerton bustled into the room and invited the guests to take their seats, Father settling at the head of the table. I sat to his right and noticed Thomas's surprised expression as he took the seat beside me. Yes, I made sure that was the case. Lieutenant Sterling now sat directly across from me, with Nelly happily by his side, followed by her parents.

As the evening wore on, I found Thomas a pleasant companion as he talked about Lucca and their shared military experiences. On the other hand, the lieutenant was immersed in his newfound entertainment— Miss Veils, who spoke and laughed as if to draw attention to her claim on him.

When the last course arrived, I was fed up with their apparent glee and angry with myself for even noticing. To make things worse, Father proposed a toast in honor of the lieutenant, a toast filled with praise and gratitude to the most courageous soldier General Contini had ever known.

I thought the lieutenant incapable of feeling timidity, but he proved me wrong when his face colored. What wasn't clear was whether the speech or Nelly's boisterous clapping had embarrassed him. When he got to his feet to raise his glass, I smiled inwardly at the sheen of nervous perspiration on his forehead. So, indeed, he was less confident than he pretended to be.

Mrs. Allerton's timely invitation to the library, where several game tables awaited, relieved the lieutenant but not me. I'd hoped to enjoy his discomfort a little longer.

"Let's go play some games," Thomas encouraged.

His enthusiasm reminded me too much of Lucca, and I felt a deep throb of loneliness. Ever since he passed away, I'd felt a little hollow inside, as if I'd lost part of my soul. "If you don't mind, I'll pass. I'm ready to call it a night."

"Are you sure? It'll be fun."

"I'm sorry."

"Will I see you tomorrow, before I leave?"

"I'll be in the garden after breakfast."

We exited the dining room.

"I shall look for you, then. Good night, Florence."

"Good night, Thomas."

He veered to the library, and I took a detour through the kitchen to the gardens. I longed for time to ponder the last hours—Thomas's friendship with Lucca, what I learned about my brother's soldier life, and Lieutenant Sterling's interest in Nelly. Why were my emotions in such disarray?

The crescent moon brought with it a dense obscurity to the night. I came into the rose garden, refreshed by the smell of the advanced spring after a long winter.

"It could be dangerous for a young lady to be out here alone." Lieutenant Sterling stood before me.

I started at his sudden appearance.

"Forgive me. I didn't mean to frighten you."

"I find that difficult to believe after our encounter in the forest. Besides, instead of worrying about me, you should get back to your new devotee." I moved toward the house.

He intercepted me under the illuminated gallery. His blue eyes sparkled as the light reached them, and my heart raced.

What on earth was wrong with me this evening? With a concerted effort, I said, "Lieutenant, you are tiresome and have a bad habit of cornering girls."

He stepped closer. "You are the first one to complain."

"Perhaps I should slap you instead."

"I wouldn't try it if I were you." He caressed my face with the back of his hand.

His touch sent my heart into a frenzy. I knew I should pull away, but with my odd mood, I allowed it.

"Your father told me many things about you."

"Surely you are disappointed, then."

"On the contrary. I'm amazed."

"Amazed at what?"

"He said you were beautiful, but you are more than that." His voice quivered, and, for the first time, his gaze looked past me into the darkness. "You captured my soul the very first time I saw you. You have bewitched me."

"You must read too many romance novels," I mocked. After the way he conducted himself with Nelly, how could he feel anything for me? I tried to leave, but he pulled me into his arms.

"I don't read romance novels. I just know the way I feel about you. Now, I would like to know what you've done to possess me so completely. I'm in love with you, and I don't know how to express it any other way than—" It took a moment for the absurdity of his statement to sink in as his lips met mine with an unforgettable desperate passion.

A sweet fire coursed through me, and I forgot my anger and sorrow—everything that seemed wrong and broken in my life. His closeness, his taste, overpowered me, and I couldn't get enough of him. Yet, somewhere along the way, my pride resurfaced, and I shoved him away. My escape was swift. My feelings for him were novel, something I'd never experienced with another man. He had the power to capture me, and that was a frightful thought.

The night would prove to be my enemy as sleep evaded me, my thoughts tossed about by his confession. Could it be? My desires lingered in his unforgettable kiss, my fears trapped in the notion that when morning came, he would be gone

CHAPTER 16
~ THE BALL ~

Time grew cruel, tormenting me with memories of Lieutenant Sterling, leaving me yearning for his presence. And I now had double the reason for sleepless nights; as the war raged on, my father's and Lieutenant Sterling's safety weighed on my mind. My only consolation lay in Father's affection for his protégé, but Father wasn't a god. He could not guarantee his own safety, much less that of the men under him.

In the meantime, I paid close attention to what Father wrote home about. He mentioned the lieutenant often, or perhaps I noticed it more. Bit by bit, I gathered a fair amount of intelligence on the young soldier's whereabouts. He spent most of his time in his flat in London, close to his military post, or at home in Landford—a town less than twenty miles away as the crow flew. It would be easy to make an excuse to visit a shop in Landford or a friend in London and maybe cross paths with him. But that would be tantamount to admitting my capitulation, and I wasn't sure I could define the true state of my feelings. Perhaps, I tried too hard to keep these new powerful emotions at bay. I knew only that my world had tilted on its axis the night of the kiss, and the only hope of regaining my equilibrium lay in seeing the lieutenant again.

With the arrival of August came a renewal within the country of optimism amid the harshness of the war. Many customary events were encouraged and kept, among them the Annual Summer Army Ball, held this year at the castle of the Countess of Brockenhurst in the heart of the New Forest. At last, I would see the face that haunted my dreams and filled my waking hours. I was elated and terrified.

The sun descended behind the trees, painting the horizon with streaks of bright orange. And there, among branches heavy with leaves, the towers of Brockenhurst Castle rose into heaven. I loved this place. With its stone walls, circular medieval towers, and exquisite gardens, it never failed to take my breath away. The Silver Ghost slowed as it entered the castle's grounds, as if in reverence. And soon it became clear we weren't the only ones to arrive early.

"Up there," Father instructed Mr. Lewis, pointing to a vacant spot near the entrance. "Make haste before someone takes it."

"Yes, sir." Mr. Lewis depressed the gas, and the car jerked forward.

Silver nabbed the coveted parking space, and before we'd completely stopped, I jumped out, eager to escape the heat inside the car. It had been a miserable, long, bumpy ride.

"Florence!" The Countess of Brockenhurst's daughter, Catherine, rushed to us.

"Catherine! It's so good to see you again." I threw my arms around her. "You look wonderful!"

A petite girl with long dark hair and green eyes, Catherine looked radiant, as always. As children, we'd spent many summers together at Brockenhurst or Forti Radici. Sadly, growing up had a way of distancing friends.

Mr. Lewis unloaded our luggage onto the steps and left to find a place for Silver somewhere on the grounds. Unnecessarily fearing the loss of our belongings, Mrs. Allerton guarded the bags like a sentinel.

"Samuel! George!" called Catherine.

Two young fellows who'd been admiring the black car up ahead, turned to look at us.

Catherine waved them over. "These are my younger cousins. Do you remember them?"

"Younger?" the shorter of the two questioned. "Only by four puny years."

"Yeah, that's right. Catherine talks about us as if we were babies," his brother added.

I studied their faces, struggling to recall them. "I'm afraid I don't."

"That's all right. I don't remember you either. I'm George," said the tall one with dark hair and brown eyes. "And this is my brother, Samuel." Samuel, a bit on the chubby side, was quite good-looking. His mischievous blue eyes looked at me from underneath a mane of blond hair.

"It's a pleasure to meet you both, or to see you again, whichever it is," I said.

"The pleasure is ours," they responded in unison, and placing one arm behind their backs, they bowed as far as possible without falling forward.

I smiled. Their fun, vivacious personalities erased the last traces of irritation brought on by the ride.

"Mrs. Allerton! Mrs. Allerton!" Catherine called. "These boys here will carry your luggage to your quarters."

"We will?" Samuel looked surprised.

"Oh, that's so kind of you!" Mrs. Allerton wasted no time in taking Samuel and George to task. She quickly loaded them up and sent them on their way.

"Well, that's how you get things done around here." Catherine laughed. "Though I have the feeling it's going to cost me. They'll find a way to get even."

It was good to be at Brockenhurst Castle again.

Catherine, Arianna Whitley, and I strolled into the ballroom as people hustled about with great industry arranging flowers, setting up tables, and cleaning the already spotless floors and windows. Thankfully, Mrs. Allerton also involved herself in the preparations, providing me with space to be myself.

"Look at this place. It's so crazy." Arianna, the daughter of the largest arms manufacturer in England, was one of the most talked about girls in the region. With dresses that showed off her curvy silhouette, blonde hair spiraling down to her shoulders, and her unbridled personality, she understood her effect on men and manipulated it to her advantage.

"If I didn't know better, I wouldn't think we are at war," I said.

"Well then, I must tell you," Catherine started, "this extreme cleansing of Brockenhurst is not solely for the ball. Next week, we turn the castle over to the authorities for use as a hospital. Being close to the south ports and railway connections, it's the perfect location."

It saddened me to think of the many who would come here after experiencing the horrors of war. The stories I heard about the battlefield ran through my head. I shuddered at the fear, brutality, and wrenching feelings of powerlessness. I ached for soldiers on all sides of the conflict. However, seeing our people rallying to help them lifted my spirits.

"My family will stay, of course," Catherine further said. "We'll help run the hospital."

"You must keep me informed," I encouraged. "I'd love to come and help. I learned a thing or two about medicine and caring for the sick during my time in India."

"I'm ashamed I know nothing about medicine or its administration. I'm more likely to kill a patient than help them," Arianna lamented. "But I'm very capable of helping with the washing and ironing. I'll call you in a few weeks."

"Thank you." Catherine smiled. "I just hope for the sake of the world, that we find a way to end the war, and soon."

"Me too. But enough of gloominess." Arianna moved to a chair by the wall of windows. "Let's focus on tomorrow night. It will be a night to remember, and we must enjoy the young men while we still have them."

While we still have them. Her remark brought the lieutenant to mind. An opportunity to see him after tonight might not happen again, especially if he was deployed, or heaven forbid, if death . . . No, I could not contemplate that awful possibility.

"Florence, there is something on your mind." Catherine observed. "What is it?"

"I just remembered my father's right-hand man, Lieutenant General Sterling. I wonder if he'll come to the ball."

"Oh, my goodness! Not you too." Ariana threw her head back and laughed.

"Me too? What do you mean?" I wished I hadn't said anything. Mrs. Allerton was right; I would never learn to hold my tongue.

"You fancy him, don't you?" Arianna gave me an amused look.

"Nonsense!"

"Come on, Florence. We can see right through that innocent face of yours," Catherine pressed.

"You wouldn't have asked if you weren't dying to know more about him," Arianna affirmed.

"He is quite intriguing, that's all," I answered uncompromisingly, but my friends weren't fooled. They were more experienced with the opposite sex. Yes, I had fallen for the coveted lieutenant.

They giggled and shook their heads at my apparent misfortune.

"So, you know him?" I asked.

"Of course I do," Arianna said lamentingly. How well did she know him?

"I've heard about him but haven't met him," Catherine informed.

"How do you know him?" I asked Arianna.

"He came to the factory to arrange some deal or other with my father —for the army, you know," Arianna explained quickly, as if wanting to move on from the subject.

"I can't wait to meet him." Catherine smiled at me. "I don't recall you being this fond of anyone before. I'm curious indeed."

"You'll be disappointed," Arianna warned her.

"Why? Surely he is handsome."

"His looks aren't the problem," I mumbled.

"No," Arianna agreed. "He's stunning, all right."

"What, then?" Catherine looked back and forth between us. "Go on, tell me."

"General Sterling has been endowed with an attractive, well-proportioned, and imposing appearance that gives one great viewing pleasure. His black hair, bright-blue eyes, and strong jaw, combined with his towering height presents a real challenge to females." Arianna recited this so adequately I wondered if she had it memorized.

"Oh my!" Catherine burst out laughing. "He doesn't sound real."

She had no idea how true her statement was.

"No, he doesn't," Arianna concurred. "To the end of making the general real, allow me to disclose the bad news."

I sighed. Everything had a downside.

"Please proceed." Catherine folded her arms and leaned against the velvet curtains, clearly enthralled by the tale.

"Perhaps it's a consequence of his looks, but General Sterling suffers from an excess of superiority and overbearing pride, which tends to give one an instant attitude of hostility toward him." Arianna shook her head as if wishing her assessment weren't true. "There, now you know."

Having barely recovered from the fit of laughter, Catherine broke into another.

Now I felt like laughing and crying at the same time.

"Let me add this: if you want to enjoy the ball, look at him from afar. As long as he doesn't speak, he is absolutely adorable." Arianna fiddled with her hair, her gaze wandering about the room. I would have loved to know what thoughts filled her head.

With a few final snorts, Catherine composed herself. "In other words, he holds himself like no girl is good enough. Indeed, I'm intrigued by the dazzling man. I can't wait to meet him."

I drew in a long breath. In one more day, I would face the cause of my turmoil, and I still had to decide on a course of action.

Every nook and cranny of Brockenhurst Castle glowed, the crystal chandeliers across the lengthy ballroom gleaming from multiple shines. And under its splendor, the staff was rarely seen now, some having receded to the grounds to welcome and direct guests, others to prepare the food they would soon serve.

Through one of the spotless windows, I observed the endless line of vehicles headed toward the entrance, headlights flickering like fireflies in the night. Before long, large numbers of guests flowed in wearing attire befitting the opulent occasion. The gentlemen sported tailored suits with crisp white shirts or crisply starched uniforms. In contrast, the ladies wore delicate evening gowns with iridescent and glimmering colors.

"Florence!" An excited voice extracted me from my contemplations.

"Thomas!" He reached for my hand to kiss it, though the gesture was rapidly disappearing from our world. "Oh, you are such a gentleman." Dressed in a brown uniform, he looked quite dashing. "How are you?"

"I'm well, thank you. It's wonderful to see you again."

"Who is your friend?" Catherine joined us, accompanied by Arianna, George, and Samuel.

I introduced Thomas, and from the corner of my eye saw the orchestra conductor raise his baton. A hush of anticipation fell over the ballroom as the first notes of music flowed like a refreshing breeze over the summer night.

"May I have the honor of this dance?" Thomas asked me, and George asked Arianna, who more than happily complied.

While we moved to the soft rhythm of the music, I searched for Lieutenant Sterling. My anxiousness must've been noticeable, for when Arianna and George danced past us, she whispered, "He'll come. Don't worry."

Thankfully, Thomas hadn't heard. I didn't want to explain. When the waltz ended, he asked for a second dance right away, a breach of etiquette, but I acquiesced. However, I soon realized that Thomas held me too close, too tight, and I wished I had said no.

"Why don't you ask Catherine?" I suggested once the song ended, nodding toward her. She stood in the same spot we had left her with Samuel, who grinned at every girl that passed him.

"Maybe Samuel should ask her," Thomas reasoned.

"Samuel is her cousin."

"Oh. I see."

"Go ahead. Ask her."

"If I didn't know you better, I'd think you wanted to dispose of me," Thomas said, leaning uncomfortably close.

True, but I also sincerely worried for my friend. "It's not good for a girl's self-confidence to wait this long to dance, especially when she's the countess's daughter."

"Right, then. We must correct that." Thomas headed to Catherine.

I waded to the edge of the sea of moving bodies. My earlier excitement fled, and I avoided looking at any of the young men nearby. I had no desire to be asked to dance.

"He's here!" Arianna's announcement startled me out of the doldrums. George stood beside her.

"Lieutenant Sterling?"

"Who else? Come, I'll show you." Grabbing my arm, she pulled me into the foyer. Through the crowd separating us, I caught a glimpse of the soldier.

"He is not alone," George said. Being taller, George had the advantage of a better view.

"Who's with him?" I asked.

"Don't know." He stood on his toes now.

"Is it a girl?" Arianna urged.

"Yes . . . yes, it's a girl. They are coming this way," George informed.

"Pretend we are having a normal conversation," Arianna suggested while George kept a running commentary on their progress.

"Almost here . . . almost here," he said.

General Sterling and his companion passed by us into the ballroom. I couldn't believe how blatantly he ignored me. Worse yet, I was stunned to see he escorted Nelly, who, as always, carried herself with overbearing self-assurance. It was obvious the kiss in the garden had been amazing only for me. I felt foolish. If anything, I had only been another feather in his cap. True, I'd turned him down, but if his confession had been sincere, would he have moved on so easily?

With my emotions raging, I yearned to confront him and express exactly what I thought of him. And, with the courage I surprisingly possessed in that moment, I wanted to give him a firm slap on both cheeks. And as far as Nelly Veils was concerned, maybe I would wipe her silly smile off her face once and for all. Thankfully, civility prevented me from humiliating myself to that extent. "*It is madness in all women to let a secret love kindle within them, which, if unreturned and unknown, must devour the life that feeds it,*" Jane Eyre's words poignantly reminded me.

"Are you sure you two met? Even if he doesn't necessarily like you, out of respect for your father, he should've said hello," George blurted.

"George, watch your tongue!" Arianna scolded.

"It's all right." I forced myself into indifference. "The lieutenant has no obligation toward me. He may do as he pleases."

"While that's true, he could do better than Nelly," Arianna opined.

"What's wrong with Nelly? She looks lush in that dress," George exclaimed. "You're just jealous."

"George!" Arianna scolded again, glaring at him. "Don't you think before you speak?"

"Sorry. Sorry." He looked down sheepishly.

Catherine and Thomas joined us. "Did you see General Sterling? Thomas pointed him out to me. I must say that Arianna described him remarkably well yesterday. Not only is he quite handsome, he seems to know how to enjoy himself."

"Sure he does," I muttered.

"You saw him, then?" Catherine asked again.

"We did," I replied.

"Florence! Florence!" Samuel squeezed through the crowd. "Your father is looking for you."

"Thanks, Samuel. I better go find him." I walked away, hoping not to cross paths with the lieutenant and Nelly again.

My father spotted me as I entered the ballroom and signaled for me to join him.

"Florence, I want you to meet the Duke of Cardiff." He introduced me to an amiable middle-aged man and his wife, who looked much older than him.

Ere long, they resumed discussing the recent German capture of Warsaw. I was so enthralled by the conversation that I failed to see Lieutenant Sterling approach.

"Good evening." His calm voice infuriated me.

"Sterling, I'm glad you made it," Father greeted. "And well accompanied, I see."

Nelly giggled. "Hello, everyone."

"General." The lieutenant nodded to Father. To me, he said, "It's nice to see you again, my lady."

"I suppose it is." I faked a smile.

Time passed, and that was the sole exchange between us, expressed by words or the look in our eyes. And while the new arrivals integrated well with the group, quite soon, the situation became galling—the obsequious way he fawned over Nelly, the adoring way she gazed up at him—and I couldn't watch it any longer.

Noticing my friends had slipped into the room, I placed my hand behind my back and signaled for help.

"Excuse me, General Contini." Catherine came to the rescue. "May I steal Florence from you?"

"Of course, Miss Brockenhurst, anything for the lady of the castle."

I followed Catherine and Arianna to the drawing room just off the main hall.

"Sterling and Nelly." I groaned. "The whole thing is preposterous. I'm going to be sick."

"Oh my." Catherine smiled. "You are helplessly in love with him, aren't you?"

I shook my head in disappointment.

"Oh, come now, Florence. Can't you see it's a farce?" Arianna asserted. "He's smitten with you. Before he joined your group, he watched you the entire time. And when he couldn't stay away any longer, he intruded to make you jealous, to irritate you."

"He did that, all right," I said, defeated.

"Be that as it may," Arianna continued, "you can't let him get away with it. If you are seriously interested in the man, you must be unflagging. All is fair in love and war."

"To a reasonable point, of course," Catherine added. We both knew Arianna employed some questionable methods when it came to romance.

"Other than to make a fool of myself, which I've been doing remarkably well lately, I don't think there is anything else to be done— especially when Nelly has him in her clutches like a bird of prey."

"We'll take care of the bird," Catherine proposed, her green eyes sparkling. "We'll separate them so you can speak to him alone."

"Yes, that's right," Arianna agreed. "At least you can find out what's on his mind and go from there."

"How? Nelly will dive down on you and scratch your eyes out."

"Nonsense," Arianna refuted. "Put on a triumphant smile and wait for us by the dance floor."

When I hesitated, Catherine urged, "Trust us."

"All right." I squared my shoulders and returned to the lively room. In a secluded corner, I waited, aware that the lieutenant and Nelly had joined the dancing couples.

Minutes later, Catherine and Arianna, accompanied by George and Thomas, came to my corner. Unlike the men, whose discontent weighed heavily in their gazes, the girls' faces glowed with irrepressible mischief.

"I don't know about this," Thomas said doubtfully.

"Why are you so worried?" Arianna asked, seemingly annoyed by his concern.

"He is my superior. He could make my life miserable."

"You are right. We shouldn't involve you in this," Catherine decided. "Please, go find some of your comrades until the deed is done."

Thomas shook his head, rejecting the offer. "Retreating is not in my blood. Besides, it's too late for regrets—even when I'm not an active participant—I'm guilty of knowing about it."

"Well, I'm the one concerned now," I stated. "The last thing I want is to put any of you in a tight spot."

"Nonsense," Catherine argued. "We do this of our own free will and choice. Right Thomas?"

"Right." Thomas made a disapproving sound.

"Ah, don't be such a bore. And stop worrying," Arianna reprimanded.

My gaze fell on the goblet filled with red punch in Catherine's hand.

"Just the ticket," Catherine said. "Come now, Arianna and George, we have a bird to catch." She skirted the room, goblet in hand. Meanwhile, the couple joined the dance.

Thomas and I were left to be anxious spectators.

Arianna and George danced their way to the lieutenant and his starry-eyed companion, their rapid approach forcing the happy couple to the edge of the crowd. And in a sudden move, George and Arianna crashed into them. Now ideally situated, Catherine waited for her opening. Appearing entirely accidental, she collided with Nelly, causing the drink to spill down the front of Nelly's cream-colored dress.

Though Nelly screamed in horror, the people around them kept dancing. And the few who did offer to help, George quickly dismissed.

Catherine's gestures indicated a profuse apology for her clumsiness. George held back the stunned lieutenant while Arianna and Catherine guided Nelly from the ballroom.

"Well, there's your signal," Thomas said and quickly strode away.

Feigning confidence, I hustled through the throng, my stomach churning with anxiety.

George excused himself once I arrived.

The lieutenant's eyes held mine, and my confidence faltered at the detachment I saw there. "I'm surprised to find you alone," I lied.

"Miss Veils had an inconvenience. She'll be back soon."

"That's unfortunate." Another lie.

"What is? That she had an inconvenience or that she'll be back soon?" The bright light from the chandelier above accentuated his face, and I had a sinking feeling I had already lost the war when it came to Lieutenant Sterling. He was embedded in each cell of my body.

"That she had an inconvenience, of course. That's unfortunate."

"Indeed. Extremely unfortunate. Lady." He turned to leave.

I had to act. I reached for his arm. "Would you like to dance?" I hoped I didn't sound desperate.

"Excuse me?" His brows knitted in surprise.

"Would you like to dance?"

"You know how to?" Did he mean to tease or insult me?

"Better than you. Let me show you."

With a flick of his wrist, the conductor raised the baton, and the first notes of "Blue Danube" filled the air. The lieutenant placed his hand on my lower back, I reached for his shoulder, and our free hands clasped. We waltzed across the dance floor, each turn and dip feeling like we had done this a million times, our synchronicity simply beautiful.

"I must say, it's an honor to dance with General Contini's daughter."

"I must say, it's amazing how fast you found a new love."

"Love? Who said anything about love?" He smiled, seeming to enjoy my resentment.

"The way you two behave is indicative."

He pulled me close to whisper in my ear. "You toss around the word 'love' too casually, Miss Contini."

"Me? I'm not the one advertising a new partner after just confessing my love to another," I fired.

"You rejected me," he fired back.

"And you readily gave up."

"I prefer surrender, not coercion." He smiled again. "It bothers you, doesn't it?"

"What does?" I dared to ask, knowing what he meant.

"That Nelly accompanied me tonight bothers you," he said calmly.

I wondered whether I should answer. His closeness made it impossible to think, and he knew it.

"Let's get some fresh air." He clasped my hand and pulled me after him.

I felt curious eyes watching as we withdrew. I would be the gossip of England for months to come if I left with the lieutenant, but too late. I had decided, my heart guiding me into the night.

We strolled through the quiet, deserted gardens, farther and farther from the castle into the darkness until we came to a thicket.

"Your love will never find you here," I noted.

"Who says I want to be found?" Because I could barely see his face in the starlight, I focused on his voice. "Besides, she is not my love —yet."

"I don't think she knows that." I leaned against a tree.

"You are blindly jealous."

"What's there to be jealous of?"

He chuckled. "If there is nothing to be jealous of, why did you have your friends ruin her dress?"

"You accuse me of such a thing?"

"You know I'm telling the truth."

"Depends how you look at it. As far as I'm concerned, we saved Nelly from a man who obviously has no interest in her."

"Nonsense. He stayed at her side all evening," he refuted.

"True, but he couldn't keep his eyes off me."

"Why are you here?" he asked, inching closer.

"I was invited to the ball."

"I mean out here with me?" His lips brushed my cheek as he spoke, sending sparks of electricity through me.

"I . . . don't know."

"You're too proud to admit how much you enjoy my company, Miss Contini. But you have a big problem."

"What can that possibly be, Lieutenant?"

"You can't stay away from me." He pressed his body against mine.

"Who said I want to?" The remaining words of Jane Eyre's statement about love came to me. "*And, if discovered and responded to, must lead into miry wilds whence there is no extrication.*" No longer able to restrain myself, I laced my arms around his neck. I expected a gentle kiss, but he poured his desire into a multitude of kisses with an intensity that stole my breath away.

CHAPTER 17
~ THE DEPTHS OF INSECURITY ~

And so Lieutenant General Alexander Sterling and I became a popular subject with the London gossips. After Nelly changed out of her ruined dress, she discovered that Alex had gone outside with me.

He'd returned to her that night, but Nelly quickly surmised that his thoughts remained in the garden. And the rumors started. The Veils insisted I stole the young general from Nelly just as he would have proposed to her. Alex laughed when he heard that. "I didn't even kiss her, let alone think about marriage," he said. "On the contrary. I tried to end the relationship since she didn't understand I just wanted to be friends, but she wouldn't listen." Since Alex had a reputation for avoiding the topic of marriage like a deadly bullet, I believed him.

The Veils's manufactured scandal was the least of my concerns for now. We would survive it. The pressing issue was the war.

Britain deployed more troops to France and Belgium, our young men dying by the hundreds each day. Would there ever be an end to the terrible suffering? My heart stopped every time the telephone rang whenever Father or Alex were on duty.

In fact, I didn't expect to see Alex until Monday, but Mrs. Allerton informed me he waited in the library. I dashed down the corridor and into his arms. "Alex!"

"Good morning, my lady." He held me tightly.

"You came back sooner than I thought."

"I hope you aren't too disappointed." He extracted a daffodil from his jacket. "There was a change of plans."

"Thank you. It's beautiful. Where did you get it?"

"Mr. Leroy's garden."

"He'll send you to the gallows if he finds out."

"I have no intention of telling him. Do you?"

"I won't tell. Did my father come back with you?"

"No, he is still in London."

"He is? Why are you here, then?" They were rarely separated these days.

"Florence, I have to go to France for a few weeks."

"France? You can't be serious."

"I'm afraid so."

"My father promised you wouldn't leave England." I pulled away.

Alex moved behind me, holding my shoulders. "General Contini didn't have a choice this time. There are important matters I must attend to in preparation for the upcoming war council. I'm sorry. I must go."

"There must be someone else who can go. You are well known. You won't be safe." I knew military orders weren't negotiable, but I had to try.

"Safety is a luxury so very few can afford nowadays. Florence, this assignment is critical. I'm honored to have such trust. I'm preparing the way for your father's arrival. He will be an indispensable part of the council's outcome."

"What? My father is going too?" I felt as if the giant bookcases lining the walls would fall on me. France was a minefield to visitors. The anguish I experienced at Lucca's death threatened to return with a vengeance. I couldn't lose Father and Alex too.

"No. He doesn't have to be there until the council takes place."

"I can't believe this is happening."

"Please don't worry. I'll be back by the end of April."

"It's a very long time to be apart." I turned around and leaned into him.

"I know. I wish you could come with me." He pressed my face against his chest, his heart pounding softly beneath my ear.

At that moment, I was certain of my path. I wanted to be his wife. "There is a way for us to secure our relationship." He looked at me curiously, and I continued. "You could marry me." I might regret it later, but there it was.

Alex grew serious and pulled away. "Life is strange. I thought I would never find someone I wanted to spend it with. I thought I would be alone forever, and then I met you. The first day I saw you, I felt as if I had known you my whole life. The attraction was so strong. What I felt and still feel for you is something I have never experienced, so much so that I didn't know how to think or act.

"That night when I kissed you and you rejected me, I was devastated. So I decided to avoid you, to avoid the pain. When I looked at you, I saw an unreachable star. After all, I've never had to chase a girl. They always chased me." He gave a wry smile. "But at the ball, you declared war, then ambushed and disarmed me—you asked me to dance with you. I could avoid it no longer. I was completely lost without you. I was completely in love with you, body and soul. Florence, I want to marry you—but I can't."

"Why?"

"Because I love you too much."

"You make no sense. How can you say you love me yet not want to marry me?"

"Florence, we are amid the greatest war the world has ever seen. I'm away most of the time, and I'm afraid this is just the beginning. Thousands of soldiers die every week. How long will it take until I'm called to the battlefront? I can't escape it much longer. What if I don't come back one of these days?" He inhaled, holding in his emotions.

"You will always come back," I assured, wishing it to be true.

"You don't know that."

"True, but I do know that if you didn't, I would forever regret not having the opportunity to be your wife."

"You say that now, but being a young widow would ruin the rest of your life. I can't do that to you. For heaven's sake, it's a miracle I'm still alive." He raked his fingers through his hair, nervously. "Please, try to understand. The deeper the bonds, the deeper the damage."

"I disagree. The deeper the bonds, the deeper the love. Listen to me, Alex, you can't be afraid. Life is just too short for that. We don't know how much time we have. That's exactly why we need to enjoy what we have left together. We can't live in fear. If we do, we might as well already be dead."

He remained silent for a moment. In his hesitation, I sensed what would come. "My heart belongs to you, but I've committed my life to our country." His words failed to comfort. Like other times, he evaded me.

"Alex, I'm starting to believe you love the army more than me."

"You know that's not true."

"Prove it, then. Or is this how it's always going to be? I'm left behind, hoping you'll return. And if you don't, I'll spend the rest of my existence dead inside, wondering what might have been. Wouldn't *that* ruin my life?" The angry words poured out involuntarily, and I wished I could recall them. It wasn't who I wanted to be. Alex deserved my support, not this, but the awful truth was that I couldn't bear the thought of never seeing him again, nor could I brush off his unwillingness to commit any longer.

"I told you I have no control over my military career. When I receive an order, I must obey it. I'm sorry. I can't commit to anything else right now."

"I'm sorry too."

"I'll be at my parents' home, but I'll come to say goodbye before I leave for London." He attempted to embrace me. I didn't let him.

"Don't bother. You might damage me."

"Florence—"

"You know what, Lieutenant? I will tell Mr. Leroy you raided his garden after all. A little less oxygen in your brain might do you some good."

He left without another word.

"Florence, it's so good to see you!" Thomas exclaimed, taking my hand.

"I was in the area and thought to stop by. I hope it's all right and I'm not imposing."

"Goodness gracious, Thomas, you're always welcome. I was going for a ride. Would you like to join me?"

"If you have a horse to spare, I'd love to. I drove here."

"I have the perfect one in mind. Old Billy will love the exercise." A stout horse with a sweet disposition and a large appetite, Billy had lived long enough to know how to enjoy life without fussing over insignificant things.

Thomas and I guided Billy and Sunny through the woods, enjoying the peaceful afternoon. After last night's downpour, the air was heavy with the scent of damp, rich earth. Try as I might, I couldn't help but think of Alex. I missed him but felt devastated by his excuses not to marry me. Love was a complicated affair. I glanced at Thomas and thought about him and Catherine. I'd heard rumors that they had been together until sunrise the night of the ball.

"How is Catherine?" I ventured.

"I'm not sure. I haven't seen her since the dance."

"Oh." Not wanting to pry, I remarked, "She's such a clever woman and always so kind."

"She sure is." Thomas was tight-lipped.

Though I yearned to know if there was anything between them, it was clear I wouldn't learn it from him, so I left it at that. Billy and Sunny marched on until we came to a clearing close to the stream I had fallen into not long ago. Sunny nodded and sniffed the air, ready for a break.

"Wait, let me help you," Thomas offered, sliding off his horse.

"Thank you. I'm fine." I dismounted before he could object. "Look at the lush grass," I said to Sunny. "Go on. Get some."

Thomas dropped to the ground, and I followed suit.

"I love the forest. There is such a calm feeling here," I observed.

"During the day maybe. It's a different story at night," Thomas noted.

"Just like human nature, isn't it? We have a bright side, full of life, and opposite of that, one filled with fear and uncertainty." Again, I thought of Alex.

"Shh, listen." He motioned with his head toward a cluster of bushes and ferns.

Sunny neared the spot. She pawed the ground and flared her nostrils, and instantly, a white rabbit dashed between her legs and vanished under a bush. Sunny let out a startled neigh and bolted through the trees.

Thomas and I jumped to our feet, staring after her. He whistled for her, but it was no use. She wouldn't stop until she reached home—that much I knew. She spooked easily. I felt for Sunny, but now I had to worry about the long walk back.

Thomas must have read the conflict in me. "It won't be a problem. I'll walk. You ride my horse."

I smiled, pleased he had a different approach than Alex to the same situation. "Thank you."

"I'm afraid Billy is not ready to leave yet, though," Thomas pointed to the horse, who hadn't been bothered by the rabbit or Sunny's outburst, thoroughly enjoying the roots he'd unearthed. "I'm surprised how tranquil he is."

"Oh yes. He's an old rascal who doesn't often jump out of his skin. Too bad I can't say that for Sunny. As you've seen, she is young and untamed." I settled on a patch of grass with a sigh, fearing Alex might think as much of me.

Thomas flopped down beside me. He was a pleasant conversationalist, if somewhat bland. His stories were interesting and well-related, but soon his military tales turned into jokes. "There was a new soldier," Thomas began, "guarding the entrance of a military base. He had strict orders not to let anyone pass without proper identification. Then, a weary general on horseback tried to get into the base." He suppressed a laugh.

"Go on." I wondered if he thought of Alex.

"The soldier asked the general for identification. The general ignored him and nudged the horse on.

"'Halt!' said the soldier. 'I have orders to shoot anyone who tries to get in without identification.'

"'Come on, Black. Move on,' the general ordered his horse.

"As the horse crossed the line into the base, the soldier spoke to the general. 'I'm new at this, sir. Please tell me: Do I shoot you or the horse?'"

Even though, or maybe because, it was one of the silliest jokes I'd ever heard, I burst out laughing. In contrast, Thomas's face drained of color, and his smile evanesced. I followed the direction of his eyes, and my smile faded as well. At the line of trees, Alex sat on his horse with a straight face, his eyes cold.

"Alex . . ." After the way we parted the other day, I didn't think he would come before leaving for France.

Alex dismounted. Thomas and I rose to meet him.

"Captain Frankfort, what are you doing here?"

"Just visiting," Thomas responded almost apologetically.

"I'm glad he came. He's always welcome," I assured Thomas, bothered by Alex's not-so-subtle disapproval of his visit. "On the other hand, I didn't expect to see you today."

"Are you disappointed?"

"I'll get Billy a drink." Thomas reached for Billy's reins and walked him to the stream.

"How did you know where to find me?"

"Mrs. Allerton said you were off riding, neglecting to mention you rode with Frankfort." Alex spoke a little softer. "I don't have much time. I must catch the evening train, but I had to see you before I left."

"Well, now you have." Childish though it was, I still couldn't forgive his insecurities.

"I'll miss you more than you think." Alex held my face and brought his lips close to mine. "I love you." He kissed me gently.

Though my entire being burned with passion, I kept the contact short.

He turned to his horse.

I wanted to tell him I loved him, too, but the lump in my throat prevented it.

Alex mounted, and a sudden awareness crossed his face. "Florence, where is Sunny?"

"I didn't bring her."

"How are you going to get back?"

"The same way I got here, of course."

"How?"

"I rode with Thomas." Thomas would kill me if he heard.

"I see."

The lie made me feel awful, but not enough to recall it. After all, he didn't have the right to question me like this. We didn't have a serious commitment, at least not on his part.

His anger apparent in every move, Alex kicked his heel against his horse's flank, spurring it into a run.

"He left in a rage, didn't he?" Thomas appeared at my side.

"That's his problem." I tried to sound uncaring, but my eyes remained fixed on the spot where Alex disappeared into the brush.

"It could become mine too. He wasn't pleased to find me here, and I don't want to be on his bad side."

"It's all right. He'll get over it. After all, he doesn't own me."

"Not yet," Thomas mumbled. "We better head back."

"I suppose we must." Alex had ruined my day, after all.

CHAPTER 18
~ AN UNBREAKABLE LINK ~

Jane Eyre lay unopened on the table. Instead of reading, I peered through the window into the gardens, where the sunshine bathed everything in a radiant glow, yet I was somber.

I heard Mrs. Allerton's entrance and subsequent bustling around the kitchen, but I couldn't get out of my thoughts. With no news of Alex, I paid the price for my haughtiness. Insecurity undermined my confidence, and I repeatedly rehearsed the things I could have done differently. He had called before embarking for France. Mrs. Allerton took the call as I was out riding with Thomas—again. No more calls came after that.

What was he doing in France besides his military duties? Would he seek amusement like the other soldiers did during their free time? Would he find another girl there? Perhaps not, but girls would surely find him.

Mrs. Allerton slipped into the chair beside me to write the week's menu. "Florence, why don't you call Margaret Sterling? She might know something."

"Father hasn't called?"

"No. He said he would be in meetings for the next couple of days. I wouldn't expect him to call anytime soon."

"If I can't reach Father, it won't hurt to try. I'll call Margaret from the library." I glanced at the clock on the counter. "Do you think it's too early?"

"Nine o'clock? Goodness gracious, no. Normal folks wake up at dawn, unlike . . ."

"Thank you, Mrs. Allerton. What would I do without your honesty?" I gave her a big smile.

"Always here to help." She smiled back.

I had met Margaret, a dark-haired woman with big blue eyes, and her tall, sturdy husband, William, last week. Alex forgot to submit a document to the army, and Father contacted the Sterlings to retrieve it. They invited us to their home in Landford to dine with them. It was a shame I had to meet them this way. Alex had never invited me home.

In the library, I went straight to the telephone on the credenza. I settled into a chair and asked the operator to connect me to the Sterlings.

"Good morning, Mrs. Sterling. This is Florence."

"Oh, Florence dear, it's so nice to hear from you."

"I'm sorry to trouble you. I hoped you might have news from Alex?"

A pause ensued.

"Margaret?"

"Well, yes. Hasn't he visited you?"

"He's home?" I almost fell off the chair.

"Well, yes, he came back Wednesday."

"Two days ago."

"He was gone all day yesterday. I thought he was with you."

"No. I haven't seen him since he left for France *three* weeks ago." I tried to keep my voice calm but could not hide my consternation. "Is he there now? May I speak to him?"

"He's out riding. I'll have him call you as soon as he returns," Margaret answered. "I'm sorry, dear. There must be a misunderstanding."

"Thank you, Margaret. Good day."

I replaced the receiver on the cradle and paced the library, processing the information. Alex got back from France two days ago. He didn't come to see me, not even a call. Was he done with me? After waiting, worrying, and even shedding a tear or two for him during his absence, I couldn't wait for the answers to fall from heaven.

I found Mr. Lewis in the courtyard, polishing the Silver Ghost.

"Good morning, Mr. Lewis."

"Good morning, miss." The chauffeur touched the brim of his hat in acknowledgment but continued to move his rag over the already shiny surface.

"Mr. Lewis, could you drive me to the Sterlings' house?"

"My pleasure, miss." A wide smile spread over his lips. Driving Silver was the highlight of his job. "When do we leave?"

"In a few minutes?"

"I'll be ready."

"Thank you." I came into the house and almost collided with Mrs. Allerton, who burst out of the sitting room.

"Are you going somewhere?" she asked.

"Yes. I'm going to the Sterlings' home to see the lieutenant." I retrieved my hat and gloves from the side table.

"He's back?"

"For two days now." I couldn't hide my disappointment, not with Mrs. Allerton. "I can't believe he's ignored me while I've been worried sick about him."

"Now, now. I understand your frustration, but surely there's a good explanation. You mustn't jump to conclusions."

"It's impossible not to," I choked. "Being a little pigheaded is fine, but he's beyond that now."

"Very well. I understand you must speak to him, but first get a hold of your emotions. You'll give him a fright if he sees you like this."

"That's the plan." I slammed the hat onto my head. "Will you please accompany me?"

"I'll get my bag."

The ride to Landford felt like an eternity, my imagination conjecturing a million scenarios regarding Alex's indifference, none favoring him. As if reading my mind, Mrs. Allerton did her best to intercede on his behalf but without success. Mr. Lewis waited in the Silver Ghost across from the farmhouse while Mrs. Allerton and I called at the door.

Margaret was home alone. If she was surprised to see us, she didn't show it. She ushered us into the sitting room, where we removed our hats and gloves and Margaret gestured toward a red sofa. "Please, make yourselves comfortable. Alexander isn't back yet. Would you like some tea while we wait?"

"Oh, that would be lovely," Mrs. Allerton accepted.

"No, thank you." The anger flowing through my blood was sufficient heat for me.

"I'll be right back," Margaret said, and just then, a clatter of hoofs came from the side of the house. Margaret moved to the window to peek through the curtains. "Wonderful. Alexander is here." She sounded relieved. "Mrs. Allerton, shall we have tea in the kitchen? And I would love to show you the common dog-violet border that has just started to bloom." The pansy-like purple flowers were a natural beauty of the New Forest.

"What a splendid idea," Mrs. Allerton responded.

The women disappeared into the shadows of the hallway.

I stood in the center of the space, my stomach churning, my knees shaking. Seconds later, the front door opened, followed by footsteps. Then Alex appeared on the threshold. His color drained as if he had seen another ghost, for surely he hadn't missed Silver parked outside.

I took in his figure, and my words left me. He wore a white shirt, brown trousers, and high boots. His hair was tousled from the ride. How could I ever forget how devastatingly handsome he was?

"Florence, it's wonderful to see you." He took a hesitant step forward, guilt written all over his face.

"Is it, Lieutenant?"

He took another step.

My hand flew up in warning.

"It's not what you think. I—"

"You what? Were you going to tell me you understand how lonely these past three weeks have been without you? And that you felt the same way about me, so when you came back to England, the first thing you would do was visit me? Well, that's not the case. But in all seriousness, Lieutenant, if dropping by Forti Radici meant such a sacrifice, at least you could have rung me."

"I didn't think you were so lonely when you had Frankfort to drag around," he snapped.

"Don't bring Thomas into this. You are the one dragging *me* around. It's been eight months since we started dating. Eight months of insecurity and avoidance. Eight months that have finally proven how shallow your commitment is."

"If that's how you think of me, you don't know me," he said defensively.

"The problem is that I know you too well. Though I love you, I can't play this game any longer. We are through. Goodbye, Lieutenant."

He remained on the spot, silent, unmoving, and unreachable.

I had to leave before he saw the rising sadness in my eyes. I passed him, exited the house, and got into the car, grateful that Mr. Lewis quickly collected Mrs. Allerton.

The Silver Ghost entered the rural road shaded by ancient trees, the ache in my heart deepening with each passing mile. I'd imagined a much different relationship with Alex. Was this really the end? I placed my head on Mrs. Allerton's shoulder and closed my eyes. Thankfully, she didn't ask any questions. I would answer them, but not now when I didn't know how to deal with the awful emotions.

"What the—" Mr. Lewis snorted.

Mrs. Allerton shifted to look through the back glass, forcing me to raise my head. "For heaven's sake! It's not a racetrack!"

I squinted to see a whirlwind of dust chasing us. "What is it?"

"A dimwit on horseback," Mrs. Allerton sputtered.

"He is in a real rush. Must be an emergency," Mr. Lewis conjectured. "We'll have to let him pass, or he'll run through us."

I turned again and saw the rider galloping at full speed, the distance between us rapidly closing. "It's Alex!"

"Nonsense. He wouldn't ride like that!" Mrs. Allerton's eyes widened. "Would he?"

"Yes, Mrs. Allerton, that dimwit is General Sterling." What on earth did he think he was about?

"Should I stop, then, miss?" Mr. Lewis inquired.

"No! Go faster, as fast as Silver can go."

"Florence, it's not a good idea," Mrs. Allerton objected.

"Just a few more yards. Go faster," I insisted.

Mr. Lewis obeyed, and the car shot forward, bouncing off every bump and rut in the road.

"Slow down! We are going to crash!" Mrs. Allerton clutched the front seat for dear life.

"He's gaining on us. Press the gas, Mr. Lewis!"

"No! Don't do that!" Mrs. Allerton cried.

Mr. Lewis ignored her. Euphoria filled his features as he tightened his grip on the wheel and floored the gas. Undoubtedly, he was thrilled to discover just how fast Silver could go—so thrilled that when Alex won the race and stopped ahead, blocking the road, it surprised Mr. Lewis.

"Stop the car! Stop the car!" Mrs. Allerton shouted. "We're going to hit him!"

Mr. Lewis slammed on the brakes, and the car squealed, struggling to slow down. "He's too close! He's too close!"

Mrs. Allerton let out a terrifying scream. I hid my face in my hands, preparing for the impact—which, thankfully, never came. Silver came to a forceful stop, skidding sideways on the road.

"This was insanity—absolute insanity," Mrs. Allerton reprimanded me and Mr. Lewis. "General Contini will hear about this. Oh yes, he will!"

"He moved out of the road in the nick of time." Mr. Lewis heaved a sigh of relief.

"Thank heaven for that." At last, Mrs. Allerton let go of the front seat.

Just then, Alex opened my door, grabbed my wrist, and hauled me out of the car. "Don't worry, Mrs. Allerton. I'll take good care of her. Go ahead. I'll bring her home."

"No. Wait," I said to Mrs. Allerton. "Don't leave me."

"I trust that you will, General," Mrs. Allerton said with a mocking smile.

"No. Wait! No!" I said in vain.

Mrs. Allerton shut Silver's door, and they drove away. My behavior infuriated her, and I would hear about it when I got home. What made love so difficult to handle? Why did it come with so many incomprehensible and sometimes untamed emotions?

Alex dragged me into the trees. "I have something to say to you."

"Let's not make this any more painful. Clearly, you want out of the relationship, and I respect your decision. I won't hold it against you." I glanced at his horse, who wandered into the brush. "Could you please take me home?"

"I will, but you must listen first."

"Please, Alex. Let's just go."

"If you don't listen, you'll have to walk to the manor."

"You wouldn't dare. It would take me all day—if I ever make it back."

"Try me." He whistled for his horse, who came almost instantly. He had left me in the woods before and would do so again.

"All right, I'm listening."

"You, lady, have a bad habit of mistreating people."

"Me?" I laughed.

"Yes, you. But that's beside the point. Now, keep your mouth shut and let me speak."

"Look—"

"No, no, no." He reached for the horse's reins.

I pursed my lips and sat down on a fallen tree trunk.

"Florence, all I've done since meeting you is think about you. Being in France was torture. I even asked to be sent home early, but I wasn't allowed. Before I left, you said we didn't know how much time we had in life and we needed to enjoy our time together. It didn't take me long to realize you were right. If I'm ever going to have joy in life, it will only be with you by my side.

"You have no idea how difficult it was to return on Wednesday and not rush to see you. But I wanted to get this first." He extracted a box from his pocket. "I traveled to London yesterday to finalize the transaction. I bought it in France, but I had them make a few adjustments, so it took longer than anticipated."

My pulse accelerated.

"I was so worked up, I stayed up all night thinking about you. I went riding this morning to organize my thoughts. I wanted to have a perfect plan to give you this. But, of course, you caught me off guard. You know, you are the only one who can do that." Alex smiled, and the love I saw in his eyes left me numb. He knelt and opened the box, revealing a ring with a large ruby in the center, surrounded by sparkling diamonds. "Florence, will you marry me?"

Beyond any emotion I had ever encountered, the happiness of that moment overcame the frustration, loneliness, and the anger of the past. "I'm sorry I misunderstood you." Tears filled my eyes. How could I have gone from desperation to this much happiness in such a short time?

"Is that a yes?"

"A resounding yes!" I dropped to my knees in front of him.

Alex placed the ring on my finger and took me into his arms, then kissed me with a deep but gentle passion. When he finished, I begged for more. Seconds, then minutes went by.

"You know, I could do this all day, but I must take you home," Alex whispered. "Mrs. Allerton might come looking for you."

"If you must." The feelings of contentment raging in me were so overpowering I had to find a way to release it. An idea formed.

Alex walked his horse over and helped me mount.

"Now that I think about it," I started, "if we are to wed, we better be on equal ground."

He looked at me inquiringly.

I pressed my heels into the horse's side, and he sprang into a gallop. Alex jumped back with a startled cry. "What are you doing?"

"I'm giving you a choice, Lieutenant," I shouted over my shoulder. "You can walk or jog back to the manor. It's your choice."

"You can't be serious!"

I laughed so hard I almost fell off the horse.

On this radiant summer day, nature bloomed in a full kaleidoscope of color—from the clear blue sky to the vibrant green of the trees and meadows to the colorful blanket of wildflowers covering the ground—perfect for a wedding.

From my bedroom window, I observed the garden where we'd hold the ceremony. The red carpet led to where Alex and I would share our vows at the base of a tiered fountain. Rows of chairs covered in gold fabric lined each side of the aisle. Some were already occupied, people conversing excitedly.

Mrs. Allerton stormed in. "Oh, dear. We must hurry, or you'll be late. Come now. Have a seat."

I moved to the chair in front of the mirror, where Mrs. Allerton's fingers swiftly wove my hair into a Grecian knot, leaving a few loose pieces around my face. She then helped me get into the ornate dress. Its delicate beads and intricate lacework made me feel like a storybook princess. Mrs. Allerton secured the slim crown holding the veil to my head and sighed. "You look beautiful. I've never seen a more lovely bride." She arranged the three-quarter sleeves of my dress one last time.

"Thank you for everything. You are like a mother to me." We clasped each other warmly. "What would I have done without you?"

"Well, enough of that." Mrs. Allerton blinked back her tears. "You already know how I feel about you, so let's get downstairs before your father comes looking for you."

Mrs. Allerton seized the train of the dress, and we descended the staircase. Father waited at the base.

"My dear daughter. I now understand the hefty price tag of the dress." With a smile, he pulled me into his arms.

"It was Mrs. Allerton's doing." I smiled back.

"Florence, there are no words to describe either the way you look or the feelings of my heart. I can only say that my joy is complete. You will be very happy with Alexander."

"Thank you, Papa." I found it difficult to say much. Father knew me. He understood. He would help me keep my emotions properly channeled on this, the best day of my life.

"Are you ready?"

"Yes." I planted a kiss on his cheek and couldn't help but wonder if he had looked this handsome in his brown uniform when he married Mother.

"Mrs. Allerton, are you composed enough to proceed?" Father asked as she dabbed at her eyes with a handkerchief.

"Of course, General." She pulled the veil over my face and turned to the ladies who would assist me. "When Florence reaches the path, carefully lower the train. And make sure it doesn't get stuck on the carpet."

"Yes, ma'am."

Father patted my hand, and we exited the house. As we approached the assembled crowd, all rose from their seats. I grasped Father's arm tighter as I looked straight ahead at the soldier awaiting me in his blue uniform.

"Florence, breathe. Smile," Father advised. "And focus on the priest."

Dressed in a deep-golden alb and matching cope and miter, the aged priest stood next to Alex. Holy book in hand, the man looked like a dove ready to take flight. As we advanced down the path, I saw many familiar faces. I acknowledged them but instantly forgot them in the excitement of the moment.

Father extended my hand to Alex, then joined Mrs. Allerton on the first row of chairs. Captain Thomas Frankfort stood beside Alex, a serious expression on his face. To my surprise, a few days earlier, Alex announced that Thomas would be his best man.

In a light, happy tone, the priest opened the ceremony. Most of his speech was a blur to me. The only clear sounds were Mrs. Allerton's sobbing. I thought I also heard whimpering from some of the young females and couldn't help but wonder how many hearts Alex had broken on his way to the altar.

"Alexander Sterling, do you take Florence Contini to be your wife,

to have and to hold from this day forward, for better or worse, for richer or poorer? In sickness and in health, to love and to cherish until death do you part?"

Thomas produced the rings.

Alex placed a ring on my finger and answered, "I do."

The priest repeated the question to me. I slid Alex's ring on his finger and answered, "I do."

"I pronounce you husband and wife, legally and lawfully wedded," the priest declared. "You may kiss the bride."

Alex raised the veil and kissed me soundly, the clapping and cheering in the background soon bringing us back to reality. We shifted to the crowd, but our eyes didn't break contact. Alex smiled, brought me into him, and kissed me again.

"Let me be the first to congratulate the happy couple," Father said joyfully.

Mrs. Allerton came forward, congratulating first Alex, then me. The Sterlings came next. They glowed with joy at the union of our families. I took in the many happy faces surrounding us, and my heart filled with gratitude for their love and support.

Through a sea of well-wishes, handshakes, and hugs, we traveled to the ballroom, where a quartet played the first strains of "Roses from the South." Alex and I moved to the happy rhythm of the music, and for the next several minutes, the world faded away. There was only the man I loved and the assurance that we would be together in life. When I returned to earth, we parted for the traditional parents' dance.

My father waited, beaming.

"Would Mrs. Sterling give me the honor of this dance?" he asked.

"My pleasure, sir."

"Florence, I'm proud of you."

"Thank you, Papa. Thank you for everything you have done, especially for inviting Alex to the house so I could meet him."

"I knew he was the perfect match for you. If anyone would stand up to your stubbornness and not flinch at your arrogance, it would be him." Father grinned.

"Your honesty is most humbling," I teased. "But I assure you General Sterling has suffered much in his conquest."

"Of that, I have no doubt, but at least I spared him from sleeping in the stables."

I laughed.

A new waltz began, and this time, couples swarmed the dance floor.

"May I steal my beautiful bride?" Alex interjected.

"I think Florence would step on my foot if I refused." Father chuckled as he kissed my cheek. "She's all yours."

"Thank you, General Contini."

"This is a dream," I said to Alex. If my feelings of joy were of any monetary value, the world belonged to me.

"One I hope will never end."

"Arianna and George are moving this way."

"With a goblet of punch?" Alex joked, alluding to the plot against Nelly's dress.

"You won't ever forget, will you, General?"

"No. I will use it to my advantage every chance I get," he said in my ear, hiding his face from the approaching couple.

"General Sterling, I must confess I never thought you would get serious with a girl, or marry one, for that matter," Arianna said with a laugh.

"Miss Whitley, life is full of surprises, isn't it?" Alex replied with an irresistible smile.

"Indeed, it is. But I must also say you have done extremely well in marrying Florence. I'm not sure I can say the same for her." Arianna chuckled once more, trying to make light of her comment, but I had my doubts she was joking.

"We agree on that much. I've married the most beautiful girl in England. George, you may have to leave the country to find someone to wed," Alex said, successfully annoying Arianna.

"Good luck, Florence! You'll need it." She rolled her eyes, taking the slight rather well. "Come, George, let's have some fun."

Once they'd merged with the crowd, Alex and I resumed our dancing, swaying in unison to the rhythm of the music.

"She doesn't like you very much." I noted the obvious. "Why?"

"You don't want to know."

"Yes, I do." I had a pretty good idea, but I wanted to be sure.

"She cornered me once in her father's factory."

"And?"

A mischievous glint crossed his eyes.

"I won't kiss you again until you tell me," I pressed.

The song ended and another started.

He held me a bit tighter. "We'll see about that. But since you are so curious, I'll tell you. Arianna said she could get me a discount on the arms order I was placing for the army. However, she required that I kiss her in exchange."

"And your response was?"

"I said I would gladly pay full price for the order. She left the office in a rage."

The image formed in my mind: Alex sitting on the edge of Arianna's father's desk, his amused eyes mocking her. Poor girl. She must've been beside herself. "You know, sometimes I wonder how you've managed to stay alive this long. However, I must ask why. She is an attractive woman. Other men would've been honored to fulfill her terms."

"I'm not other men. I dislike girls who throw themselves at a man. It's not proper or fun."

"Proper?" I let out a startled laugh. "You, of all people, chased me in the most improper manner. Even more so considering I'm your superior's daughter."

"That's different, my lady. Men always chase, and an easy catch is not worth keeping."

"Thank goodness I didn't chase you."

"You did something worse. Mrs. Sterling, you tortured me. Although I rather like being tortured at your hands."

The evening wore on, the dream continuing. Soon, we would be on our way to Alex's flat in London for an undetermined length of time. Only a few guests remained when an out-of-breath Colonel Swinger, my father's aide-de-camp, burst through the front doors in an agitated state. All eyes turned to him. He was late for the wedding and party. I wasn't sure he had even been invited, for that matter. A large, bearded man, Swinger always presented a calm exterior, and so his panicked appearance spoke volumes.

Addressing Father and Alex, he said, "Gentlemen, we have problems."

CHAPTER 19
~ THE HUNT IN THE FOREST ~

The night advanced rapidly, squashing any hopes of a departure for Alex's flat and our honeymoon. In minutes, Forti Radici underwent a radical change. Hours ago, it had been filled with music, smiling guests, and excitement. But with the sudden appearance of Colonel Swinger, the atmosphere turned grim. Father asked the house staff and guests to leave, soldiers and guns replacing them.

Mrs. Allerton hastily helped me out of my dress and into my riding clothes. Before rushing out of my room, I glanced at the white fabric, now carelessly heaped on the floor. Hopefully, it wasn't a portent of what was to come.

A sense of urgency and tension filled the office as Father, Alex, and Colonel Swinger hovered over a map sprawled across the Victorian desk. Alex had changed into combat clothes, a pistol at his side. I joined their circle.

"Florence, we are under attack," Father said matter-of-factly. "You and Alex will leave Forti Radici at once."

"Under attack?"

Father threaded his fingers nervously through his mustache. "I want you and Alex out of the country."

"What are you saying?" I hadn't even processed his command to leave the house, and now I was to leave the country?

The telephone rang from the back of the room, stretching our nerves.

"I must answer. Colonel Swinger, go ahead." Father signaled for him to explain the situation.

"A while ago, a Belgian cargo ship docked at the Southampton port. Since they arrived later than scheduled, they had to wait until morning to unload." Colonel Swinger pointed to the spot on the map. "However, the Royal Navy's request for a routine check forced them to search the ship, which they found had been hijacked, the crew neutralized by German soldiers. Those aboard were arrested, but they aren't cooperating. The good news is I'm here with a few men, and reinforcements are coming."

"And why are you here? Why are reinforcements needed? What is the bad news?" I was utterly confused.

"A group of soldiers disembarked before the ship was searched, and our efforts to track them down suggest they are headed this way." Swinger tapped his finger on Breamore on the map.

The news, coupled with Father's voice booming as he argued with whomever he spoke to on the telephone sent my head spinning. "Coming here? Why? Why here?"

"General Contini helped mastermind last year's Treaty of London. The repercussions hit Germany hard," Alex explained. "And he possesses highly classified war documents. We could lose many battles and lives, even the war, if our enemies get hold of them. Your father was to deliver the documents to the upcoming Security Council in France."

The information hit me like a bolt of lightning. "Are these documents here at the manor?"

"Yes." Swinger ran the back of his hand across his forehead, wiping at the beads of sweat there. "Somehow, somewhere, information leaked, and the enemy knows."

"How long do we have?" I feared the answer.

"At most an hour," Swinger answered.

Father hung up and returned to us. "Our enemies don't want me to attend the council. They don't want the information delivered, so we must see that we do." From a secret compartment in his desk, he retrieved an envelope. "Gentlemen, these documents are more important than our lives. General Sterling, I fully trust you to carry out this mission." Father extended the envelope to Alex.

Alex's face filled with wariness. Suddenly, he looked twenty years older. "Florence, the fastest way to get the documents to safety is to bring them to Hurst Castle. For that, we'll have to cross the forest on horseback. The fortress is safe, and it's only a few hours of sailing to France."

"Yes. Yes." Swinger nodded reassuringly. "Even if you have to wait for a ship, you and the classified information will be safe there."

I understood: any other route meant suicide. Spies and assassins hid among our own, and they would stop at nothing to obtain the documents.

"We have tried to get a message to Hurst Castle without success. We'll keep trying. They'll be expecting you." Colonel Swinger sounded convincingly optimistic about the success of our mission.

"General Sterling, one last word before you leave," Father said.

Clearly wanting me out of earshot, the three men drew near the window. I pressed my finger to the map, tracing the distance between Breamore and the South Sea. It would be a long horseback ride.

All of a sudden, an earsplitting explosion rocked the house, windows shattering into a million pieces, fragments of glass catching the light as they scattered in all directions. I screamed. Colonel Swinger shrieked and collapsed to the floor, holding his leg as a quick succession of gunshots came from the grounds.

"Get down, Florence!" Alex sprinted toward me.

"Come on! Come on!" Father cried, dragging Colonel Swinger to the security of the wall.

Alex pulled me behind the desk, shielding me with his body as the house shook with more explosions. I pressed my hands to my ears, struggling to process the chaos. A short while ago, I'd been dancing at my wedding. Now, the enemy attacked my home and all I held dear.

"We need to move Colonel Swinger to safety," Father shouted to Alex as the shooting momentarily subsided.

"Stay down," Alex ordered me and crawled to the men. He slipped his arms around the colonel's upper body while Father grabbed the man's feet, and they brought him to safety, a trail of blood left across the office floor. Swinger scooted up against the desk.

"Colonel, hold still." I yanked the scarf from my neck and tied it around his leg to stanch the bleeding.

"Thank you." Colonel Swinger managed a weak smile and turned to Father. "Sorry, General. I miscalculated their arrival."

"There's no way we could've known for sure, Colonel. But it sounds like your men are giving them a hell of a welcome. Now, you stay put. I'll be back for you. Alex, we must get Florence to safety."

We shuffled out of the office into the hallway, safe for the moment with no windows in sight.

Mrs. Allerton emerged from behind the staircase. "Goodness gracious, Florence. Are you all right?" She dropped the military bag in her hand to embrace me. "Oh my, you are shaking." She also shook with panic.

"Colonel Swinger is wounded."

"I'll see to him," Mrs. Allerton decided.

"No. It's not safe. The colonel will have to wait," Father objected, stopping her. "Mrs. Allerton, didn't I order you to leave?"

"I'm sorry, General. I couldn't do it while Florence remained here."

I reached for her hand. "You shouldn't have."

"We better get them out of here now," Alex growled. "But how? We can't expose them to the grounds."

We stood motionless for a moment while the severity of our predicament held us captive. Suddenly, the gunfire increased. Almost unconsciously, we moved farther back into the corridor.

In the gloom near a corner, a figure appeared. Alex shoved me behind him and drew his pistol. Father reacted next, pointing his gun at the man. Mrs. Allerton shrunk against the wall.

"Don't shoot! It's just me!"

"For heaven's sake, Mr. Leroy! What the devil are you still doing here?" Mrs. Allerton exclaimed disapprovingly, even though she was guilty of the same crime. "You should have gone with the rest."

Mr. Leroy smiled at Mrs. Allerton. "I won't leave without you."

"You foolish man!" She shook her head.

"I'll find a way out," Alex said. "Stay here. I'll scout the perimeter."

"No, Alex, wait! The tunnel!" Father exclaimed.

"What tunnel?" Alex looked perplexed.

"There's an underground passage that leads deep into the forest."

"The tunnel." I had forgotten about it, but it seemed like an answer to our prayers.

"Of course! That's the ticket!" Mrs. Allerton agreed.

Mr. Leroy grabbed the military bag off the floor. Father took point, and Alex brought up the rear, guarding us as we hastened to the kitchen. Father opened the door to the larder, and we stepped inside, Alex helping him to lift a rug out of the way. They then removed several boards with a little effort, revealing an opening just big enough for one person at a time. The top of a ladder was the only visible thing in the darkness below.

"An ancestor of ours in Cromwell's time built it as a precaution. I had a feeling it may come in handy someday," Father explained.

"Besides us, no one knows about it." Mrs. Allerton attested to its security.

"The tunnel travels roughly 150 yards and exits by the hedgerow past the south lawns. That should give you enough cover to get to the protection of the forest. When you come out, head south and don't stop until you are far away," Father instructed.

"The farther, the better," Mrs. Allerton emphasized.

"I'll contact London from Hurst Castle," Alex said.

"Florence, I trust Alex with your life. Do what he says," Father advised, almost pleading.

I nodded. "But you must promise me you'll stay alive." I searched my dear father's eyes for a spark of hope.

"I will most definitely try." He smiled, but it was a lifeless gesture.

"Don't you ever forget who you are and how much we love you," Mrs. Allerton pointed to the silver bracelet on my wrist. When Lucca and I were born, my mother had two identical bracelets engraved with our names to remind us that our family's love would live forever in our hearts.

"You aren't coming with us?" I choked on the words.

"Oh, my dear, I would only slow you down," Mrs. Allerton responded lovingly.

"They are leaving next," Father assured, referring to Mrs. Allerton and Mr. Leroy.

"Oui, oui, miss. I'll take care of Mrs. Allerton, don't you worry," assured Mr. Leroy.

"General Sterling, don't fail. Bring her back home. That's an order," Father commanded, handing him the bag.

"Yes, sir. I swear on my life."

I hugged my father, Mrs. Allerton, and Mr. Leroy.

Mr. Leroy handed Alex an oil lamp, and Alex started down the ladder.

Before descending into the uncertain darkness, one last time, I looked up at the faces I so dearly loved.

One more minute in the tunnel, and I'd have fainted. The narrowness, stale air, and scuffling of unseen creatures felt suffocating. When we finally emerged into a maze of trees, I inhaled deeply. With the lamp left behind, the starry night was almost as dark as the underground. It was also eerily silent, magnifying our movements and heavy breathing as we struggled through the dense vegetation.

"Are you all right?" Alex asked.

"Never better," I joked breathlessly.

"At least no one would ever guess where the exit is." Alex looked back at the thick brush. "Come on, lady. We must move."

The relief of being in more favorable terrain didn't last. Aware of the enemy in our wake, Alex assumed a brutal pace. Amid our ordeal, he remained levelheaded. His serenity forced me to focus on the task ahead, to forget for now what I couldn't change or accept. Like hunted creatures under the dark canopy of the trees, we traveled south. Determined not to hinder our mission, I marched without complaint, although my muscles soon screamed and my side cramped.

With the first light of dawn, our arduous escape finally caught up with me. My head spun, and I staggered every few steps. To our right, I saw that we had been walking along a road but yards from it. Staying off the main path meant staying out of sight, but the uneven ground, thick grass, and dense foliage there obscured our vision and slowed our journey.

"How are you holding up?"

"I'm fine," I lied, the stitch in my side nearly undoing me.

We heard it simultaneously—a rumbling like thunder from the north. At the sound, my weariness became a burst of energy.

"Horses!" I cried.

Alex grabbed my hand, and we broke into a run. I struggled to keep up with his long strides, fearing my newfound energy wouldn't last. The sound of the horses' hooves became distinguishable, beating evenly, like the striking of drums. You must keep moving, I told myself, and just then, Alex yanked me to the ground on the steep side of the road.

"Shh." He pressed his finger to his lips reinforcing his command.

I lay flat in a sea of stocky grass, scared of my own breathing for what felt like ages.

When I fidgeted, he mouthed, "It's all right," placing a comforting hand on my back.

The clamor diminished, the horses having slowed. I raised my head just enough to see the road, where ten riders in dark combat clothing jumped off their horses and began to search the area. Their voices were rough, their words foreign.

Alex pushed my head to the ground. "German soldiers," he whispered.

The soldiers shouted to each other in apparent disagreement. Amid the chaos, I picked up two words—Contini and Sterling. There was no doubt. They were after us. And the longer they lingered, the more likely they'd find us. The desire to flee, to put distance between the threat and us, seized me. I wriggled, considering the idea.

Alex must have read my thoughts, for he warned, "No. Don't move."

I obeyed, and at length, one of the men barked something like an order. The horses huffed and nickered as our pursuers moved out. The stomping of the animals became distant, eventually fading altogether. I rolled onto my back and let out the breath stuck in my chest.

"Wait, Florence, wait." Alex stopped me from sitting up. A long, frightful moment passed as he intently studied the trees, his head barely above the ground. "We are being hunted."

My heart skipped a beat. "How do you know?"

"Three horses were riderless when they left. The riders are on foot. They know we are here. I think they are on the other side of the road. Listen, we have the advantage of the sloped terrain." Alex's fingers tightened on the bag he had carried since we left. "We'll slide down as far as we can, then run. All right?"

"All right."

"Florence, if we get caught, you run. Do you hear me? You don't wait for me. You run." Alex looked at me with a mix of love and desperation. We knew this could be the end of our journey.

With my heart pumping in my ears, we scooted down the slope through the boscage, branches and twigs mercilessly scratching my skin as we did so. Today, I wasn't fond of the woods.

Once we hit the bottom of the drop, we ran like mad. Three, four, five yards, and then Alex abruptly halted, dropped the bag off his shoulder, and changed direction. "They've found us," he hissed.

Keep moving. Keep moving. Pulled by Alex, I did my best to keep up, not daring to look anywhere but straight ahead. I blinked, and before I knew what happened, a soldier jumped into our path and hit Alex in the head with the butt of his rifle, knocking him to the ground. Alex scrambled to his knees, and our gazes connected. The assailant read Alex's concern for me in his eyes. In that moment of hesitation, Alex grabbed the soldier's weapon and threw himself backward using gravity to wrench it from his opponent's hands. Simultaneously, he kicked out with his legs, catching the soldier in the groin. With a hoarse cry, the latter buckled in agony.

"Run, Florence!" Alex ordered.

Without looking back, I sprinted away. Soon, I could hear Alex's boots crashing against the ground and knew he was catching up. In a flash, someone yanked me by the hair, jerking my head back, my scalp burning with the force. Then, arms wrapped around me. It had not been Alex.

"Stay still, and I won't hurt you," another soldier said in heavily accented English. "Make a fuss, and I'll kill you."

I stopped wrestling, though I growled a few not-so-pleasant words. I glanced sideways and spotted the first soldier moving stealthily through the trees. *He must be hunting Alex.* But where was Alex? Somewhere along our run, he must have hidden to get the advantage. If I was correct, I had to distract my captor despite his threat. Without another thought, I twisted and turned in his grasp, striking him with my heels even when I knew there was no chance of escape. He was far too strong. But every moment I could buy for Alex might make the difference.

When my captor's arms tightened viselike around my chest, I threw my head backward, hitting him in the face, blood splashing onto my hair. I'd injured his nose. He swore with a viciousness I'd never heard and smacked the side of my head, the blow sent me reeling to the ground. While I writhed in pain, the hunter materialized not too far from me. He crouched behind a clump of shrubs, his rifle aimed at a target I couldn't see. *Alex.* A gunshot echoed through the forest. The hunter let out a groan and fell dead. Alex had found him.

On shaky legs, I rose in a weak attempt to escape, but my captor quickly restrained me, his arm tightening around my neck. I gasped for air, my fingers digging into his skin to loosen his grip.

"The more you writhe, the faster you'll asphyxiate," he said coldly. And it happened as he spoke, my strength plunging as rapidly as the oxygen. I froze. "The game is over, Sterling. Come out!"

There was no sign of Alex.

"Come out, or she dies!" Using his free hand, the soldier drew the pistol from his holster. He shot twice into the air and then placed the muzzle on my temple. I jerked at the heat.

"Let her go!" Alex's voice sounded distant, yet his proximity must have startled the man, who flinched.

"Drop your weapon!" The soldier squeezed his arm around my neck. An immense amount of pressure rushed to my head, and I fought the darkness as my vision blackened around the edges. I had to stay conscious.

"Right, then." Alex came into view. "I think we are done here."

He lowered his rifle to the ground, never breaking eye contact with the enemy.

No, no, no. Don't give up. He'll kill us both.

My captor shoved me aside, and I scrambled over to a tree, my hands clutching my neck. I coughed and choked, the air burning as it entered my lungs.

Alex rushed to my side. "Are you all right?"

I nodded, unable to speak, as my thoughts spun in confusion. Why had the man let me go? Alex had only dropped the rifle. He'd tucked the pistol and other weapons inside his clothing. And why had Alex given up so quickly when surrendering wouldn't help us?

The explanation came soon enough. Like snakes slithering silently through the vegetation, soldiers emerged from every direction. They forced us into a clearing at gunpoint, giving way to a rider who broke through the tree line, maneuvering his horse with much dexterity. As he came to a hard stop, the look in his eyes chilled me. Although I knew nothing of this man, I felt the evil; he was a sadistic man who took pleasure in the suffering of others.

"Krause." Alex said the name as if it left a vile taste in his mouth. "What do you want with us?"

Krause dismounted with such roughness I held my breath in fear. "We have unfinished business, General," he said in a raspy voice, his English surprisingly clear.

Alex sidestepped, sheltering me from the man. "Very well, then. Let the girl go, and we can settle this like gentlemen."

Krause let out a terrifying laugh. "The famous General Sterling thinks he can fool me! Do you think I don't know who she is? She's more valuable to me than you are."

One of them said something in German, which I comprehended all too well in the unbridled excitement I saw in his eyes. The rest laughed.

"I'll kill you if you touch her!" Alex charged at him only to be suppressed. They pinned his arms behind his back and patted him down, taking his pistol and knife, then dragged him away.

I attempted to near Alex, but one of the men interceded, keeping us apart.

Krause's face was inches from Alex's as he sputtered, "I don't think you understand the severity of your situation, General. Let me help put it into perspective." He slammed his fist into Alex's stomach, then his face. Alex struggled to stay upright as his head swung back and forth under the force of the blows. "Now, there must be a powerful reason for you to have fled into the woods. Otherwise, you wouldn't have abandoned a battle." He searched the inside of Alex's clothes, retrieved the classified information, and looked at it briefly before concealing it in his jacket. "As I suspected."

"You got the documents and me," Alex said between clenched teeth. "Let her go."

"Touching, but not convincing. Now, don't you worry. We'll take care of Miss Contini, all right. Oh, forgive me, it's Mrs. Sterling, isn't it? Death is too easy for an arrogant man. I'll break you first. Watching your wife enjoy our company will do just fine." Krause leered at me and caressed my cheek with the back of his hand.

"Don't you touch me!" I flung my head backward to pull away.

Krause seized me by the hair and forced a kiss on my lips. I spat at him, hoping to rid myself of the vile taste, but he laughed, unfazed by my retaliation.

"You bloody coward!" Alex growled. "Leave her alone."

With one swift movement, a soldier threw his elbow at Alex's ribs, the latter wailing in pain. The soldier lost no time and forced Alex to his knees.

"All right—enough," Krause decided. Sterling, I came here to kill you, and since your mission is over, let's get to it. I will then have my fun." He snatched a rifle from one of his men.

"Don't make her watch this evil," Alex said through gritted teeth.

"You wretched beast. My father will hang you!" I raged and cursed Krause in the foulest words the English language had to offer, words I had never uttered.

"Silence her!" Krause repositioned himself, aiming his rifle at Alex.

A soldier pulled me to his chest and covered my mouth with a gloved hand. Alex lowered his head, avoiding my gaze. I could almost hear his thoughts: the agony of failing to save me was worse than losing his life.

Don't! Please! Don't! I looked away. My heart stopped beating. I waited for the shot that would end Alex's life and the light in my soul.

The blast rang through the woods, followed by multiple shots, and I felt as if my heart had exploded into a million pieces. Then Krause collapsed to the ground, his eyes rolling back in his head, his body jerking before going still. A few of his men dropped like flies. The remainder ran for cover, including the ones who had restrained Alex and me. Alex. He was alive.

His gaze fixed on mine, and he darted in my direction. We took cover behind a fallen tree. Lying on his stomach, he reached for the rifle of a dead man and opened fire. I covered my ears with my hands and did the only thing I could—pray.

After what felt like forever but couldn't have been more than minutes, the shots grew sporadic, then stopped altogether.

"What's happening?" I asked.

"Stay down. It's almost over. They're surrendering," Alex answered.

"General Sterling! Where are you?" a familiar voice called.

"Over here, Captain Frankfort," Alex called back.

Thomas.

"Wait here." Alex walked into the open.

I sat up. In the center of the clearing, British soldiers had the surviving Germans on their knees. At once, the severity of what had just taken place hit me. I was horrified by the scene of death, stunned that Alex and I were alive, and grateful for our saviors. And though the assailants showed no mercy to us, I felt for them. Somewhere under the same heaven, they had families awaiting them. I feared I would never understand the atrocities of war.

"Frankfort, it's good to see you," Alex said.

I then spotted Thomas's red hair.

"Where is Florence?" He looked about.

"Right here." My voice was strangely calm.

"Florence, I was so worried." Thomas visually inspected me. "Are you hurt?"

"I'm fine."

"I'm sorry we took so long."

"You were right on time," Alex assured. "Have your men collect the scattered weapons and search the trees for our bag. We'll then interrogate the prisoners."

"Sir, if I may ask, do you know who he was?" Thomas motioned to the leader.

"Oskar Krause. He visited the New Forest before the war. He knew exactly who we were and where to find us."

"He is under General Richter's command, right?" Thomas noted.

"Yes. Richter's right-hand man." Alex spoke to me now. "Richter is one of the most powerful German leaders. This was a brazen move, and I fear it won't be over until we've neutralized Richter himself."

Alex took the envelope from the dead man's pocket. His mission wasn't over after all.

CHAPTER 20
~ A BEACON OF HOPE ~

A group of soldiers left for London with the prisoners, the extra horses, and Oskar Krause's body as evidence. Alex and I rode south with Thomas and the rest of his men.

Instinctively, my hand went to the tender skin on my neck, and the memories flooded me—the desperate run for our lives, the enemy's indescribable brutality, and my terror when Krause almost took Alex's life.

The audacity of the German soldiers to come onto British soil was remarkable. Their masterfully designed plan had almost succeeded. After disembarking the Belgian vessel, they'd headed to a farm where an accomplice waited with horses. And since the forest wasn't a stranger to the training of troops, their presence went unnoticed. They planned to assassinate my father, retrieve the classified information, and return to the ship under the cover of night. Notwithstanding, the Royal Navy's inspection, the arrival of Colonel Swinger, and the secret tunnel foiled their plans.

Now, my focus was on discovering the outcome of the encounter back at home. According to Thomas, reinforcements hadn't reached Forti Radici when he left. I hoped Father managed to hold out a while longer.

"Their number wasn't the challenge. The surprise attack gave them the advantage," Thomas said. "As you know, we had no time to prepare, and then your father ordered me to take some of Swinger's men and come after you."

The sinking feeling that I might never see my father again made my heart ache. I swallowed the lump in my throat and blinked my eyes dry. I had to be strong for him.

At last, we crossed into Keyhaven, a fishing hamlet near Hurst Castle. Alex brought his horse level with mine. "We'll camp here. The fortress is overrun by soldiers. I don't think you'd be comfortable there."

I smiled. "Sleeping in the open is not appealing either."

"Don't worry about that. I have something in mind." He winked and urged his horse forward, retaking point.

The atmosphere grew warm and muggy as we neared the sea, my exhaustion increasing. I felt heavy and stiff, my senses slow. When my body slipped too far to one side, threatening my balance, I patted my face and refocused. I couldn't fall off the horse.

"Florence, do you see it? Just beyond those trees." Alex pointed to an obscure silhouette. At first, it didn't look like much, but as we drew near, it formed into a bedraggled cottage that had seen better days. Shut in by trees and safely concealed, it looked like heaven.

"Find a good spot to set up camp," Thomas ordered the weary soldiers.

"It's not much, but I'm glad it still stands." Alex extended his arms to help me dismount. And as nightfall chased away the remaining daylight, he extracted a torch from the sack on his horse. "I haven't been here since I joined the army. Let me make sure it's safe."

"I haven't come all this way to sit out here." I stumbled after him, relieved when my legs didn't give in.

"If you insist." Alex pushed the door open. It screeched in complaint, sending a plume of dust through the space.

We stepped into a large room. In the semidarkness, I could see a stone fireplace, a table, and two chairs. Alex shined the torch on a ladder in the corner.

"Here, Florence, hold the torch." He lifted the ladder to a square opening in the ceiling. "Do you want to see up there?"

"Certainly."

The ladder protested under Alex's weight but stayed in one piece. I followed him into the attic. He moved to a window with shutters and opened them, letting in a fresh breeze. Except for an enormous trunk with shiny hasps and a metal bed, the space was empty.

"It's too dark now, but you can see the sea from here," he said.

I peered into the woods. "How can you possibly see anything through that jungle of trees?"

"You'll be surprised. We are a lot closer to the water than you think. Listen. Can you hear it?"

I listened. "Yes, barely. I hear waves washing on the shore."

"Look! That's Hurst Castle's beacon." Beyond the treetops, a beam of light circled the sky. "The lighthouse has been a guiding star to wandering vessels for generations."

"My father brought Lucca and me to see it when we were little. I hardly remember it, though."

"My family came here all the time during hunting season. It was my grandfather's cottage. But after he passed away, the tradition slowly went away."

"That's too bad. It must have been amazing in its glory days."

"It was. Now, it's the perfect hideout."

"Is it?" Fear suddenly struck me. "What if there are more German soldiers in the forest? What if they track us here?"

"Not likely. They wouldn't come this far. It's too close to Hurst Castle."

"But what if—"

"Don't worry, my lady. If that happens, I'll send Thomas to fight them," he joked.

"Very amusing, General."

"Ah, very nice. You called me general."

"You are impossible."

He chuckled and pulled me into him. His lips brushed against mine, but a voice called from below the window before we could enjoy the moment. "We are ready, General."

"I'll be right down," Alex told the soldier, then spoke to me. "I'll go to the fortress with a few men to secure a ship and send a report to London."

"Do you think there is a ship already here?"

"I hope so, but it's not likely."

"Are you going to send a message to your parents? I'm sure they've learned about the attack by now."

"No, I can't. Until the mission is complete, I exist only in the army. My parents know how it is. They'll be fine."

"Could you inquire about Forti Radici and my father, then?"

"I'm planning on it."

Aided by the torch, I found a lamp among the artifacts in the main room. And while waiting for Alex, I freed the cottage from dust and aired the bedding in the trunk. I looked about me, pleased. It wasn't the honeymoon I envisioned, but being together was all that mattered.

I heard horses approaching, followed by voices, and soon Alex came through the door.

He looked around the space. "You've been busy."

"I just got rid of the spiderwebs."

"What did the spiders ever do to you?" he teased, setting a sack of supplies on the table. "No matter. Look what I got."

"I should send you shopping more often."

"No, let's not make a habit of it." He unwrapped a package of bread, cheese, and some fruit.

It looked delicious, but I lacked an appetite, even though I hadn't eaten all day.

Alex noticed. "Are you unwell?"

"No, I'm just not hungry."

"It must be the stress of the past day, but you must eat something." He handed me a piece of Manchet bread. "At least eat this. We might be here for a bit, and I don't want you to get sick."

I tore a piece of the bread off. "Any news of home?"

"Very little." His eyes held mine with a measure of compassion that worried me.

"Tell me."

"The reinforcements ended the battle quickly, but they were unsuccessful in locating General Contini. He is missing."

"Missing? What do you mean missing?"

"Please don't panic. The military continues to comb the woods surrounding the house. They'll find him soon enough."

"He could be wounded." A rising sense of desperation crept into my heart.

"Your father is well trained, and he's come through worse scrapes. I'll check again tomorrow."

"There must be something we can do." In my mind, I pictured the places I'd search. "No one knows the manor and its vicinity as I do. I should be there. I should be looking for him."

Alex moved his chair closer and took my hands into his. "Do you trust me?"

At that moment, I felt as if Father stood beside me, his hand on my shoulder, reminding me of his advice to trust Alex. "I do."

"The best thing we can do for General Contini is to complete the mission he assigned us."

"What about Mrs. Allerton and Mr. Leroy? Did they get out?"

"I haven't heard about anyone else. Please, Florence, we must stay focused."

"It's so hard." The uncertainty and fear would consume me if I let them, but he was right. I had to keep a cool head. This wasn't just about me. The classified information we carried had the potential to end the war and save lives. The thought felt empowering and somewhat comforting.

Alex encircled me in his arms, bringing me into his chest. "If it cheers you up, know that the soldiers at the castle had a good laugh at my expense."

"They did? Why?"

"Have you seen my face?" He raised an eyebrow. "They called me ugly." The bruising and swelling were getting worse.

I laughed. "How rude."

"Quite rude, but I won't take it personally." He reached for the blackberries. "Shall we try these?"

I ate a handful of the sweet, juicy berries, followed by a piece of cheese, chewing slowly so as not to upset my stomach. Minutes later, the meal was over. Our conversation died down, and Alex extinguished the lamp. With my thoughts and emotions racing in different directions, we ascended the ladder to the attic.

The night was warm and still, the only noise coming from the natural creaking of the wooden structure. We stood in front of the window, watching the bright moonlight travel across the treetops and into the room, bathing our skin with a soft glow.

With a gentleness that had my heart pumping out of rhythm, his fingers slipped down to the buttons of my blouse. One by one, he unfastened them, sliding the fabric off my shoulders and letting it fall to the floor. "Oh, heavens, you are beautiful."

I smiled, realizing this moment would change us forever.

"I hope you will never regret the decision to marry me," he said.

"When I married you, it was the only time in my life when I knew what I wanted."

"That's wonderful because I want to be with you forever. I can't imagine life without you."

I helped him out of his shirt, and even though I knew of his muscular physique, the shape of his chiseled arms and chest surprised me. Then, I saw the dark contusions spreading from his shoulders to his waist. "I'm sorry about this." I brushed my fingers over his skin.

"My lady, for a single moment like this," he spoke softly, his cool lips tracing my cheek, "I would take the beating all over again."

Daylight touched my face, and birdsong called me out of a deep sleep. I refused to open my eyes, fearing the peace I felt would disappear. Being with Alex, even if just for a while, had lifted the anxiety and uncertainty from my heart. I stretched my arm across the mattress, searching for him, only to find the bed empty.

"Florence, come down for breakfast."

I smiled. I loved his voice. "Only if you make me."

With a groan, he climbed the ladder. I hid my face underneath the pillow, but that proved to be a bad idea. Alex tickled me until I nearly suffocated with laughter.

"Are you coming now?"

"Not convinced yet."

"My lady." He faked a serious voice. "I'm starting to understand what poor Mrs. Allerton went through all these years."

"She served me breakfast in bed," I said, mimicking his tone.

"Well." He looked into my eyes, and I saw the deep love there. "I've already tried persuasion, so you leave me no other choice but to—"

"To what, General?"

"Force you to come down." He swept me off the bed and swung me into the air before letting my feet touch the floor.

"You know, General, if you want me to be obedient, all I require is a kiss."

He laughed. "Why didn't you say that before?"

Our lips connected, and the world around me faded. Breakfast would have to wait.

The afternoon sun filled the forest with life. It was the first time since we left Forti Radici that I noticed the beauty of nature with its many shades of green, full of vitality. The trees didn't seem so dark and dense anymore. They now stood like giant warriors, there to protect us instead of harassing us. And the wildlife that had seemingly been concealed now emerged from everywhere.

"Hurry, Florence. Come on!" Alex called as he ran up the path to the sea.

Through a break in the brush, the shining blue water beckoned. I lengthened my steps and exited the woods to join Alex on the sand. He dropped the bag from his shoulders and unlaced his boots. To my surprise, he went on to remove his clothing and plunge into the ocean.

I took off my shoes, dipped my toes in, and gasped as the freezing water touched my skin.

"Come on, Florence!" Alex waved for me to get in.

I shook my head decisively.

"Come on! Come on!" he insisted, his voice lost in the sound of the waves.

"You are mad!" The thought of being wet, cold, and miserable convinced me to stay on the beach.

I strolled along the shore, soaking up the warm sunshine. The expansive fortress established by Henry VIII stood fully visible from here, guardian of our shores for over three hundred years. Its enormous wings sat majestically on the narrow strip of land stretching out into the sea.

My memories transported me back in time. One after another, images of the day Father brought Lucca and me here flashed through my recollection. I closed my eyes, tilting my head toward heaven, my feet still moving. It had been years ago, yet I could clearly see us riding up to Hurst Castle.

I remembered Father's boring history lesson on our journey across the New Forest. I thought of Lucca walking across the courtyard, his face beaming with pride as he dreamed of becoming a soldier.

Alex hugged me from behind.

"You are wet!" I exclaimed the obvious.

"Where is my lady going?"

I had wandered off without noticing, closer to the fortress than anticipated.

"Would you like to go inside?" he asked.

"No, not today."

"If you change your mind . . ."

"I won't. And you, General, will catch a cold."

"You sound like my mother."

"I am Mrs. Sterling, after all."

"I better dry off, then, Mrs. Sterling." Alex took my hand and broke into a run, pulling me along with him.

"You are going to break my legs!"

"Is that so?" Before I could react, Alex scooped me into his arms and resumed his run. "How about now?"

"Much better." I laughed wholeheartedly as his face contorted with the strain the movement caused to his body.

"You are heavier than you look." Out of breath, he set me beside his clothing.

"And you are stronger than you look, General."

With a grin, he lay down on the sand, his eyes fixed on the sky. I unpacked our bag.

"Would you like an apple?" I offered.

"Not hungry."

The waves danced on the ocean's surface. Like a kaleidoscope, they reflected a mesmerizing amount of light. I took the last bite of my apple and realized the silence had stretched on too long. I glanced at Alex. He seemed deep in thought. "What is on your mind?"

"Do you remember what the priest said?"

"During the wedding ceremony?"

"Yes. Do you remember?"

"Some of it. Maybe. I'm not sure. Why?"

"He said we would be together until death separates us. Truly, Florence, have you ever thought about what happens after death? Will we be together again or is this life the end? In the forest, I came too close to losing you. And just the thought of being without you drives me mad."

"I'd much rather believe there is life after death—that a supreme power watches over us, giving us the gift of love. Love, I think, is the most powerful force in the world. It must last longer than a lifetime."

Alex opened his mouth to say something but didn't.

I observed the sun, almost behind the west skyline now, and recalled Mrs. Allerton's words. "After my brother passed away, Mrs. Allerton told me that difficulties come into our lives to shape us and strengthen our character. She said that what matters is the way we handle our trials— that we design our destiny through the things we do and believe during hard times. She was sure there is more than we can see and feel right now. This life is just a temporary trip, she used to say." I smiled at the thought. She wasn't here, yet I felt her presence through her influence.

"Do you believe her?" Alex held my gaze, holding me accountable for my answer.

"I do. Even when I get discouraged, the hope of seeing my brother again someday, keeps me going." I read an unusual sadness in his eyes and realized death frightened him. Though he was fearless when confronted by it, he feared losing those he loved. "Alex, promise me that no matter what happens, you'll hold on to hope." I held his gaze now, holding him accountable for his answer.

He considered my petition for a moment. "All right, my lady. If it makes you happy, I promise."

"Very well, General. We have an agreement, and we also have this time together."

"Well then, we better use it wisely." His eyes took me in with a desire that made me blush.

I stole a quick kiss and jumped to my feet. "I'll race you back to the cottage!"

"Wait! What about all of this?" His eyes darted over the items scattered on the sand.

"That's your problem, General. I need a head start!"

He shook his head, watching me merge with the woods.

"General Sterling, sir!" Thomas called from just outside the window. The sun had barely risen.

"Is he seriously calling this early?" Alex yawned, turned onto his other side, and closed his eyes.

"General Sterling! News, sir!" Thomas insisted, louder this time.

"This better be good, or I'll shoot him." He jumped out of bed and pulled his shirt on.

"That's a bit too drastic." I groaned, unable to shake off the haziness of sleep. Exhaustion had finally caught up to us both.

Alex pushed open the shutters. "Captain Frankfort, what's the rush?"

"The ship, sir. It has arrived." Thomas's words jolted me awake. Change had come.

"I'll be right down."

"Yes, sir."

Alex gazed out into the forest for a long while, clearly disturbed by something he might not have considered previously.

"How soon do we have to leave?" I asked.

"Right away." He slipped into his uniform, his thoughts still far away.

"Should I start packing?"

"No, not yet. We'll talk about it when I get back."

We'll talk about it? What is there to talk about?

He hurried down the ladder.

"It's a French Navy ship." Alex avoided my gaze. "Only four of us will go."

"Am I included?"

"Florence, I'm sorry. You can't come."

"What? You can't be serious." I seized his arm, forcing him to face me.

"Please don't make this any harder on me than it already is."

"Hard for *you*? You're not the one left behind."

"Listen, Florence." His voice rose, his frustration evident. "I wouldn't ask you to do this if it wasn't best for you."

I sank onto the bed, heartbroken. How could he leave me?

He sat next to me, his hands fisted.

"Why didn't you tell me this from the beginning? I could've gotten used to the idea by now," I said.

"This wasn't the plan. I'd never leave you out here alone. But when Thomas showed up, I realized there was more than one reason your father sent him."

"You're going to blame it on my father now? He did order you to take me to France, didn't he?"

"Before we left, your father ordered that if the situation permitted, I wasn't to risk your life. The ship could be attacked, or worse, there could be traitors aboard. You'll be safe here. You have Hurst Castle's protection. And apart from the military, no one knows you are here. If you came with me, I might be forced into a situation where I must risk the lives of my soldiers to protect you or risk yours to protect theirs. Please try to understand how I feel. What happened in the forest is nothing compared to what could happen."

"I might be safe here, but what about you? What if I lose you?"

"There is a slight chance of that, but I'm more likely to succeed if I travel alone."

I understood the wisdom in his plan, but it didn't help the anguish of being apart, of worrying about his safety. But I could do nothing except to hold on to hope, as I had preached to him. "I suppose I better get used to you leaving."

"Please don't be sad. To me, you represent what the lighthouse is to wandering vessels. I'll always look for you, always come back to you." His tight embrace left no doubt he spoke the truth.

"Every night when I see the light shining into the sea, I'll remember your promise. As long as it shines, I'll be waiting for you." I drew in a long breath, absorbing his warmth and familiar smell, fearing this might be the last time I might do so.

He placed his finger under my chin, guiding me to look at him. "Florence, I love you."

"I love you more." The tears behind my eyes betrayed me and rolled down my cheeks.

"I won't be gone long. I'll deliver the documents and head back as soon as possible. If anything changes, I'll send word to Hurst Castle for you to return to Breamore." He brushed the back of his hand across my face, wiping away my tears. "Unless you want to go back now, but I would rather you stay here. I don't want to risk anything happening to you. Besides, the manor is still a crime scene. You would have to stay in the inn."

"I can't go back if Father is not there. And I suppose there is no news about him or Mrs. Allerton and Mr. Leroy?"

"No. However, I found out that Colonel Swinger survived the attack. He's in the hospital recovering."

"That's wonderful." I felt happy for Swinger and at the same time beyond distraught about Father. Too much time had elapsed. If he was alive, he would have surfaced by now.

Before long, Alex was ready to depart. I tried to be strong and let go, and, to a certain degree, I succeeded, but on the inside, I withered. We said our final goodbyes, and he walked away, taking my heart with him.

CHAPTER 21
~ STANDING STILL ~

For a long while, I stared out the window, watching the gentle breeze blow through the trees. My eyes wandered from the sunset to the sliver of blue sea in the distance. My heart ached. It had only been a day, but the void Alex left ate at me, consuming my thoughts and energy.

"Good evening, Florence. I need to speak to you," Thomas called from the ground.

"I'll be right down." Dreading what he had to say, I climbed down the ladder and invited him inside.

He looked pale and unlike his calm self. Fidgeting with the buttons on his shirt, he said, "Please, Florence, have a seat."

"What's wrong? Is it Alex?"

"No." Thomas settled across from me. "I'm sorry to be the bearer of such terrible news. They found your father's body in the woods north of the manor."

Thick silence encircled us, and time stood still, my thoughts and feelings suspended as I grappled with the surreal news.

"Florence, breathe." Thomas slid his chair closer. "You look like you are going to pass out."

I inhaled and exhaled in a concerted effort, but each breath drew more than it gave, leaving me more faint by the second. "What about Mrs. Allerton?"

"They found her, too, along with Mr. Leroy. The priest identified their bodies." Thomas reached for my hand.

His warm touch confirmed this was worse than a nightmare. It was a reality from which I couldn't wake up. "Tell me all you know." My words came out broken but determined.

"Are you sure you want to know?"

"Sooner or later, I have to know."

"Later might be better."

"Please, Thomas."

His gaze dropped to the floor as he spoke. "They found General Contini concealed in a thicket, shot several times. No one could've survived that. My guess is that someone pulled him to safety after he went down."

"And Mrs. Allerton and Mr. Leroy?"

"They were shot in an underground tunnel. I'm so sorry."

"The tunnel . . ." I imagined my dear Mrs. Allerton and Mr. Leroy being chased like animals. In my mind's eye, I saw their desperation to move faster, their assassins gaining on them. I could see Mrs. Allerton being struck by a bullet and collapsing to the ground, Mr. Leroy trying in vain to help her, and, finally, bravely dying by her side. He wouldn't have left her behind.

Like a shroud, grief enveloped my soul and shattered my heart. My shoulders slumped forward, my head fell into my hands, and I wept. The agony carried with each sob echoed throughout the cabin like a haunted soul unable to flee. Yes, I had to be strong and hold on to hope—hope that I would be with them again in the afterlife. Father would expect that much from me. Howbeit, it would take time—time to forget and forgive, time to heal.

"They were great people. They'll live in our hearts forever." Thomas knelt in front of me, and I fell into his arms.

I wasn't sure how to describe it, but I felt strength in his sincere desire to help—as if, for that instant, he carried part of my agony. I held on to him, to the feeling of being rescued from a free fall.

When I shed the last tear, I felt lighter in body and spirit. Thomas released me, and I looked at my bracelet, remembering Mrs. Allerton's final words. *"Don't you ever forget who you are and how much we love you."*

"It's late." Thomas rose, and before darkness engulfed the cottage, he lit the lamp. "If you need me, you know where to find me."

I watched him near the door, and the demons of fear and grief threatened to wreak havoc on me again. "Thomas, don't leave me. I can't face the night alone."

"I can't stay inside. General Sterling will shoot me or, worse, send me to the gallows. I have no choice. I better go."

Thomas was right. I couldn't ask this of him. Still, for the first time in my life, loneliness weighed heavily on my heart. My loved ones at the manor lay dead, and Alex remained far away. I quickly made up my mind. "You might not have a choice, but I do. I'll stay outside with you."

"You might regret it. It's not very comfortable."

"I'll manage." I followed him out with a blanket in hand.

On this clear summer night, the stars shone like glittering jewels, a stark contrast to the darkness of the woods.

"I'll stand guard tonight." Thomas dismissed the soldier, taking his post under a giant sequoia.

I secured the blanket around my shoulders and joined him, leaning against the tree trunk—its harshness instantly stabbing my back. No matter. It was better than the desolate indoors.

"Listen, Forti Radici is still in custody, but now that everyone is accounted for, I'm sure they'll release it to you." Thomas propped his gun on his lap.

"I can't face it just yet."

"We'll wait for General Sterling, then?"

"Yes."

"I sent a message to the priest," Thomas said tentatively. "I hope it's all right."

I nodded, encouraging him to go on.

"He'll keep the bodies in the mausoleum until the funeral. He'll also notify Mrs. Allerton and Mr. Leroy's families."

"Thank you." *The bodies.* I pushed the image away. "I don't have the heart to think about those things right now."

When morning came, Thomas suggested we go to the beach. The sea was eerily calm except for a few roseate terns gliding above its tranquil surface—so free, so uncaring about the world's troubles.

"Which one would you like to read first?" Thomas kneeled on the sand, holding up two books he had brought from the fortress.

I took the one titled *As You Slept*, but the words on the pages blurred, and my attention wandered.

"I wish I would've met you before you met General Sterling," Thomas suddenly said, flipping through the pages of his novel.

"Why do you say that?" My gaze darted to him.

"Because I feel like an intruder in your life."

I didn't know where he was headed with the conversation, but I feared he liked me more than just a friend. I hadn't missed how he looked at me or avoided me now and then. If my suspicions were true, I had to be tactful. While I respected his feelings, there could never be anything between us other than friendship, and his friendship meant the world to me. "An intruder? Do you realize that if it weren't for you, I would be dead?"

"I did my duty."

"Risking your life for the safety of others is more than doing your duty. It's a noble deed." I made a mental note of how much my view of the world had changed since meeting Alex.

"Florence, I—"

"Please, don't say anything. Just know I'll never forget what you've done for me."

Thomas's saddened eyes found the sea, and after a moment, he said, "He will come back, you know."

"What if he doesn't?"

"He will. General Sterling always makes good on his promises."

I observed the lighthouse in the distance. It reminded me of Alex's words before he left. "*To me, you are what the lighthouse is to wandering vessels. I'll always look for you. I'll always come back to you.*" With a sigh, I switched the discussion back to Thomas. "What are you going to do when the war is over?"

"Take a long vacation."

"You know, if you haven't been in touch with Catherine, you should ring her. I'm sure she would love to hear from you."

"I think I will, but don't hold your breath. I hardly have time for a personal life, and I don't foresee a vacation in the near future."

"Do you think you'll stay in the army?"

"Yes. I like the discipline and the opportunity to serve our people." I sensed a profound patriotism in his statement. "Without people like us, more lives would be taken, not just those of young men but women and children. The cruelty would have no end." His words reminded me of the evil I witnessed in the forest.

"I wish it was different."

"So do I, Florence. So do I . . . in more than one way."

At Thomas's insistence, I accompanied him to the fortress. Though I had been hesitant to visit, in a strange way, I now wanted to be here. It was an illusion, I knew. But here, I felt closer to my father.

"Captain Frankfort, miss," an older soldier greeted in a somber voice as we passed him in the courtyard.

"Stand here, Florence," Thomas instructed excitedly. "Look across the yard to the far wall. What do you see?"

"Am I supposed to see something other than the wall?"

"Right in front of it."

"Wait—are you talking about the posts?"

"Yes, yes! Do you know what they are for?"

"Why would I know that?"

"It's a shooting range! The posts are the targets. The wall catches the missed bullets."

"Oh." I looked at him inquiringly. "What's exciting about that?"

"The officer in charge permitted me to teach you how to fire a rifle."

"I'm not sure that's a good idea." I was a terrible shooter. "I know how to use a pistol. That's more than enough."

"A pistol? In our current world, you won't get very far with a pistol. We are at war, Florence. You must know how to handle a rifle. Besides, it's for the sake of us all."

"This is a result of the other day, isn't it?"

The memory rolled through my head: Thomas handed me his rifle while he gathered firewood. A fast-approaching, thundering noise caught us off guard, and he instructed me to be ready to shoot. Fearing it might be a threat, he instinctually prepared for the worst and hoped for the best. My reflexes were too slow, and thankfully, the frightened horse ran past us by the time I lifted the weapon. But then the rifle fired, sending Thomas diving to the ground for cover. The earsplitting boom brought the soldiers from camp, frantically searching for us.

"Put it down!" Thomas yelled in distress. "You almost shot me!"

"I'm sorry. This thing is too heavy for me to handle."

"I noticed."

"Oh, thank heaven I didn't shoot the horse," I stammered, still shaken by the whole encounter.

"Better me than the horse, I see!" Thomas scoffed in disbelief. "And thank goodness it wasn't an enemy, or both might be dead."

We hadn't talked about the incident since it happened. Evidently, he had no intention of forgetting it.

"Truly, Florence, if you can't handle a rifle, you are pretty much defenseless," he now observed.

Unconvinced, I beheld the soldiers strolling about the courtyard. "Seriously, Thomas. I may manage to wound or kill several of them before I ever hit a post."

"Don't worry about them. As soon as you position yourself, they'll seek shelter." He smirked.

"All right, all right." I frowned. "If it makes you feel better and me less guilty about my clumsiness with the rifle the other night, I'll do it."

After a lengthy bit of instruction, Thomas helped me steady the rifle as it went off. Eventually, I withstood the blast without stumbling, although my shoulder burned. Then he taught me how to aim. I was amazed at how easy it was to miss and ever so grateful the wall took the brunt of my mistakes.

Night arrived, and I welcomed it, craving the relief of sleep. Though I did my best to stay busy and distract myself from thinking about my family and Alex, their absence was almost unbearable. Thomas's friendship was an anchor in the storm. And though I'd forever be indebted to his kindness, he could never fill the emptiness in my heart.

I lay in bed, suspended somewhere between sleep and being awake. My body went numb, but my mind wouldn't settle. What if Alex didn't come back? Had he succeeded in his mission? Should I go back to Forti Radici without him? Was I any more prepared to do so? What was happening with the war? I wrestled with the unanswered questions until I heard a muffled creaking. The door from below had been opened. I held my breath and listened closely.

There. Another creak. Then another.

I swung my legs over the edge of the bed and sat up. It was dark in the attic, but I could make out shapes. The noise came again. This time, it sounded rhythmic, purposeful. Footsteps. Someone moved about the cottage. The awareness came at once. I was trapped. The window was too high for an escape, and it faced south. The soldiers camped to the north. Yelling would be a disadvantage as it would warn the intruder, accelerating his purpose. Perhaps the intruder had killed the night guard.

My heart hammered against my rib cage so hard I thought it would break through it. I had to get to the rifle Thomas insisted I keep with me. It was visible against the wall a few paces away. But it might as well have been miles, because with every step I took, the floorboards groaned louder than ever. *Whoever is here now knows I know.*

I had one chance to do this right, for, no doubt, the intruder had no honorable intentions. Shrinking at the idea of shooting someone, I gripped the weapon and backed against the wall behind the floor opening, my fingers squeezing the forestock. One efficient blow should give me the needed advantage.

The ladder complained as a figure surfaced from the darkened hole. I froze in fear as the intruder turned toward me. I swung the rifle, but he intercepted it in midair.

"Whoa! Whoa!" He tried to yank the weapon out of my hands. "Florence! It's me!" The voice sounded familiar but faint amid the struggle. With one final pull, he took the rifle and sent me flying against the wall. Then he jumped onto the floor and grabbed my arms, holding me in place. "Florence, it's me." He spoke softly, soothingly.

Alex! In the moment it took to process it, I felt my heart might explode. I fell into his warmth and wept.

A new day spread over the forest, rays of light infiltrating the attic through the gaps in the wood. I opened my eyes. Alex lay beside me, facing the window. I shifted closer and squeezed my arm under his. It hadn't been a dream. He was here with me.

"You almost killed me last night," he whispered.

"Me? I don't think so. You almost killed me with fear."

"I was going to call up to you, but I wanted to surprise you." He rolled over, his blue eyes sparkled in the daylight.

"You did that, all right. You scared me stiff."

Alex chuckled.

When his voice died down, the words I had wanted to avoid a little longer stumbled out, "I know what happened at the manor. I know they are dead."

He rose on one elbow and looked at me with profound tenderness. "I wish I could make it all go away. I'm sorry I wasn't here when you got the news. I'm sorry I had to leave you. Forgive me. I had to."

"The abandonment was brutal, Lieutenant. Regardless of being the right thing or not, I will hold it against you," I said playfully, softening the soberness of the conversation.

"I know you will."

"I still can't believe you left me with a group of soldiers in charge."

"I left Captain Frankfort in charge."

"Same difference."

"Leaving you with Thomas wasn't an easy decision. He loves you." Alex's words carried an undeniable truth. "Because he would die for you,

I knew you were safe with him. And I also knew I could trust him to be honorable."

"He is a good man and quite a protector." I felt no need to elaborate. Instead, I went on to the question that weighed on my mind. "Tell me. How was your mission?"

"Not *too* complicated."

"So there were complications?"

"When we disembarked, a vehicle from the French army picked up my men as a decoy. I took off on foot, dressed in civilian clothes, of course. But I knew from the minute I left the ship that someone pursued me."

Alex was here with me, safe and in one piece. Still, my heart raced at the story.

He continued. "I guided him to a deserted alley, where we worked it out."

"I'm glad your face is not bruised again." I brushed my fingers across his cheeks, noticing that even when there were no fresh wounds, the vestiges of the beating remained.

"I was sure lucky. I went on to deliver the documents and found out they'd also followed the car carrying my crew. They engaged in gunfire. One of my men lies in the hospital, recovering from a gunshot wound."

"I'm so glad no one died."

"Me too. It's a great relief. The mission was a success. Hopefully, the information will help stop the madness."

"Thomas told me a few things he heard at the fortress about the war, but it wasn't much."

"The conflict just got worse. We engaged in an offensive to relieve pressure on the French at Verdun, which neither your father nor I agreed with and hoped would never happen. It'll simply be another manslaughter and won't get us anywhere." Anger flashed in Alex's eyes. "We need to leave right away. I can only stay in Breamore for the funeral before moving to London. I'll be spending much of my time at headquarters. Now that those documents are safe, there will be many meetings to reevaluate our situation."

"Are you going to leave me at Forti Radici?"

"No, unless you want me to. My plan is for us to stay at my flat."

"The famous flat. I'll finally get to see it." I slipped off the bed and raised my arms over my head to stretch my back.

"Where is my lady going?"

"For a stroll. My muscles are ungiving."

"I can help with that." He pulled me back into the bed. "You know, now that I think about it, I will miss this place. The little time we spent here together was our time. Let's enjoy it a little longer." His fingers weaved through my hair, releasing the bun I'd made before going to sleep. "I love you." His voice trailed off, his lips gently trailing kisses down my neck.

CHAPTER 22
~ DESOLATED ~

The green fields surrounding Forti Radici unfolded along our path. I urged my horse into a fast gallop, leaving the group of soldiers behind. The manor came into view, and my heart sped up. I was home. However, the sight tricked me into a costly illusion. For a moment, I could see Mrs. Allerton in the garden, chastising Mr. Leroy for not pruning the vines the way she liked them and Father helping Mr. Lewis to shine the already beaming Silver Ghost while discussing the latest news. Sadly, those were memories of a past that would never repeat itself.

I dismounted near the water fountain where my wedding took place. The once meticulously tended flowerbeds had been trodden under men's feet. I observed the ribbons Mrs. Allerton had dressed the garden with now scattered among the debris, and my chest constricted.

Alex caught up with me at the door. "It might be worse than you think," he warned.

"I'll be all right. I need to do this by myself."

"I'll check out the stable, then."

I sighed and stepped inside, then made my way from room to room, accompanied by the presence of death and destruction. Furniture lay strewn about, windows had been shattered, and bloodstains painted a vivid picture of the sanguinary conflict that took place. The profound sense of loss gripped me anew. Forti Radici had gone from being my haven to a place haunted by the deaths of those I loved. Though I'd had time to prepare for this, it felt surreal now that I stood here. I couldn't wrap my mind around it.

I fled to the stable in a trance. *Thank heaven.* It had been spared from the destruction. The aisles remained unobstructed, and the hay lay neatly stacked to the sides as Mrs. Allerton liked it. Alex and a few others moved busily about in preparation for the night. They inspected the horses, readied the stalls, and brought in fresh food and water for the horses.

"I'm sorry you had to go through that." Alex pushed a water trough across the aisle.

"Me too."

"We'll clean the house as soon as we are done here. It shouldn't take long with all of us helping. You'll feel better once it's done. But for now, check out the stall at the far end."

"Why?"

"Someone is waiting for you there." He smiled. "Come on. I'll show you."

I felt ashamed not to have thought about her and elated to see her again. "Sunny!" I kissed the bridge of her nose and laced my arms around her neck. "It's good to see you. So good."

"The rest of your horses must have fled during the skirmish. We'll ask around. Someone must have found them."

"Well," I said to Sunny, "I'm happy you know your way back home."

We were thorough in the cleaning process—washing and airing the house, restoring the furniture to its proper places, and discarding the broken items.

"Florence, come with me."

Alex's voice gave me a little start. So concerned about not ruining Mr. Grant's French bread recipe was I that I failed to hear his approach. "Can it wait?" I dropped the dough on the counter and rubbed my hands together to free them of the sticky clumps.

"Not really. The helpers from my parents' house have arrived. I would like you to meet them."

"Any word from our staff?" I missed them. They were part of the family, and their return would bring a sense of normalcy.

"Not yet, but don't worry. They'll pop up soon enough."

I observed the dough with pity. Mr. Grant would be disappointed. Unlike his, mine was thick, heavy, and flat to the touch.

"Are you coming?" Alex insisted.

"Yes, yes."

I washed my hands and followed him to the foyer, where a man and woman waited. The man was tall and slender with brown hair and large dark eyes that stared at me like a distrustful owl. The woman was good-looking, with short blonde hair and a nice figure. But when her gaze turned to me, I was taken aback by the coolness I saw there.

"Mrs. White, Mr. Vines, this is my wife, Florence Sterling."

"Nice to meet you both," I greeted. "Welcome to Forti Radici."

"Thank you," said Mrs. White curtly. "We are thrilled to be here."

"It's a pleasure to meet you, Mrs. Sterling. The Sterlings told us many great things about you." Mr. Vines shook my hand.

They would fill in for Mrs. Allerton and Mr. Leroy, though it felt strangely disrespectful to have these newcomers take their place. Although, Mr. Vines made it clear he was no gardener. He would only help around the house as a repairman.

"I don't recall meeting you." If I had, no doubt, I'd have remembered them.

"That's right. They weren't at my parents' home when you visited," Alex said. "They only work part-time."

"Most unfortunate." Mrs. White smiled awkwardly.

"Well then. Welcome again. I hope you'll feel at home here." I didn't miss the sharp glance Mrs. White gave me as I weaved my arm through Alex's.

"I'm sure we'll like it very much." She smiled again.

"Thank you for coming at such a short notice," Alex said. "I trust you'll know what to do around the place."

"Indeed, we do," Mr. Vines assured. "Leave it in our hands."

Portraying confidence and a sense of urgency, Mrs. White and Mr. Vines marched down the corridor.

I stared after them. Something about them set me on edge, something I couldn't place. "Are you sure we can trust them?"

"They have worked for my parents for years, and we never had any problems."

"Hmm . . ."

"I know it's hard to hire new people this soon. But let's give them a chance. Oh, I almost forgot. I have a surprise for you in the library."

"You do?"

"Yes, come on."

Alex stepped to the side, letting me in first. Joy filled me when I looked at the man staring at me from across the room.

"Miss Contini!" He strode over to me.

I threw my arms around him. It was so good, so terribly good, to see him again. "Mr. Lewis, I'm glad you are back!"

"Oh, Miss Contini. Excuse me, I should say, Mrs. Sterling, I'm thrilled to be back." He glanced at Alex, who lingered on the threshold, looking pleased with the reunion.

"Where have you been, Mr. Lewis?"

"When the guests were asked to leave, I drove the Sterlings home. And they insisted I stay with them."

"I found out when I called my parents after we arrived." Alex moved to the window and signaled me to look through the broken glass into the yard. "Mr. Lewis brought another surprise with him."

"Goodness gracious! It's so wonderful to see it again!" I exclaimed, gazing at the Silver Ghost. My father loved the car, and it was now a connection to his memory.

"Still a beauty," Mr. Lewis said with pride. "Still a beauty."

———

"I didn't see a ring on her finger. Is she married?" I asked Alex as we sat in my father's office.

"Married? Who?"

"Mrs. White, of course. She's a pretty woman. Don't you think?"

"What's bothering my lady?" Alex put down the newspaper he had been reading.

"I wish I knew her better, that's all."

"With time, you will. But if it helps your curiosity, Mrs. White is a widow. Her husband, Frederick, used to work for my parents too. He passed away a few years ago."

"He did? He was quite young, wasn't he?"

"Late thirties, I think. Always sick, always in pain, he suffered from a rare disease. Poor fellow. Death was a relief to him."

"That's awful. I can't imagine what Mrs. White must have been through." I sympathized with her. However, the thought of the woman hovering perpetually in the background, as her duties would dictate, left me disquieted. I could only hope that in time, I would grow more accustomed to her presence.

We held two separate funerals, the first for Mrs. Allerton and Mr. Leroy. Saying goodbye to them was one of the hardest things I ever did. I missed them terribly. The following day, a bright Sunday morning, we paid our last respects to my father. Attendees flooded the parish grounds, having traveled from every corner of the country to bid farewell to General Marcus Contini.

A dozen soldiers dressed in crisp blue uniforms stood around the freshly dug grave. The ceremony opened with a series of shots that reverberated through the sky in respect for the fallen leader. The priest spoke briefly, followed by Alex's eulogy. Margaret and William Sterling remained at my side, providing emotional and physical strength as I wept and my knees buckled.

I watched as Alex and Colonel Swinger reverently retrieved the flag covering the coffin, then folded it over and over upon itself. My father's life had been like that folded flag—layer upon layer of knowledge, wisdom, and love—all of which had gone with him. All, except for the piece of his heart left with me through his affection and teachings. Alex extended the flag to me with tenderness in his eyes.

Among others, General Sterling, Colonel Swinger, and Captain Frankfort helped lower Father's coffin into the ground. General Contini would now rest peacefully next to his dear wife and son.

The final shots, saluting the great general, echoed through the air.

"Until we meet again," I whispered and pressed the British flag Father had so loved against my chest.

<hr>

We were ready to depart for London. Thomas and Catherine, who had graciously stayed after the funeral to keep us company, left early in the morning. Only Alex's parents remained.

"Are you feeling better, my dear?" Margaret asked as we enjoyed the afternoon in the garden.

"I am. The funerals were heartrending, but my parents are together, and so are Mrs. Allerton and Mr. Leroy. I'm sure they are happy."

"Well said, darling, well said. Funerals are always hard, but we all need closure." Margaret reached for the teapot, and her gaze found the flowers on the other side of the evergreens. "Oh my, are those wild gladioli?"

"Indeed."

"They are so rare in these parts."

"It was Mrs. Allerton's favorite garden." Thankfully, it survived the attack.

Mrs. White came from around the hedge of evergreens. "Mrs. Margaret, I thought I would see if you need anything."

"Thank you," Margaret responded. "We are quite all right for now, right, dear?" She addressed me.

"Yes. Thank you, Mrs. White."

Margaret left her chair. "I must get a better look at the gladioli. They are so beautiful."

"Mrs. White," I called as she shifted to leave.

"Yes, Miss Contini?"

"Please, call me Mrs. Sterling or Florence," I reminded her for the second time.

"Yes, of course."

"Would you please tell Alex to join us for tea?"

"Certainly, Mrs. Sterling."

"Thank you."

Margaret returned from admiring the flowers. "Isn't she marvelous? Always so helpful. I don't know what I would've done without her. She nursed me back to health more than once. She is an angel in disguise," Margaret praised the housekeeper.

I smiled to be polite. Mrs. White might be an angel, but what kind remained unknown. The more I got to know her, the more I feared she had a dark side—and worse, that she disliked me.

"I must say those plants are priceless. Mrs. Allerton did an extraordinary job with them," Margaret observed, settling back in her chair.

I glanced longingly at the plants. I could almost see Mrs. Allerton wandering through the flourishing garden, quietly nodding in approval at the vibrant colors.

"I'm sorry, dear. I've saddened you with memories."

"Don't worry. It's all right."

Margaret took my hand in hers. "You must know that William and I always wished to have a daughter. And now we do. We love you as our own and are overjoyed to have you in our lives."

"Thank you, Margaret. I consider myself blessed to belong to your family."

"I must confess that there were moments when I worried Alexander would never marry."

"I know what you mean."

"Florence, he loves you more than anything in the world. You make our Alexander so happy, and I can't imagine how wonderful it will be when you have a baby."

"A baby—oh! I'm not ready for that."

"When the time comes, you will be." She sipped her tea, then spit it out. "Oh my, it's cold."

"Am I missing something?" Alex stepped into the garden.

"Just cold tea," I replied.

"We were talking about you two having a baby." His mother smiled at him.

"Sounds like a good idea." He winked at me.

Margaret giggled and shifted in her chair, ready to continue the discussion.

I quickly changed the subject. "I would offer you tea, but you won't like it. It's gone cold."

"I could use another cup. I'll heat it." Margaret left, teapot in hand.

"Were you asleep?" I noticed the hollows under his eyes.

"I was."

"I'm sorry. I didn't know. You look like you could have slept a little longer."

"The exhaustion from the past weeks is finally catching up with me, but two hours was a good enough nap." He dropped beside me. "But seriously, Florence, if you want me down here, you don't have to be so drastic."

"Drastic? What do you mean?"

"Mrs. White traipsed into the bedroom before I had time to react."

"She didn't knock?"

"She must've forgotten that little detail, but I would rather think she did knock, and I didn't hear her."

"What happened?"

"I was getting dressed."

"She must've enjoyed that," I retorted.

"She didn't mind it, for sure."

"Stop playing games and tell me," I pressed.

"No, seriously. She stood there, and I hid behind your folding screen."

I laughed, but it wasn't funny. "I see. Your soldier reflexes came to the rescue."

"Thankfully. It was quite uncomfortable."

Our time in London was blissful despite Alex attending to his military duties. I couldn't deny that the past still haunted me, but the healing balm of the love between us helped me endure. After a prolonged absence, primarily out of obligation, we returned to Forti Radici for the weekend. Alex went to the study to work, and I strolled the gardens.

I rounded the corner of the house and froze. Was this real? I stared at the bare wall for a long while not believing my eyes. Then, out of the blue, the need to check on Mrs. Allerton's wild gladiolus gripped me. Again, I was dumbfounded. "I must've lost my mind." I blinked and blinked, but what I saw remained unchanged. I stormed inside, indignant.

Mr. Grant, Lucy, Mrs. White, Mr. Vines, and the new groundskeeper, Mr. Sawyer, assembled the luncheon in the kitchen. They looked up, startled, as I entered.

I met Mr. Sawyers's disconcerted stare and said, "Explain why you cut down the vines on the east wall and destroyed the gladioli garden?"

"Mrs. Sterling, I—" Stopping short, he found Mrs. White's eyes.

"I'm waiting."

"Mrs. White asked me to. I'm sorry, Mrs. Sterling. I simply followed her orders," Mr. Sawyer stammered.

"You!" I tried to keep my emotions under control, but my anger got the best of me. "Why the devil did you order such a thing?"

"Mrs. Sterling, I suggest you lower your voice. It's not appropriate for the lady of the house to behave like a wild creature in front of the staff," she answered.

"I'll tell you what is inappropriate—inappropriate is for you to lecture me. Or worse, do whatever you think is best in *my* house. Now, answer me. Why did you have Mr. Sawyer ruin the plants?"

She tried hard to hide her contempt for me, but her face betrayed her. "General Sterling told me to do it."

Lucy gasped. Mr. Grant dropped his fork. The groundskeeper looked at the stove.

"He would never do such a thing," I scoffed. "How dare you accuse him."

"If you don't believe me, ask him," she taunted, hands on her hips.

"I will, and while I do, you'd better gather your things." I left the kitchen, telling myself to breathe, to think about this. But I simply couldn't. It hurt me deeply to have lost the plants that Mrs. Allerton and Mr. Leroy loved so much. They had been a sanctuary to me—a place where I could recall happy memories and feel their influence. I flew down the corridors and into the study.

Alex sat at the desk, completely focused on a stack of papers.

"Did you order Mrs. White to cut down the vines and destroy the gladioli?" I said with an edge.

"Did I do what?"

"You heard me. The vines are gone, along with Mrs. Allerton's plants."

He met me halfway across the room. "Florence, calm down." He placed his hands on my shaky shoulders.

"You haven't answered my question. Did you or did you not?"

"I . . ." Awareness crossed his face. "Well, when we hired the new gardener, I told Mrs. White to trim the damaged plants so they'd grow back stronger. I wasn't thinking about the vines or the gladioli. It's just a misunderstanding."

"How can it be a misunderstanding when neither plant was damaged? Besides, she knew how fond I was of them. I find it hard to believe she didn't do it on purpose." I shrugged his hands off.

"We'll replant them. They are just plants," Alex said.

"Just plants!" I stared at him in disbelief. "How can you be so insensitive?"

"Florence, you are taking this too far. I'm sure Mrs. White meant no harm."

"Of course she didn't, just as I don't intend any harm by not dining with you tonight and not allowing you to stay in *my* room!"

CHAPTER 23
~HIDDEN TRUTH ~

When had the suspicion taken hold of me? I didn't know. Perhaps it wasn't a moment I could single out but the result of many subtle incidents. Somehow, I could overcome her questionable actions, even the atrocity she committed with the vines and gladioli. Although I hadn't forgotten it, out of pure consideration for Margaret, I forgave Mrs. White. As for Alex, his innocent insensitivity to my feelings hurt, but I loved him too much to stay angry. However, this new awareness haunted me.

It had been an uncomfortable drive back to the manor from London. We arrived late in the evening, and after supper, we retreated to the drawing room.

"What's wrong, my lady? You hardly touched your food tonight." Alex took the armchair by the crackling fire.

"I'm quite tired. It's been a long day." Not wanting to alarm him, I did my best to hide how frail I felt. Alex had recently been appointed to take my father's place in the army. His responsibilities amid the war vexed him mentally and emotionally, and I didn't want to burden him with my health. However, for the past week, nausea and a sensation of dizziness replaced my appetite, challenging my pretense.

"You look pale. Maybe we should ring for the doctor."

"Nonsense. I'll feel better in the morning." I lay down on the sofa across from his chair. "If I fall asleep, carry me to the bedroom." I smiled.

Alex grabbed the coverlet and tucked it around me. "I sure will." He kissed my cheek and returned to his seat to read the newspaper.

Soon, my eyelids drooped. The warmth from the fire enveloped me, and I drifted into a light sleep. But it wasn't long before I heard the door open, followed by footsteps. I knew those almost imperceptible footsteps too well by now. Mrs. White sauntered across the room to Alex and placed the tea tray on the coffee table.

Too comfortable to sit up, I remained as if I were asleep, watching her through my eyelashes.

She poured a cup of tea and handed it to him.

"Thank you, Mrs. White." Alex didn't look up from his reading.

"It's a bit dark in here." She turned on the lamp behind him.

"That helps. Thanks." He thumbed through to another page.

"Would you like a blanket for your legs?" she asked.

"No, that's not necessary."

"Well then, allow me. The fire is dying down," she offered.

"Please, don't bother. I can do it." Still, Alex didn't look at her.

"It's no bother at all." She propped a log on top of the embers and waited for it to catch before adding another.

None of this would've seemed out of the ordinary except for the way she executed it all. The way she moved around him, the way she bent over the fire, the way she leaned above him alarmingly evidenced her desire. Only my presence prevented her from touching him. And she grew more brazen with each passing day.

My stomach twisted in revulsion. "I'll have some tea as well." I bolted upright.

Startled, Mrs. White stepped away from Alex. "Yes, of course, Mrs. Sterling." She reached for the teapot.

"I'll do it myself. You may leave now," I said brusquely.

"My lady, did you get any rest?" It was the first time Alex's attention left the paper.

"Not much."

Mrs. White withdrew with a dark expression. Jealousy, perhaps?

This incident solidified my suspicion. Mrs. White loved Alex. Would he believe me if I told him? Not likely. He would laugh. Could I prove it?

No. She would never admit to it. Would I allow her to stay? Margaret would be offended if I let Mrs. White go without reason. Would I confront her in private or ignore her actions? I didn't know.

Snowflakes coated the windowpane. Behind me, a crowd interacted joyfully. Forti Radici hosted a Christmas party once again. The year 1916 had come to an end, and the New Forest lay under a blanket of snow. It had been the best and worst year of my life—a year I gained and lost more than words could express.

I reflected on the experiences that willingly or unwillingly were mine. The deep wounds in my heart had molded my soul. The scars were permanent, but time had been merciful, and the hope of being with my loved ones in the afterlife helped me manage the grief. Nevertheless, every time it surfaced, I found refuge in happy memories of my loved ones.

Positivity took over as I concentrated on how lucky I was to have had my brother, Father, Mrs. Allerton, and Mr. Leroy in my life. My heart filled with gratitude instead of misery. It also helped me enjoy what I now had, with Alex at its center. His love was the anchor in my life. So, as the new year approached, I was blessed with peace, inside and out. The physical discomfort of the past couple of months left me, and I finally knew its source, which added to my happiness.

I strolled to the library and joined Alex on the piano bench. To the admiration of our guests, he played some of Beethoven's best pieces.

"Your playing is heavenly," I whispered.

"I know," he replied a little smugly. "I owe it to my mother, who chased me with a stick if I didn't practice."

"Thank goodness for Margaret." I glanced at the women in the room and saw they were spellbound. "I also imagine you know the effect your musical skills have on the ladies."

"It's not just my musical skills. It's my looks."

I rolled my eyes. "You are insufferable, Lieutenant."

"I know. But you are distracting me, and I must keep up the entertainment."

"I think I'll continue to distract you. I don't like the attention you are getting."

"Are you jealous, Mrs. Sterling?"

"I wouldn't be human if I wasn't."

Suddenly, his fingers froze, and the piano fell silent. He took my face into his hands and kissed me soundly, stealing my breath. The crowd cheered and applauded. I knew I blushed because my cheeks were on fire.

"Do you feel better now?" A wide smile spread across his face.

"Much better. Much better." I hoped he caught the sarcasm in my voice. His gaze took on that shine I had come to love so much, and fearing that he would kiss me again, I stood. "I won't distract you any longer. Do continue."

Pleased with himself, he resumed. I headed to the dining room, where the large table overflowed with Mr. Grant's best pies, vegetable dishes, and desserts, all ingredients locally grown. And even with my hearty appetite, I found it hard to decide.

"You should try the lemon cake." Thomas had a good variety of goodies on his plate.

"Ah, it's always a great choice." I picked up a piece.

"It's wonderful to see you so cheerful."

"Thanks, Thomas."

"Everything is delicious." He swallowed another bite of trifle. "You have done a marvelous job with the party."

"I'm afraid Mrs. White planned most of it."

"Knowing you, that's hard to believe." He smiled.

"I may have helped a bit."

"How are you getting along with her?" Thomas motioned toward the hall, where Mrs. White went from room to room, watching over the guests and ensuring they were well cared for.

"Why do you ask?" I finished the lemon cake and placed a slice of fruitcake on my plate.

"She doesn't strike me as the friendly type. She seems uptight, like a feline ready to pounce."

Interesting assessment.

As if sensing that we spoke of her, Mrs. White glanced at us. Her eyes had recently grown cooler than usual. I faked a smile, and she moved on. Even though I would've loved to, I refrained from telling Thomas how much I distrusted her, especially because Alex, his superior, had hired her.

"She is efficient at her job. That's all that matters, right?"

"If you say so." Stepping closer, he softly asked, "How are you truly doing?"

"The truth? I thought I would never feel balanced again, but I am getting there."

"I'm thrilled to hear that," Thomas said around another mouthful of trifle.

"Though I still miss them." The words flowed naturally, sincerely.

"I can imagine. General Contini's absence is greatly felt in the army. It takes time."

"I hope General Sterling is not disappointing at headquarters."

"He is managing well, and judging by what I have seen here today, he is also succeeding at home."

"I can't complain. But enough of us. What have you been up to besides work?"

"Not much." He avoided my gaze.

"Not true," I accused. "Tell me."

"Sounds like you already know." He was right. I had heard comments here and there. "Yes, it's true. Catherine and I are seeing each other."

"That's great news! You make a perfect couple."

"Shh. Not so loud. People will hear."

"What is wrong with that?"

"Rumors spread like wildfire, and people will be planning my wedding before I know it."

"And there is no wedding?"

"Not yet. It's too soon."

"Speaking of Catherine, where is she? I wish she had come."

"In London with family for the week."

"I see."

Thomas filled his cup with fresh lemonade and gulped it down. "Florence, there's something different about you, something unusual." He contemplated me for a moment. "I'm not sure how to describe it."

I was surprised he perceived the change taking place in me, but I couldn't tell him until I told Alex. "I think it's called peace. Thomas, I am quite content."

Christmas day arrived with a blinding light. The sun's rays glistened off the blanket of snow and filled the woods with a celestial glow. I shifted from the window and returned to bed, where Alex slept on. 1 brushed my fingers across his back, my stomach twisting with anticipation. He shifted to his side, and I slipped into his arms.

"Happy Christmas." He kissed my forehead.

"Happy Christmas to you."

"Do you want to know something?" he asked.

"I don't know. Do I?"

"Yes."

"Tell me, then," I said.

"I love you."

"Ah, I did know that."

"You take advantage of that, don't you?" He pinched my waist playfully.

"Quite soon, you won't be able to do that."

"And why is that?" He got up and pulled on his shirt.

"General, you are going to be a father."

He beheld me in awe. "Are you serious? Are you sure?" He jumped back into the bed on his knees.

"I've waited two months to tell you to be absolutely sure."

"Florence, that's wonderful. I can't believe it!" He placed his hand on my belly.

"If I've calculated correctly, the baby will come in July."

"This is the best Christmas gift." He planted a kiss on my lips. "Thank you."

"You are welcome." I returned the kiss. "Your parents will be thrilled, especially your mother."

"I can't wait to tell them." Alex's gaze wandered dreamily beyond the room. "If it's a girl, we'll call her little lady."

I laughed, knowing it didn't matter. Either way, this child would be our greatest joy.

By June, Dr. Jones prohibited me from riding horses. I had pushed his decision far enough and could avoid it no longer.

"It's too dangerous in your condition," he had said. "You're done riding for a while." I felt as if my legs were cut off, but I strictly obeyed.

Since my belly had grown considerably, making it difficult to move about, I hunkered down at the manor while the war raged on, and Alex continued to spend most of his time in London. I'd missed the last two trips to with him and depended more and more on Mrs. White to handle any needs that arose. Her apparent dislike for me and my distrust toward her hadn't diminished, but having been away as much as we had in the past year helped me cope with the situation. I still didn't have a tangible reason to let her go.

The tiny person inside me became more active than ever. Every day, I felt his little legs pressing against my ribs and his little fists waking me up in the morning. Though I couldn't see him yet, our connection transcended the physical realm. He flourished within my womb, soaking up the love and excitement I held for him, and in turn, I thrived, experiencing his growth and sensing his innocence. His company eased the loneliness of Alex's absences, especially when sleep eluded me.

Tonight was one of those nights. Yesterday, Alex left for London to arrange a leave from the army so he could be here to receive our child. I lay on my side, a pillow propped under my belly. Outside the open window, a symphony of cicadas and crickets brought the night to life.

Though there was no breeze to chase away the stifling air. I turned to my other side, but nothing helped. I was hot and restless.

"*A cup of milk will help you relax*," I recalled Mrs. Allerton's counsel when as a child I feared the dark. It was worth a try. From deep within the house, the grandfather clock, a relic from the 1800s, struck twelve times.

My swollen legs felt heavy and slow as I left my bedroom and descended the staircase, holding my tummy. *One step at a time, Florence.* I stepped onto the landing and heaved a breath. I followed the winding corridor while the baby kicked against my ribs as if possessed. Taking another deep breath, I paused, hoping to dissuade him from another kick. Two more kicks, and he finally relented. I resumed my march and noticed a sliver of light coming from the kitchen's partly open door. Then, voices reached my ears. It was odd. Who could be up at this time of night? I inched closer.

"You are a fool!" Mrs. White hissed.

"The only fool here is you. Why won't you accept it? You are wasting your life, and for what? In pursuit of the impossible," Mr. Vines cried angrily.

"He is young and stubborn, but sooner or later, he'll accept his love for me."

"How can he accept something that doesn't exist? Something which will never exist?" Mr. Vines refuted. "Free yourself from the obsession and give me a chance."

"Don't be an idiot. One doesn't let go easily when love is so deep."

"Why won't you allow me to prove you wrong? You know how I feel about you." His voice softened. "I've been faithful to you through it all, even Frederick."

"Don't you dare threaten me." Her voice vibrated with something more than anger. Was it fear?

"I'm not threatening you. I'm trying to help you see how strongly I feel about you."

"Well, you know how I feel about him. Just like you are willing to wait for me, I'm willing to wait for him."

"You can't ignore that your situations are completely different. He will never be yours. He has everything a man could ask for—a career, a beautiful wife, and soon a child. He has a family."

"Well then, if he is not with me, he might be better off alone." My blood froze at the viciousness in her words. "You know very well that I won't hesitate in removing any obstacles."

"Deborah, for heaven's sake!" he cried.

They spoke of Alex. I had been right all along. She'd fallen in love with him. Remove the obstacles? What was this woman capable of? I made the decision in a split second. For now, they couldn't know I had overheard their conversation. Without Alex, I was unsafe and vulnerable under my own roof. With my heartbeat thumping in my ears, I retraced my steps to my bedroom, locked the door, and climbed into bed, but I knew sleep wouldn't come. My physical discomfort paled in comparison to the threat of the woman obsessed with my husband. *"If he is not with me, he might be better off alone."* Her words pounded in my head. My child and I were in danger.

"Alex, you must come home at once," I said over the telephone.

"Lady, what is wrong?"

"Last night, I heard something alarming that changes everything. I can't tell you over the phone."

"Are you feeling unwell? How is the baby?"

"We're fine." Not wanting to sound hysterical, though I was, I said, "I need you at home." I had managed Mrs. White thus far; I could do so a bit longer.

"Florence, are you sure you're all right? Are you sure you don't want to tell me what's bothering you?"

"I'm sure. We should discuss it in person."

"I have a meeting I must attend, but I'll leave right after. I should be home this evening. Florence, I love you."

"I love you more."

A shuffling of feet called my attention to the corridor. I replaced the receiver and hurried to the doorway. At the bend of the intercepting hallway, I caught a glimpse of a shadow scurrying away. Someone had listened to my telephone conversation.

I needed some fresh air. Thankfully, I hadn't seen Mrs. White this afternoon, and Alex would be home in a few hours. I moved with purpose to the stable, needing the love and companionship of my faithful friend.

Six horses watched me from their stalls, their big, wide eyes shining in the semidarkness. I passed them, noticing they had plenty of hay and water, and came to the one I was here for. Sunny. She swung her head over the short door separating us and gently nudged my arm. I pressed my cheek against her cold nose. "I'll be able to ride you again soon, you know. You and I will watch this baby grow. We'll watch him run through the green fields in the summer and play in the snow in the winter. He will love you as much as I do."

I picked up a brush from a bucket and stepped inside her stall, where I ran the brush over her brown mane, drifting into pleasant dreams of the days ahead.

Sunny neighed as her attention was drawn to the entrance, her black eyes widened, her nostrils flared. There, Mrs. White held a burlap sack. She traveled down the aisle, her dark gaze sweeping over the horses. They recoiled, nickering and shifting from one foot to the other as she passed them. Even Billy, who wasn't easily frightened, let out a snort and shuffled restlessly in his compartment.

Mrs. White planted herself before Sunny's stall, radiating a malevolent energy. "You love horses too much."

"They are faithful and trustworthy, unlike some humans," I said calmly, though I knew she would not miss the meaning behind my words.

Mrs. White stepped closer to the short door. "Perhaps, but you fail to acknowledge the one thing horses have in common with humans."

Sunny neighed and rocked back and forth in the limited space, growing increasingly agitated.

"Remind me," I said to the housekeeper, and to Sunny, "It's all right, girl." I stroked her neck, but it did nothing to reassure her.

"Fear, darling. Fear," Mrs. White spat the words with venom. My blood ran cold. She was right, especially in Sunny's case. In the blink of an eye, Mrs. White dug her hand into the sack, retrieved an adder snake, and threw it at Sunny's feet. I screamed and shrunk against the partition wall.

The silver-grey reptile with black markings launched into frenzied swirling between Sunny's legs. Sunny pounded the ground, desperately attempting to subdue the threat, but the snake moved quickly, hissing and striking at the horse until it bit Sunny's thigh. I was trapped. I couldn't get past the horse, but I had to protect my baby. He deserved to meet his father, to love and be loved.

I turned from the terrified Sunny and the snake to the wall, shielding my unborn child. From the corner of my eye, I saw the snake strike again. Sunny reared up on her hind legs, her hoofs slamming into my back. There was an audible crack as my spine snapped. Dimly, I registered Mrs. White's diabolical laugh.

"My baby!" I cried and collapsed to the floor.

Through spasms of agony, I heard Mr. Vines shout, "Deborah, what the devil are you doing?" before I lost consciousness.

CHAPTER 24

~ THE SILENT ANGEL ~

The pressure on my abdomen awoke me. Where was I? What was happening? Struggling to get out of my head, I forced my eyelids open just enough to see my surroundings. Mrs. White stood beside the bed, her arms locked, her hands on top of my belly. Lucy came into view, moving busily about with towels and other items. Next, I saw Dr. Jones at the foot of the bed, his face etched with exhaustion and worry. Bewildered, I tried to move my head to see more.

The memory came quickly, mercilessly—Sunny kicking with ferocity, me turning to save my baby, the sensation of my spine snapping, the panic and pain, and everything going black. I focused on the doctor again, and it hit me. *I'm giving birth.*

"Keep trying, ladies. We must get the baby out," Dr. Jones urged as Lucy joined Mrs. White in her efforts to force the baby out.

"She's losing too much blood. There's no use," Mrs. White said in a weary tone, but she continued to work.

"We must get him out, or they'll both die." Catching my eye, the doctor said, "Mrs. Sterling, can you hear me? We need you to push. Can you hear me?"

His voice faded as my mind slipped away . . .

·   ·   ·

A muffled whimpering pulled me from the edge of unconsciousness. Little by little, it grew into a strong cry. My child. I fought against the heaviness that trapped me. I wanted to see him. However, while my mind sharpened, my body felt strangely disconnected from the world.

"He won't survive without her," Mrs. White stated pessimistically.

"He is a little fragile but looks healthy," Dr. Jones observed.

A baby boy. I had been right all along.

I had to see him. I might never have the chance again. Mustering every ounce of strength I had, I turned my head. The figures formed slowly. Mrs. White held a bundle in her arms. I spotted his tiny head and hands. I yearned to hold him, to see his face. I tried to speak, but no sound came out.

My gaze followed Mrs. White as she left the room. I stared at the door for a long while. My son would never return to me—that much I knew.

"We are losing her! Bring more towels," the doctor cried. "Have you found General Sterling?"

"He is en route," Lucy responded.

My eyes became unbearably heavy, and everything went black once more.

How much time elapsed I couldn't tell, but long enough for Alex to have arrived. I felt him holding my hand. I wished he could take me into his arms and comfort me, take my suffering away as he always did, but, physically, I felt nothing.

"There must be something you can do," Alex implored the doctor.

"I wish there was, but she has lost too much blood, and her spinal cord is injured beyond repair."

"We must take her to London."

"General, moving her would only hasten her passing."

"There must be something you can do! There must be!" Alex choked out in agony.

"I'm deeply sorry. All we can do is make her last days, perhaps hours, as comfortable as possible." The doctor's voice broke.

"I don't understand. How did this happen? It doesn't make any sense." The ache in Alex's voice deepened my own. I was leaving him, but how could I?

"We are lucky Mr. Vines found her when he did," said the doctor.

"Something must have scared Sunny. It's not in her nature to be wild."

"She might have tried to ride her." Mrs. White's unexpected words made me aware of her presence.

"Nonsense! She wouldn't do that," Alex defended.

"I agree with the general. Mrs. Sterling wouldn't do such a foolish thing," Dr. Jones said.

At last, I opened my eyes and focused. I tried to speak, but only guttural sounds issued forth.

"Florence, I am here. Everything is going to be fine. Can you hear me?"

I stared into my husband's eyes, desperately wanting to communicate with him, but my voice refused to obey.

"I shouldn't have left. I'll never forgive myself for leaving you when you needed me most. If only I had come back sooner."

My gaze searched his, inquiring about our baby.

He understood. "Oh, Florence, I'm so sorry. Our baby. . . he was too frail." Tears rolled down his cheeks.

Our precious baby was dead, the reality of it too immense to comprehend. At last, my agony won the battle. I couldn't fight it anymore.

"Florence, please don't leave me!" Alex pleaded.

In my mind, I spoke the words my traitorous voice refused to. *Alex, I wish I could stay, but my body is already gone. My life is slipping away. I ache at what has been stolen from us. I long to feel your sweet embrace, share our tears, laughter, accomplishments, and disappointments, and spend our days out in the sun together. All of that, along with bearing children, I can't offer you anymore. I pray that in time you'll find someone who will fulfill your needs and that you'll love and be happy again. I want that for you. But I also want you to know I will always love you, and I will always be thankful to have known your love.*

"We better let her rest." Mrs. White approached the bed, interrupting my farewell. My thoughts turned to her. Oh yes, I remembered.

Alex groaned. "I'm not going to leave her again."

My gaze met hers. "*You are responsible for this.*"

"*You are thinking about me,*" her eyes seemed to respond. "*Yes, what you're thinking is true. I'm responsible for your misery, and you'll take the truth to your grave. No one will ever know. We played, and you lost.*"

"*I didn't lose. I won. I'm taking Alex's heart with me until he finds an honorable woman to love. But one thing is for sure, he will never love you because you are wicked,*" I willed her to hear.

A shadow of fear crossed her face, and she retreated to the corner of the room.

My attention returned to Alex. He would forever be the love of my life. I didn't know how or when, but we would be reunited. For now, I just wanted to rest. *Alexander Sterling, I love you. I will always love you.* I closed my eyes and felt the light pressure of his lips one last time.

"I love you, my lady," he whispered.

It felt like I slipped into a peaceful sleep, but an instant later, I found myself standing across from Alex in my spirit form—those in the room were totally unaware of my ghost—their eyes and ears denied the gift of seeing and hearing the otherworldly.

Alex fell to his knees beside my lifeless body. He rested his head on my arm and softly cried.

Dr. Jones, who had patiently watched the unfolding scene, approached and took my pulse. "I'm sorry, General." He shook his head and, in a gesture of respect and compassion, left the room.

"Come, come now," Mrs. White said. "There's nothing else you can do. You must rest."

"Leave me, please," Alex said.

"You need the energy for the days ahead," she insisted, reaching for his shoulder.

"Leave me. Now." Alex shook her hand off. Nothing would separate him from my remains.

Defeated and perhaps offended, Mrs. White complied.

At that moment, the room grew a shade lighter as if a light switch had been flipped, and the knowledge of my entire existence illuminated my understanding. I'd regained the memories of my life before I was born in New York. But why had I been given a chance to live again? Why was I a part of Alex's life a second time? While my thoughts left me feeling confused, some things were crystal clear.

Mr. Sterling grieved for *me* back in New York, the same Florence Contini whose husband he was. The memory of what happened haunted him. His love for me still burned brightly. No wonder he had been so perplexed and tortured by my presence. The idea of a duplicate of his lady brought both hope and madness to his troubled soul. And I didn't just look like the old Florence; I was an exact copy with the same name, born when she died. How could he even attempt to explain those things to me when they made no sense? It was indeed madness.

Alex broke into deep sobs, oblivious to anything in this separate sphere. I stood so close to him, yet he did not sense me. My heart shattered for him, and as I attempted to draw near him, the scene changed to another place and time.

In front of me, people dressed in black gathered around a grave in the cemetery behind the ancient parish in Breamore. The priest withdrew first, and then, one by one, the rest, until only one remained. I moved to the figure crouched on the loose dirt. Alex stared at the newly placed headstone, frozen with grief.

Florence Contini Sterling—
Forever My Lady—
1894–1917

Alex had dreaded the idea that death might separate us, and now he faced his worst fear. I noticed the tiny grave beside mine, confirming my suspicions. It was death's biggest sting.

Sterlings' beloved baby boy,
sleep in peace under the nurturing

love of your dear mother

"Why did you have to leave me? What am I going to do without you?" His voice broke. "Whatever happens to me, I promise you'll always be my lady."

When Alex rose, I saw the change in him, the light and joy in his eyes replaced by despair and detachment. He strode off, his shoulders slumped as if he bore the weight of the world. Death had defeated the great General Sterling.

Just then, the guide who'd taken me back in time reappeared.

I looked more closely at his lively brown eyes, his loving smile, and the anguish I had harbored since his death, like chalk erased from a blackboard, vanished forever. He pressed me to his chest, and my heart burst with joy.

"Lucca, I can't believe it's you!" Happy childhood memories flooded me.

"Florence, you know me! It's wonderful to be recognized." Lucca smiled.

"I have missed you so much!"

"I never left you."

"There are no words to express my gratitude. Though, I must say, you gave me a few good frights at Oak's Place."

He chuckled. "What can I say? Being a ghost has its fun side."

"Lucca, please help me understand. How am I able to live again? To find Alex? I died in adulthood, yet I was a baby the very same year that I died. How?"

"Because you now know who you are, I can connect the pieces for you. This is not the first time we have met since my death. I came to you when you passed away." He held my hand and said, "Remember the space between your death and your second life. Remember."

Mrs. White had thrown the snake into the stall. Sunny had injured my body beyond repair. I had died yet existed in another form, a spirit form.

And suddenly I found myself in an oppressive fog. A sense of anguish, endless isolation, and loneliness washed over me. The suffering my mortal body had experienced under Sunny's attack was minuscule when compared to this new level of grief. I felt trapped inside a box without oxygen and that death would never release me.

"What have I done to deserve this misery?"

"Absolutely nothing," my dear brother said.

"Lucca—Lucca!" The joy of seeing him again, of realizing that Mrs. Allerton had been right all along and there was an afterlife where our dear ones awaited us, was indescribable. I fell into his loving arms, and the fog evaporated like dew beneath the morning sun. We were now on a brightly lit path. The ground beneath us gave off a luminescent glow, separating the darkness behind us from a powerful light that stretched across the horizon. I looked back into the gloom and shivered at the shadows that moved about restlessly.

"Those demons feed on our deepest fears and failures, making us miserable," Lucca explained. "Your spirit is suspended between the living and the dead, allowing you to make an eternal choice. Because you've briefly, and to a lesser degree, experienced darkness, your decision can be just."

"A choice?"

"You lost your life prematurely, causing this imbalance. To satisfy justice, you may reenter mortality to correct some of that. Grief consumes Alexander, and he doesn't deserve a life of misery. You can restore his joy. The love you share connects your souls. Only you can accomplish this, for you own his heart. You can also bring justice and send Mrs. White away from him, for she is bound to cause more damage."

I looked at the inviting warmth of the light on the horizon, then back at the obscurity. "How can I go back? I can't return to my physical body."

"No, your former body is broken beyond repair. If you choose to return, your mortal remains will be reorganized in a new life. It is the only way. And yes, your memories will be wiped clean. The veil of forgetfulness is part of the price you must pay. Love will be your guide and greatest ally."

"A connecting link between our souls . . . guided by love, my greatest ally," I repeated. "Wouldn't that prevent him from ever loving another woman?"

"A woman formed with her own remains is the same woman. And he will not have to fall in love again. His love for you runs through his veins and simply needs to be reawakened. You'll also retain any personal belongings buried with you." He shot a glance at the spiritual bracelet on my wrist. "Furthermore, you'll be reborn in a place where your path crosses his at some point. Now, you'll suffer consequences if you fail to listen to your heart and choose not to be with him. The price for failure after reentering the mortal realm is separation. You won't be with him after mortality, nor will your memories be restored, ever."

I felt as if a hand from the obscurity had stretched out its dreadful fingers to grab me.

"There will be no help from this side of the veil. We are not allowed to interfere unless, through no fault of your own, evil jeopardizes your mission. Only then will we help you see how to balance justice. Nonetheless, if you decide not to take this chance, you'll be instantly drawn into the light, where our loved ones anxiously await you. If you stay, you'll be safe in their company forever."

I considered staying with Lucca, reuniting with the mother I yearned to know, Father, Mrs. Allerton, Mr. Leroy, and my dear baby boy. My heart ached to be with them again. "My loved ones . . . all except for him. Without Alex, the light will be darkness to me. I will take the chance. I will reenter mortal life."

I was back at the cemetery, and the memory of the choice I had made after my death receded to the back of my mind while knowledge settled within me. "It would have worked. Alex and I would have been happy again, even if we did not know the truth. But Mrs. White separated us with her lies, and that's why you came, and I have the chance to go back in time—to remember, to balance justice," I summarized.

Lucca smiled. "I couldn't have said it better myself."

"Alex . . . he is now fighting for his life back in Geneva." I remembered how I had dismissed Zaira's call after I fled Oak's Place, and my thoughts spiraled in desperation. She didn't think he would last the night. "Lucca, he can't die. I must return to him. He must know the truth."

Again, Lucca clasped my hand. I blinked, and we were back where we started—in my room at the monastery in 1938. My mortal body lay peacefully on the bed, just as I left it.

"When you return to your body, it will be the same hour as when we left the room—give or take a few minutes. From then on, you are running against time," he warned. "Do you understand?"

I nodded. "I'll forever be indebted to you."

"My beautiful sister, don't fail." His arms engulfed me, filling me with confidence.

"Our family . . ." I thought of those who were gone, longing to know about them. "How is the next life?"

Lucca smiled brightly. "Better than you can imagine."

"I'll miss you."

"I won't be far." He raised his hand as if saying goodbye, and the next thing I knew, I was back in my body, and he was gone.

Fueled by the intensity of returning to flesh and bone, the heaviness of losing my baby, and leaving Alex behind, I bolted upright, gasping for air. The profound love I felt for them was woven into my body's fiber and sinews.

Many things were still far from my grasp, but I knew my Alex was still the same and we belonged together. How would I explain who I really was? Would he believe me? I had a good chance since my name and likeness to the deceased Florence and the bracelet had paved the way. But for now, it mattered only that I was here for him, and he wouldn't feel alone or defeated any longer. Our past, future, and entire existence depended on me reaching him in time.

CHAPTER 25
~ BREAKING POINT ~

I jumped out of bed and flew downstairs to the kitchen and straight to the telephone. My fingers trembled, making it difficult to dial Oak's Place.

"Zaira! It's me, Florence."

"Florence, I didn't think you'd call."

"Please tell me. How is Alex?"

"Mr. Sterling is fading fast. I'm afraid it's just a matter of time."

"Zaira, tell him I'll be there soon."

"He is unconscious."

"Tell him anyway."

"You are seriously coming?" Zaira questioned.

I understood her incredulity. From her perspective, it had been a short time since I said Mrs. White could care for him. I blamed myself for my willingness to believe in her hateful tale without giving Alex the benefit of the doubt. "Yes, I'm coming. Zaira, please forgive me for what I said earlier. I was confused, but I understand things now."

"It's all right. No harm done."

"Were you able to find a doctor?"

"No. No one will drive out to Geneva until tomorrow."

"I'll find someone. Zaira, please watch over him. I'll be there as soon as I can."

"Florence, he—" Her words were cut short, replaced by Mrs. White's cold voice.

"You have nothing to do here," she hissed. "You would do well not to set foot in Oak's Place again."

"You're wrong. You're the one who should have nothing to do with Alex. I know what you've done, and I'm coming to settle the debt."

"You're a fool!" She hung up.

I heard the clamor of voices outside. The sisters had returned from the fundraiser. The door flung open, and they entered, chatting merrily. Thankfully, they didn't linger. Granny and Sister Callahan came inside last.

"Granny! Alex is deathly ill. Dr. Petersen is out of town, and no one else will come until the morning. We must find Dr. Ferns."

"What's going on?" Sister Callahan asked from where she rummaged through the pantry, probably for a late snack.

I ignored her. "Please, Granny, help me."

"Calm down, child." Granny took hold of my shoulders, her eyes fixed on mine. "If he is so ill, why didn't you stay with him earlier?"

"I can't explain right now. We must find Dr. Ferns."

"I don't think he practices medicine anymore." Granny would've insisted on an explanation any other time, but perhaps because of the urgency in my voice, she desisted. "He is quite aged, I fear, and at this time of night—"

"That's exactly why we need to find him. We need his experience."

Granny shifted to a cupboard. "Well, he might make an exception." She pulled out the phone directory and flipped through the worn pages. "It won't hurt to try."

I moved around impatiently, listening to the ticking of the clock on the counter, mercilessly giving time the advantage over me.

"Oh, child, he is not listed here, and I don't know where he lives."

"I have to get someone." A sob formed in my throat.

"Whining won't solve anything. Yes, yes, you need a doctor. Mr. Sterling is severely ill, and it's late at night." Without encouragement from us, Sister Callahan entered the conversation. "There is one person who surely knows where to find Dr. Ferns. He is well-informed on all that goes on in town."

"Who?" Granny and I asked in unison.

"The priest, of course."

"Yes, yes. Friar Thompson is a good friend of Dr. Ferns," Granny exclaimed. "Why didn't I think of that?"

"Of course he is. Priests and doctors often converge at people's deathbeds," Sister Callahan added.

I didn't appreciate the significance of her statement, but it was undeniably true.

"We just left Friar Thompson at the parish. He should still be awake," Granny said encouragingly.

"Let's call him," I urged.

Granny picked up the receiver. After several tries with no answer, she hung up for good.

"He leaves us no option but to visit him." Sister Callahan readjusted the veil on her head ready for action.

"You are right," Granny concurred. "Friar Thompson won't mind. He is such a dear."

"Right, then. Fannie, stop fiddling while Rome burns and go start the car," Sister Callahan ordered.

Minutes later, we were on our way to the parish. The wind howled through the deserted streets, causing the trees to bend and sway while dust and debris swirled through the air, clouding our path.

"Be careful," Granny cautioned as I parked the Buick alongside the curve by the church. "There are lots of things flying around."

"Do be careful," Sister Callahan echoed.

"I'll be back soon."

Pushing into the wind, I skirted the building, fighting the branches of the overgrown vegetation on the way. Evidently, Friar Thompson wasn't fond of gardening. I came to the portico and tapped on the door. Seconds passed. No response. I knocked again. Nothing. Perhaps he couldn't hear my knocking above the wind.

A hand descended on my shoulder, and I spun around with a gasp.

"Allow me," Sister Callahan said, using surprising force as she called on the door.

"We had to check on you. You took too long." Granny joined us, her black habit swirling about her in the wind.

"He might not be home," I said.

"Fiddlesticks. He was here when we left the fundraiser. Besides, where would he go at this hour?" Sister Callahan pounded on the wood. "Either he sleeps like a rock or is as deaf as a post."

After yet another pounding, light shone through the window. The lock turned, and Friar Thompson formed in the doorway, looking dazed.

"Father, please forgive the disturbance," I said promptly. "We need your help."

"What's the matter?" His gaze jumped from me to Sister Callahan and back to me.

"We must find Dr. Ferns. Do you know where he lives?" Granny stepped into view from behind Sister Callahan.

"Sister Dolores," Friar Thompson exclaimed, "you shouldn't be out in this weather. I thought you were back at the monastery."

"I was—"

"Let's not deviate from the topic." Sister Callahan interrupted. Dressed in her red habit, she appeared quite menacing. "Dr. Ferns. Where does he live?"

"Why do you need Ferns?" Friar Thompson glanced at his watch and raised an eyebrow as if to say, "This late at night?"

Sister Callahan sighed, growing impatient.

"Mr. Sterling is extremely sick. Dr. Petersen is out of town, and anything else will take too long," I explained hurriedly.

"Dr. Petersen is out of town? Are you sure? I saw him this morning. He didn't mention anything about leaving."

"That's the information we have," I replied.

"Right, then," the priest relented. "Ferns lives on the outskirts of town, close to the lake."

"On the outskirts?" Granny repeated. "I thought he lived nearby."

"He moved after he retired. It won't be easy to find his house if you've never been there, especially at night," he cautioned.

"You'll have to come with us, then," Sister Callahan declared, "and why don't you answer your phone?"

"The phone line is down." A sudden awareness crossed his face. "Oh, I see. You must've tried to call me. That's why you came."

"Yes, yes!" Sister Callahan threw her hands in the air as if thanking heaven for finally opening the priest's understanding.

"Will you show us to Dr. Ferns's house?" I asked. "Please?"

He observed us for an instant. "Come in. I'll grab my keys and cloak. You can follow me there."

We stepped into the waiting area.

Time presented yet another challenge. I had to get to Alex. "Granny, could you bring the doctor to Oak's Place? Do you think Friar Thompson would mind? I don't want to lose another minute."

"He won't mind," Sister Callahan assured. "We'll ride with him."

I smiled for the first time that night. Sister Callahan would ensure the priest cooperated. She was becoming my hero quite rapidly—a hero who knew how to succor others, even in unconventional ways. Like Granny had said, Sister Callahan, though a bit rough around the edges, could teach us a great deal. My soul filled with appreciation for her.

"Of course, child. Go ahead," Granny said. "We'll catch up with you once we find Ferns."

"Thank you." I gave Granny a heartfelt hug, and though I worried that Sister Callahan might squeeze my ribs, I hugged her as well.

Without the sisters in the car, I drove wildly, gas pedal to the floor. It wasn't long until the heavens opened, and rain pelted the windshield. The wipers produced a devilish screech, unable to keep up with the downpour. I had to slow down. *Hang in there, Alex. Please. Don't you dare leave me.*

Though I had no doubts about my previous life or our relationship, I still found it difficult to wrap my mind around all of it. Not in my wildest dreams would I have thought anything like this was possible. However, it was, and I soon would face the person who'd murdered me and my baby in a most ruthless manner. Confrontation wasn't probable; it was certain. We could no longer exist under the same roof.

Her audacity floored me. Indeed, she'd plotted to get rid of me again since I first arrived at Oak's Place. My resemblance to the woman she had killed must have stunned her beyond reason. Now that I thought about it, letting me step into the foyer that morning must have been one of the hardest things she ever did. And since Alex knew my name from my call with Zaira about the ad, though Mrs. White tried, thanks to Mr. Vines, she couldn't send me away. Ultimately, she had woven an astonishing, credible story to separate us that would have worked if not for supernatural intervention. I winced at how skillfully she manipulated the situation to simultaneously deceive Alex and me.

I could not help but think how Alex must have felt—a broken man who allowed himself to dream, to love once more, only to have his heart broken again. When Alex had come into my office and saw my tears, along with the pictures in my hands, he'd assumed Mrs. White had told me the truth, that he believed me to be his deceased wife, pushing me to think he was on the brink of madness.

And then there was Mr. Vines, her faithful accomplice. In a way, I felt a twinge of pity for him. He was caught in a pernicious love. Unfortunately, he, the only person who could back my allegations, would die before betraying Mrs. White. The word *die* nauseated me. She was capable of killing.

"*He was always sick, always in pain. Poor fellow. Death was a relief to him.*" Alex's words about Mrs. White's husband, Frederick, struck me full force. My mind went blank for a few seconds, allowing the new idea to form. Alex had described *his* illness.

"*I've been faithful to you through it all, even Frederick,*" Mr. Vines said the night I overheard their dreadful conversation at Forti Radici.

"*Don't you dare threaten me!*" Mrs. White had retorted.

Had Mrs. White murdered her husband? Was she slowly killing Alex the same way? Perhaps with a poison administered in moderation to avoid suspicion? It could be. Since the crash of the stock market, killing by poison had become more common.

Moreover, I knew it was also preferred in England. I just had never imagined it could happen close to me. Although, after my awakening, nothing seemed far-fetched anymore. With this new insight, I threw caution to the wind and floored the pedal once more.

When at last the Buick jerked to a halt in front of Oak's Place, my adrenaline surged. I ran for the shelter of the porch and thankfully found the door unlocked. I burst into the foyer, and the wind gusted through the corridor to where Mrs. White stood with Mr. Vines, both with suitcases in hand.

"You vile woman!" The memory of the snake in the stall hit me, followed by Sunny's desperate thrashing. I dashed at her, consumed with rage. "How dare you lie to me!"

I had seen many expressions on her before, but her current look of terror trumped them all. The time to confront the past had come. And as impossible as it seemed, she must have feared I was indeed the same woman she'd murdered. At the very least, she must be conscious of what she did and the lies she told me.

Reacting on pure instinct, I pushed her with a force that surprised us both. Her head bounced off the wall, and for a moment, her eyes lost focus. She dropped the suitcase, locked eyes with me, and lunged. We struggled back and forth, each movement a calculated motion of attack and defense. And amid the wrestle, my fingers caught her rosary. The string snapped, the black beads splashing onto the floor.

Mrs. White gasped as if I had disassembled her soul instead of the rosary.

"Don't worry. You'll need more than an organized set of prayers to atone for what you've done," I sputtered.

"Restrain her, you fool," she barked at Mr. Vines, who watched with perplexity.

When I glanced at him, she managed to free her arm and clocked me with an open-handed blow. My skin burned, and my head spun, but I was happy to return the favor with even more force.

"Mr. Vines! For goodness' sake! Do something!" she cried.

With one swift movement, he wrapped his spindly arms around my waist, wrenching me away.

"Alex didn't kill his wife. You did! You threw the snake in the stall to scare the horse." I twisted to look at Mr. Vines, seeking an ally. "You know. You were there. You must stand for the truth!"

Shock registered in his eyes, but his loyalty held him bound.

"Enough of this," Mrs. White hissed, regaining control. "You have lost your mind."

"Yes, but unfortunately for you, I have regained it."

"Whatever your delusions are, you are too late. Mr. Sterling is almost dead."

"How can you be so cold-blooded?" I twisted in vain to break free of Mr. Vines. "But I shouldn't be surprised when you killed your husband!" I took a shot in the dark, but I knew I'd hit the mark when I saw the astonishment in her face.

"Don't you speak of Frederick. He has nothing to do with this."

"You killed him, didn't you?" I accused, sensing her weak spot.

"You have no idea the hell I lived in knowing there was no cure for his illness. My heart died a little each time he groaned in pain, each time he cried for help—help that would only come one way."

"Deborah, stop! Don't say anything else," Mr. Vines urged.

"Don't you tell me what to do," she responded. "For the longest of time, my dear Frederick begged me to free him from his misery. *'It's a noble deed, my dear Debby, what you do for me. I'm sorry I've become so useless. I'm sorry you have to do this,'* he would say. So yes, judge me all you want. I poisoned him to end his torture."

"If you understood how terrible it is to lose a spouse, why did you kill m—Alex's wife?" I corrected for the sake of clarity. "Why?"

"The rotten creature had it all and appreciated nothing. General Sterling deserved better. My Frederick always said Alex would be the perfect match for me. For years, I waited. I even convinced him to move to America, hoping he would forget. Then you came along, unearthing the past. You gave me no choice but to finish what I started. You forced my hand."

"You are poisoning Alex. Why? He has done nothing to you." I continued to attempt to free myself of Mr. Vines. I wanted to get to her, but he wouldn't allow it.

"I've given him the best years of my life, yet he doesn't even notice when I enter the room. I suppose I'm not good enough for him, not pretty enough, not young enough, not rich enough! Never enough!"

"You can't force love. It's not his fault. Your obsession consumes you."

"Frederick said the general was the right man for me, and my Frederick was never wrong." She closed her eyes and sighed as if her words were liberating, as if she had waited eons to let them out.

In a heartbeat, I saw what had eluded me all this time. Lunacy. Was it a product of her suffering early in life or of her wicked acts? Perhaps both. Within the inmost parts of my soul, my anger turned to compassion, and I pitied her, this miserable, lamentable soul.

"Florence, what's the matter?" Zaira popped into the corridor, and her gaze swept to Mr. Vines. "What's going on here?"

"Let go of me." I gave one harsh pull and finally broke free. "It's a long story, Zaira."

Like a rat from a sinking ship, Mr. Vines picked up the suitcases. "Come on, Deborah. Let's go."

Never breaking eye contact with me, Mrs. White squared her shoulders and laced her arm with Mr. Vines's. She smiled scornfully. "Of course, you have no proof. And there are things you don't know and will never know."

They walked out the door into the night.

Part of me, the part that would have been happy to get even with Mrs. White and maybe even get in a few more satisfying blows, wanted to charge after her. But a wiser part let her go. Right now, just as she said, I had no evidence of her crimes, and I needed to get to Alex. Sooner or later, in this life or another, possibly both, Mrs. White would face justice. And that knowledge was enough for me.

Zaira locked the door behind them. "Florence, what just happened?"

"I think Mrs. White and Mr. Vines poisoned Alex."

Zaira's eyes widened in horror, and her hand flew to her mouth.

"Granny will be here soon with a doctor. Please watch for them."

"You really think they poisoned him?" Zaira choked on the question.

"I'm afraid so." The thought that they might return swirled through my head. "Where is Mr. Snider?"

"He retired to the cottage for the night."

"Go get him. We need him in the house."

"I'm not sure that's possible."

"Why not?"

"I'm sorry I didn't tell you, but it didn't feel right to divulge Mr. Snider's problems. Considering everything else, I guess it's the right time."

"Quick, please tell me." I had to get to Alex.

"He suffers from severe war trauma. It usually hits him at night, and more often than not, he is heavily intoxicated—it's his way of dealing with it."

"Intoxicated with what?"

"Whiskey, rum, vodka, you name it. He has bottles stashed all over the grounds. That is why Mrs. White fights with him but can't let him go —because Mr. Sterling won't allow it. On the contrary, he's often tried to get Snider the help he needs."

"And that's why his wife left him, isn't it?" I felt for him.

"I'm afraid so. Anyway, I just came from the cottage, and, I'm sorry, but he is legless."

I should have known. The morning I went to the cottage looking for Zaira, I found Mr. Snider hung over. That's why he'd tripped over things and looked so disoriented. "No matter. Bring him to the kitchen and pump him with coffee until it flushes the alcohol out."

CHAPTER 26
~ MERGING ~

Upon entering Alex's room, I felt like I had traveled back in time again—as if we hadn't been separated, the knowledge of the hidden past erasing all unfamiliarity. Alex slept, his ashen countenance heartrending to behold. The hollows under his eyes spoke of the fatigue and strain of his long, upward battle. His heart was broken yet still beating, still filled with love for me.

I sat on the edge of the bed, took his hand in mine, and shuddered at the coldness of his skin. "Alex, I'm here. I'm here to stay." I pressed my cheek to the scar on his chest left by the bullet he had taken for my father so long ago. No wonder it impacted me when I saw it the day of the storm. Not only had I dreamed of it, but I had also seen it many times as his wife. I just couldn't remember it then. "You, General, who unselfishly saved so many lives, deserve the chance to live. It's only fair."

"Florence, the doctor is here," Zaira announced from the threshold.

"Please, show him in." I glanced at the clock on the dresser—almost midnight.

Zaira returned with Dr. Ferns. "I'll be in the kitchen if you need me."

"Thank you, Zaira." I signaled to the doctor. "Please, come in."

Dr. Ferns had seen quite a few winters. The small-framed man had silver hair and thick spectacles. He moved slowly across the room, medical bag in hand.

"I fear he has been poisoned," I said.

"Yes, Zaira told me of your suspicion. And I took the liberty to ask her to search the house for any poison." He studied Alex with keen awareness. "We need to know what we might be dealing with. For now, Miss Contini, please explain what you know about his symptoms." Taking a few medical instruments from his case, he started the examination while I answered his question. "Yes, yes, very interesting," he said in reply.

"I'm afraid that's all I know," I concluded.

"Very well. This will take a minute longer. If you don't mind, have a seat." Politely, he excluded me from his working space.

While he continued to check his patient with much care and thought, I retreated to the far wall. Alex made a few soft, groaning sounds but otherwise remained inert. I forced myself to be still, to not distract the doctor, for I had the feeling that if I did, he would banish me from the room. Nonetheless, a whirlwind of emotions churned inside me. Would Mrs. White succeed in taking Alex's life? Would he be the one standing in spirit form near me now, unable to comfort me? Each passing second stretched indefinitely as I fought to stay positive. Alex had to live. We had a bright future.

At length, the doctor informed me, "I have a partial diagnosis," while returning the instruments to the briefcase. "Without further testing, I can't be 100 percent sure, you understand. But yes, I'm afraid you are correct. Mr. Sterling has been poisoned."

"I can't believe I was so blind."

Zaira hustled in, held the doctor's gaze, and shook her head. "We searched everywhere. We didn't find anything."

My stomach turned. Mrs. White had carefully covered her tracks.

"Thank you, young lady," Dr. Ferns said, and she withdrew. "Well then, we must work with what we know. His symptoms suggest the poison was administered in small doses over an extended period, slowly shutting down his system. Does Mr. Sterling have any close relatives?"

I flinched at the implication. "No, he doesn't. I'm the closest to a relative he has. We contemplated marriage." I omitted that I had broken the engagement the previous day.

"In that case, you'll have to decide. I'm going to send a blood sample to the hospital right away to determine the kind of poison we're dealing with. But it will take time—time we don't have." Dr. Ferns reached for Alex's hand, finding his pulse. "If he is going to survive, we must give him the antidote without delay. Now, not knowing which toxin is in his system—the medicine, instead of healing, might help to kill him."

"It's too dangerous."

"It is. However, if we don't give it a try, he'll die in the next few hours. He needs the antidote right away," the doctor affirmed. "And, thank heaven, I brought some with me. It's used for myriad things, you understand."

Gambling with my soul would be easier than this decision. If I chose wrong, it would weigh on me for eternity. I looked at Alex's pale face, and my heart constricted. "Give him the medicine."

"I'll take the samples to the hospital," Friar Thompson, who had graciously driven the nuns and Dr. Ferns to Oak's Place, kindly offered.

"I'll go with him to speed things up," Sister Callahan decided. "And I suppose with Mr. Sterling having been poisoned, we must alert the police."

The priest gave her a look of apprehension but proceeded politely. "Yes, yes, Sister Callahan, and I will take care of it."

"There are no words to express how grateful I am for your help," I said sincerely.

Sister Callahan smiled. "Don't mention it, Fannie."

With a nod, the priest gathered his cloak and hat and hurried out into the stormy night, followed by the irrepressible Sister Callahan.

I turned to the doctor and insisted he stay in the guest room. I wanted him to be rested and sharp.

"Very well," Dr. Ferns agreed. "I'll check on Mr. Sterling every few hours. Please don't hesitate to call on me if anything seems out of the ordinary."

Mr. Snider, Zaira, and Granny were determined to keep watch in the kitchen.

"Miss Contini, I'll keep the ladies company. We'll be here if you need us." Mr. Snider shifted on the chair, a bit jittery from all the caffeine Zaira forced into him. As if reading my mind, she veered from the stove with a fresh pot of coffee and refilled his cup to the brim. At this rate, he would have insomnia for months.

The lamplight cast a warm glow over the bed, creating a soothing atmosphere. I lay beside a silent Alex to keep him warm, rain falling faintly in the background.

"General, remember the days in Keyhaven? You promised you'd always come back. You better make good on that promise now. And so you know, I have always loved you. Remember the first time you came to Forti Radici? When we saw each other in the field?" His heartbeat grew louder. I went on.

"Remember the night you followed me out into the gardens and kissed me? Your kiss haunted me until the night of the ball. When I saw you with Nelly, I almost went crazy. Your indifference cut deep into my pride, exposing my true feelings for you. And when we ran out into Brockenhurst's grounds, I had no choice but to accept that I was your prisoner. Remember the happy time we spent in the flat in London amid the war? The world was upside down, and my family was dead, but we had each other and a deep desire to help end the conflict. You did incredible things for our country and those who fought for freedom and their families."

I lost myself in the memories. Minutes and hours crawled by, and my voice became almost inaudible, then stopped altogether.

I awoke with a start. The silence was too thick. Alex lay deathly still. I put my hand on his chest and gasped. I couldn't feel his heartbeat. I dashed into the darkened corridor, shouting for Dr. Ferns.

Zaira, Granny, and Mr. Snider met me just outside the kitchen.

"What is the matter, child?" Granny asked in alarm.

"Alex's heart stopped! Get the doctor."

"I'll get him." Mr. Snider hurried to the guest room.

I rushed back into the bedroom, hit the light switch, and gasped at the white figure on the bed.

How could I have fallen asleep? My eyes burned with tears of guilt.

Dr. Ferns hustled in with the agility of a wildcat, a fierce determination in his eyes. Mr. Snider, Zaira, and Granny trailed behind.

The doctor examined Alex's eyes and pulse. "Quick, turn him onto his stomach. We need him face down," he ordered.

Mr. Snider was fit for the task. I did what I could to assist. Granny and Zaira observed the scene from a safe distance.

"Turn his head to the side and raise his arms. Rest his face on the palms of his hands. Quickly!" the doctor instructed as if commanding a platoon of soldiers. And at once, he applied upward pressure to Alex's elbows, slightly raising his upper body off the bed. He then firmly pressed Alex's shoulder blades with both hands.

The constant motion went on, accelerating my heartbeat instead of Alex's. Dr. Ferns's hands worked steadily, but it wasn't enough. It was taking too long. I held my breath, suppressing a sob. My eyes found Granny's. She remained composed, giving me hope.

"Allow me," Mr. Snider said.

Dr. Ferns wiped the perspiration from his forehead and, with a nod, acquiesced.

Mr. Snider's larger hands had more power behind them. After three tries, Alex let out a sigh, followed by a choking sound.

"Turn him around and bring him to a sitting position," the doctor said.

I arranged a stack of pillows against the headboard, and Mr. Snider set Alex against them.

"Would you mind?" Dr. Ferns pointed at Alex's shirt, and I

unbuttoned it. With his stethoscope, he listened attentively to Alex's chest. "Good. Very good. He has a steady heartbeat."

"Thank goodness." Granny looked up as if thanking heaven.

"That was too close, too close indeed." Zaira held Granny's hand in reassurance.

Mr. Snider smiled, a rare occurrence with him.

"Is Alex going to be all right, then?" I desperately wanted an affirmative answer.

"Miss Contini, I think this was his body's natural reaction to the conflict between the poison and the antidote. I'm happy to say the antidote won." Dr. Ferns took off his spectacles and stood a little taller, clearly pleased with his work.

I collapsed into a chair, relieved that my worst nightmare hadn't come true.

Sunlight poured in through the east window, and birds chirped excitedly over the new day.

Alex's health continued to improve in the following hours. Though he hadn't woken, his heartbeat remained strong, and his skin gradually regained color.

The doctor walked in. "I spoke with the hospital. We won't have the results back until tomorrow, but I think it is safe to say Mr. Sterling is reacting well to the medicine. I'll proceed with a second dose if you agree."

"Thank you for all you did last night. You've saved his life."

"My pleasure, Miss Contini. But now there is a more pressing matter. The police have arrived and would like to speak to you."

I glanced at Alex, not wanting to leave his side.

"I need to check on Mr. Sterling anyway. No worries, I'll watch over him until you return," assured the doctor.

I kissed Alex's forehead. "Stay put. I'll be right back, General."

Two police officials and a detective conversed with Zaira and Granny in the kitchen.

"This is Inspector Stanley," Zaira said. "We have told them everything we know about Mrs. White and Mr. Vines."

After a brief set of questions, the handsome, olive-complexioned, middle-aged inspector said, "There is only one thing that doesn't fit. We don't have a motive for the lady in question to want to dispatch Mr. Sterling. Without a motive, we can't accuse her. Anyone could've done it. In fact, each of you is guilty until proven otherwise." His gaze wandered suspiciously from face to face.

I hadn't thought about it that way. I felt pretty sure it was the other way around. People were innocent until proven otherwise, but I knew enough not to cross him. However, it complicated matters. I had no proof against Mrs. White. That she might be in love with Alex was in her favor, and comments on her mental state would play against me, for it was my assumption.

"I'm afraid you're right. We have no evidence against her," I stated, "except for the poison."

"That explains Mrs. White's fixation with overseeing Mr. Sterling's tea. That's how she did it," Zaira deduced.

"That's exactly how she did it," I agreed. She mixed it with his drink, just like she did to Frederick. "And the poison had to be bought somewhere."

The inspector rubbed his chin thoughtfully. "Once we get the results from the hospital and know with certainty what we are dealing with, we can act. If it's a controlled substance, someone prescribed it. Zaira mentioned a Dr. Petersen, so we'll start there."

"Then, of course, it could be something simple as a household poison used to kill rodents or undesirable plants," Granny reflected.

"Yes, of course," the inspector agreed. "We'll check with the local stores."

"You must do it quickly, before she is halfway around the world," I said to the inspector, anxious to see her put safely away. This woman with a murderer's heart had escaped justice for way too long.

"Wait." Zaira's eyes brightened with excitement. "She went to New York City when Mr. Sterling was in England, remember?"

"Yes, but he's been sick longer than that," I argued. "Besides, if she bought anything there, it would be impossible to find out. The city is too big."

"Not to mention how many shady transactions go unnoticed," the inspector added.

"I'm thinking about a motive," Zaira said. "I'm not sure if it's relevant, but when I searched Mrs. White's room for the poison, I found several newspapers. They caught my attention because she circled quite a few places in New York."

"What types of places?" I was instantly interested.

"I'm not sure. I didn't think much about it until now, but it could be helpful. I'll go grab them."

"That's interesting indeed." Granny poured herself more coffee.

Inspector Stanley settled at the table, eagerly jotting down notes.

My thoughts raced in many directions. Could this be what we needed for an arrest warrant?

"Here they are." Zaira resurfaced and dropped the newspapers on the table.

We all took a paper to examine it.

I flipped through the pages, hoping to find something useful. "Solicitors offices."

"Same here," Inspector Stanley said.

"Here too," Zaira and Granny echoed.

"A legal matter is the only reason why she would contact a solicitor," the inspector reasoned. "Any ideas what it could be?"

"No. As far as I know, she has nothing back in England that requires that type of assistance," Zaira affirmed.

"There is one way to find out." I held the inspector's gaze. "We must call them."

"While it might be a good idea, I can't do that," he stated. "I can't meddle in personal affairs without a valid reason. I mean, for now, I only have an employee who left."

"I'll do it, then." I dragged a chair close to the telephone, calling one number after another. My anticipation dissolved when I dialed the last number with the same result. No one had a client by the name of Deborah White. I shook my head in disbelief, frustrated to have wasted this much time. I needed to return to Alex. I abandoned the chair, my sense of defeat weighing on me.

"I'm sorry, child," Granny offered.

"Let's take another look at the papers to make sure we didn't miss anything," Zaira proposed.

The telephone suddenly rang, everyone stirring to attention.

"Yes, this is Florence Contini," I said into the receiver. "Yes, I called a few minutes ago. Yes, I'm Mr. Sterling's secretary."

"You spoke to my colleague, Mrs. Green. She said you called on behalf of Mrs. Deborah White." The man on the other end provided his name and office information.

"Oh yes." I gestured for Zaira to hand me a pen. I wrote everything he said in the margins of a newspaper. "She's been a bit busy lately and asked me to contact you."

"I was planning on reaching out today to finalize the paperwork. I apologize that it took longer than we planned. But as you might know, testaments and wills can be a lengthy process, more so when dealing with overseas assets."

"A will, you say?" My gaze darted to the inspector.

He signaled for me to keep them speaking.

"Mr. Alexander Sterling's will," the man informed.

"Oh yes, of course. Is it ready, then?"

"That's correct. Mrs. White can stop by to pick it up at her earliest convenience. Please remind her that, by law, Mr. Sterling must sign it in the presence of at least one witness."

I swallowed the lump in my throat. Mr. Vines would have served the purpose well. I fished for more details. "And Mrs. White is the sole beneficiary, correct?"

"As requested, yes."

"Thank you for your call. I'll let her know." I turned to the inspector. "Looks like we found our motive. She wanted to steal Alex's fortune. All she needed was his signature."

"In his condition, it would have been easy enough to have him sign without knowing what he signed," Granny remarked.

"Is there any chance Mr. Sterling might have been in on this?" the inspector questioned.

"None. Why would he give away everything he has when just yesterday we planned to marry and start a life together?"

"Just when you think you've heard it all." With a loud sigh, Zaira leaned against the counter, seemingly, like the rest of us, trying to reconcile herself to the jarring reality.

Perhaps last night, when I told Mrs. White over the phone, "*I know what you've done, and I'm coming to settle the debt,*" she thought I had discovered her attempt to steal from Alex. Thankfully, the completion of the will had taken longer than expected. I shuddered to think how she must have timed his death to the minute.

"I'll take your word on this for now, but I'd like to speak to him as soon as possible." Inspector Stanley copied the information I had written on the newspaper. "I must get in touch with these people. And we'll track down Dr. Petersen, see what he knows."

"I'll let you know as soon as Alex is well enough to speak with you."

"I'll leave my men to search Mrs. White and Mr. Vines's quarters." With that, Inspector Stanley left Oak's Place.

"It's been a long night." *A long night of twenty-three years of recovered memories.*

"Why don't you rest awhile?" Granny suggested. "I'm afraid Dr. Ferns will have another patient if you keep going like this."

"I'll rest beside Alex."

"I'll prepare a hearty breakfast," Zaira decided. "We can all benefit from that."

"I'll help you, dear." Granny swiftly moved to the stove.

I walked out of the kitchen with deep gratitude for these women in my life.

CHAPTER 27
~ CLEAR REALITY ~

I found Dr. Ferns perched on the chair by the window, a peaceful look on his face. "He is much better. He woke a while ago, and I explained the poisoning."

"Thank you, Doctor. Zaira is working on breakfast. Please have something to eat."

"Don't mind if I do." He withdrew, humming happily beneath his breath.

I moved to Alex's side and intertwined our fingers. His eyes fluttered open, and a faint smile crossed his lips. Our gazes met, the oneness that had been ours returning. Our experiences, happiness, and suffering were all there in that connection—no secrets, no confusion. We knew each other fully.

"Hello, General. About time you came back to me."

"Hello, my lady."

"You haven't called me that in a long time."

"You know . . ."

"I do," I said.

"So do I."

"I'm so glad you're back. I was terrified to lose you."

"You were the one who left, twice. First in the New Forest and then yesterday."

"I'm sorry. I love you, Alex." I crawled beside him and kissed his cheek. I was anxious to find out how he knew it was me, but fearing his health was too frail, I didn't ask.

"When you first came to Oak's Place, I thought I'd gone mad. I was filled with fear and wonder. Remember when I went back to England?" he started.

"You were healthier when you returned. I understand why now. Mrs. White wasn't there to poison you. But perhaps we should wait to speak about this."

"No, I have waited long enough." He cleared his throat and tightened his arms around me. "I went because of my struggle to grasp reality. You were my deceased wife, yet that was impossible. I saw you die. I buried you. However, here you were, the same young woman I lost twenty years ago, the same beauty, the same softness, and this." He touched my bracelet. "I buried it with you. So, in a frenzy to prove to myself that you weren't her, I had your grave dug up, your coffin taken out."

"You did what?"

"I know. I can hardly believe it myself. And so you know, I even rummage through your purse that time when you asked why I'd come to your office. I denied it, but I did."

"I knew it!" I could laugh about it now.

"I'm sorry. I was so out of my mind trying to find an explanation for the resemblance that I did foolish things."

"I already know there wasn't anything of interest in my purse, but what did you find in the grave?"

"Nothing. It was empty, with no evidence of foul play. Scotland Yard made sure of that. I couldn't explain it, but I knew then that you were my lady. My voyage back to America took an eternity. I couldn't wait to see you, to be with you. You have no idea how difficult it was to squash the impulse to embrace, to kiss you. Worse, I couldn't bring myself to tell you the truth because the truth was unfathomable. I feared you would think I was off my rocker, and I would lose you again."

"I know why the coffin was empty." I first told him about Mrs. White's elaborate story concerning his and my past—how she had me believe Alex had killed my father and the nanny had gone into exile to save my life. Furthermore, she told me he'd traveled to England to search immigration records. I also disclosed how she used the photographs to back up her lies. "I'm so sorry. I believed that wretched woman instead of giving you a chance to explain. But after you hear me out, perhaps you'll agree it turned out for the best." I told him of my encounter with Lucca, my journey back in time, and the truth behind my death.

"I knew something must have scared Sunny. I knew it." Anger laced his voice. "How could I have been such a fool? I should've known. There was so much going on with the army and the war that I failed to see the enemy in my own home! I should have let her go when she destroyed Mrs. Allerton's garden."

"Don't blame yourself. There were things we didn't know nor could've ever imagined." Not wanting to further overwhelm him, I briefly shared the opportunity I had to live again, thus explaining the empty coffin. "I couldn't accept the idea of leaving you behind to live the rest of your life grieving, especially with Mrs. White still around."

"I don't know what to say. I'm as astonished as the first time I saw you here at Oak's Place. I'll forever be thankful that you took the risk, and it worked out. I shudder to think of what might have been. And the hardest thing to forgive myself for is to have allowed White to play me this long. To control me, she controlled my health. Now I see that she began poisoning me in England to convince me to move here. Thank goodness it backfired on her."

"You know, in her own twisted way, I think she loved you."

"Love doesn't do the unspeakable things she did. She only loved one person—herself."

"Be that as it may, we mustn't let her take any more time from us. For now, we are together, and that's all that matters." Was she mentally ill or brilliantly dangerous? We might never know.

"Tell me, am I still dreaming? Is this real?"

I looked up and kissed him. "You are not dreaming, General."

"Florence, your empty coffin is not the only thing that convinced me of your identity. I had a dream." He paused, clearly overcome by his emotions again. "After Mrs. White lied to you, you left in such a rage I was sure you would hate me forever. I thought she told you that I believed you to be my deceased wife, which I did, that I was insane, and that I would never love you for who you were. I thought you would never come back, never understand, and I couldn't change my past or my feelings for you.

"I didn't want to live. I was ready to let my life slip away, then I heard you speaking to the doctor. You were here. You didn't abandon me. A sense of great peace came over me, and I dreamed as if I was there, but I knew I was in bed. You stood on a riverbank, dressed like you used to in the New Forest. I stood on the other side and couldn't get to you. You had to come to me, and for that, you had to cross the water. You went completely under, and when you emerged, you were dressed as you do nowadays. We embraced, and at that moment, any lingering doubts about you were removed. And I found the strength to fight for my life and come back to you."

"The end starts at the beginning and the beginning at the end. That is our story. It is hard to grasp. Perhaps we never will. But I have learned that there are powers at work in this world and the next that we have no idea about. Powers that strive to help our families succeed—for that, I'm eternally grateful. The chance to be with you again, Lieutenant, is a priceless gift."

Alex's laughter was a welcome sound. "I hated it when you called me lieutenant."

"I know. That's why I did." My heart swelled with gratitude that he was still the man I always loved, the man who enjoyed teasing me and taking care of me. The man who completed me.

Forty-eight hours later, Alex was well on his way to recovery. The lab results came back positive, though the type of poison was still being determined. The police detained Dr. Petersen under suspicion of prescribing unlawful substances pending an investigation. Meanwhile, the search for Mrs. White and Mr. Vines intensified.

"Where do you think you are going, General?" I met Alex halfway across his bedroom.

"To look for you. This belongs with you." He extracted my wedding ring from his pocket. "Please, don't throw it at me again." He gave me a crooked smile.

"I'll do my best," I teased.

"I love you." He placed the ring on my finger.

"I love you more."

"Does America feel like home to you?"

His question took me by surprise, but the answer came out naturally. "No, not after remembering it all."

"Would my lady like to return to Forti Radici?"

"I'd like that very much." The prospect of seeing the manor again, of visiting the graves of my parents, Lucca, Mrs. Allerton, and Mr. Leroy felt right. Returning to my roots would bring me full circle. Forti Radici, the name struck me full force. Strong Roots. My ancestors had wisely named it.

"Florence, stay tonight. Stay with me." Alex brought me into him. Before I could respond, he kissed me with the same ardent passion he had twenty years ago, pouring his desire into every stroke of his lips against mine.

I managed to pull away, heaving a breath. "I see you are feeling much better."

He buried his face in my neck. "Please."

"I'm sorry, General, but I must leave." It took all my willpower to say it. "You are much better. There is no reason for me to stay overnight."

"You are joking."

"I'm not. It's not like I can tell Granny and Zaira the truth. So, it's not proper for me to stay, especially when I would be staying in this room."

"I could visit you in the guest room."

"Nice try." I started for the door, and he reached for my hand. I evaded him.

"Florence, you're my wife."

"No, in this life, I am not your wife. If you want me to stay, you must marry me again."

"I'll bring the priest to the monastery first thing in the morning."

"I'll be waiting." I stepped into the corridor. "Good night, Mr. Sterling."

He shook his head in dismay, but a smile crossed his face. "Good night, Miss Contini."

Though I didn't show it, walking away was one of the hardest things I would ever do. Dreams would have to suffice for tonight, but tomorrow Alex and I would be wed for the second time, and I'd never leave his side again.

———

Thank you for reading! Did you enjoy? Please add your review because nothing helps an author more and encourages readers to take a chance on a book than a review.

And don't miss part two of *Shadows of a Forgotten Past* with ALIVE by Marcia Armandi available now. Turn the page for a sneak peek!

Also be sure to sign up for the City Owl Press newsletter to receive notice of all book releases!

SNEAK PEEK OF ALIVE

The New Forest, Hampshire, England, 1939

Amid the complexities of life, one truth I knew without a doubt: the beginning is the end, the end is the beginning. Even when the tombs at the Breamore cemetery told a different story, one story—my own—attested to my conviction.

Florence Contini Sterling—
Forever My Lady
1894–1917

Standing before my grave, I wondered if anyone could ever understand how dreamlike this moment was. Twenty-two years ago, I had been laid to rest here. This burial ground witnessed Alexander Sterling's grief. It also provided a mysterious ray of hope when it later proved to no longer hold my remains. The empty tomb revealed an unfathomable truth: I had been released from the bonds of death.

Soon after I awakened to my past identity, Alex married me once more. With little notice from the world, Father Thompson performed the ceremony at the monastery in Geneva, New York. Reading from an ancient manuscript, the priest taught, "The souls connected with perpetual love have no cessation. They live on forever." If only he'd known how profound that statement was, his world would have turned topsy-turvy.

The setting sun deepened the twilight, and shadows spread across the graveyard. My gaze drifted to the headstone beside mine.

Sterlings' beloved baby boy,
sleep in peace under the nurturing
love of your dear mother.

My baby didn't have a name.

The knowledge of my past life was a blessing, yet it could not reconcile my grief for the departed nor ease my longing for what might have been. True, after my brother Lucca's visit, I found comfort in knowing that the spirits of the dead indeed dwelled in another realm and that, someday, I would join them. Still, the ache of their absence lingered.

Then, in contrast to the memory of my loved ones, thoughts of Deborah White, the cold-blooded murderess who remained at large, set my nerves on edge. She had stolen my son at birth, robbing me of the opportunity to behold his face. Her obsession with Alex, her resolution to end my life, and her callous indifference to my baby's fate haunted me. Had my baby died of natural causes, or had Mrs. White taken his life to sever the ties between Alex and me? That she was an iniquitous woman was beyond question, but would she go that far?

I didn't know what transpired after she took the baby. On more than one occasion, I had almost mustered enough courage to ask Alex, but the fear of reopening old wounds stayed my tongue. After all, there was no reason to wander back through years that were gone or chase something not meant to be. Still, the memory of my son's birth refused to fade, and I yearned to learn more about his death.

"I'm sorry, miss. I don't mean to intrude," a raspy voice broke the stillness.

Startled, I spun to face the cemetery keeper. Pale, dressed in black, and jingling a ring of keys on his belt, he looked as though he'd risen from one of the tombs he tended.

"The cemetery is now closed," he said. "I should've locked the gate twenty minutes ago." As if to underscore his words, the last rays of the sun slipped below the horizon, draping the graveyard in shadows. The closure of another day obscured the names, lives, and memories of those who lay asleep here.

"Do forgive me, Mr. . . .?"

"Morris, miss. Morris is the name."

"I apologize. I'm afraid I lost track of time."

"Indeed, you've been here for an awful long while." He gestured to a copse of trees beyond the Elmores' Victorian mausoleum. "See, I've been watching you from over there."

"You have?" I felt uneasy.

"Goodness, yes," he replied with a crooked smile. "I thought you were a haunt at first."

I supposed he could have. The nudge to come here had been so compelling, I hadn't bothered to change into riding clothes. My white dress, in the diffused light, likely made for a peculiar sight. And apparently, I wasn't the first ghostly figure Mr. Morris had seen on these grounds.

"You aren't from these parts, are you?" He gave me a measured look. "At least your accent is not."

"I'm from America."

"Hmm, a recent arrival, then?" he said with a hint of skepticism.

"That's right." A recent arrival to my previous life, I thought wryly. Had Mr. Morris known the Contini family? I didn't remember him from the past. "Have you worked in the cemetery long?"

"Since I was a young lad. I know these grounds and everyone who lives here like the palm of my hand."

Lives here. Interesting choice of words. To settle my curiosity and deflect suspicion, I turned toward my grave and asked, "Did you know her?"

"Florence Contini?"

"Yes."

"Saw her once or twice from a distance. Very refined lady, she was." He fidgeted with his keys. The sound drifted across the tombs as if summoning their inhabitants to rise. "Are you related?"

"Me?" I smiled nervously. "Well . . . no, not really."

"Hmm." His gaze bored into mine. "I'd have sworn you were family."

His words held truth, mine deceit—but then again, what choice did I have? I couldn't very well tell him I *was* the deceased.

"The way you looked at her and her child's grave, you know," he continued. "This place is acquainted with sorrow. I recognize it whenever I see it."

"Ohh." Relieved he wasn't referring to a physical resemblance, I offered a half-truth. "You see, I married Alexander Sterling—her husband and the baby's father."

"Ahh." He nodded slowly, as though my presence finally made sense. "It was but yesterday I heard talk of the general's return to the forest. So, it's true, after all these years. Who would have thought he would ever marry again?"

"Why do you say that? He is young. Besides, it's never too late, is it?"

"Oh no, don't misunderstand me. It's just that their story is so tragic. For years, he came to see her rain or shine. He spent hours kneeling beside her, sometimes weeping, sometimes staring into space. It was heartrending to behold."

If I weren't his late wife, I might have worried that Alex would never love me as much as he had loved her. As it was, I marveled at the wonder of my current existence, of being with him again. My heart had belonged to him ever since I first saw him in the fields of Forti Radici. Despite my childish antics, insecurities, and grief, he stood by me with undying affection.

"He moved to America after he retired," Mr. Morris concluded, breaking my reverie. "Of course, you knew that already."

"That's where we met."

"He visited not too long ago, though." Mr. Morris rubbed his chin thoughtfully. "Even now, I'm not sure what took place that day."

"What day? What took place?"

"It was early morning . . . winter it was. The ground was frozen." He motioned to my headstone, shifting uneasily on his feet. "Scotland Yard ordered me and another chap to dig up her coffin."

"You don't say!" I feigned astonishment but remembered Alex's sudden trip to the New Forest while I worked at Oak's Place.

"Nasty business, I thought."

Had he seen the empty coffin? "I'm sorry you had to see that," I said, hoping for a little more information.

"No, miss. We didn't see anything. Me and the other chap were dismissed after we unearthed the box. Scotland Yard, the local police, and the general himself were the only ones who saw inside. I don't know what they were looking for. Some presumed it might have been valuables buried with her," he said with a shrug.

"Do you believe that?"

"Not for a moment. He loved his wife too much to disturb her rest for something so trivial. And besides, the man does well enough regarding money."

I clasped the bracelet around my wrist, the only thing that had been buried with me. Even that, they hadn't found in my coffin.

"I must say," Mr. Morris continued, "Scotland Yard's secrecy flustered me. They came here in their well-pressed overcoats and polished badges, yet didn't have the decency to explain why on earth we were digging up corpses. 'It was a family matter,' they said, and left it at that. In other words, they hushed it up." He looked at me intently, as though he expected the general's new wife to elaborate.

As the last hints of day dissolved into night, I seized the opportunity to end the discussion. "I'm sorry to have kept you this long, Mr. Morris. It was nice chatting with you."

"I'll walk you to the entrance, or exit, same difference. It can get spooky after nightfall." Before I could object, he added, "I need to lock the gate anyway. Not that anyone with half a brain would wander in at night, but protocol is protocol."

We started on the pebble path. In addition to the click-clack of our shoes and the clink of his keys, the evening was filled with unspoken things—about the graveyard, about me, and about my family.

When the iron gate materialized ahead, I lengthened my steps.

"Thank you. My horse is just by the trees."

"Your horse?" His gaze flicked over my attire. "You didn't drive here?"

"I prefer to ride."

"A woman shouldn't be riding alone through the woods at this hour."

"I'll be all right." I stepped through the gate into the glow of a nearby lamppost.

"I'll say!" His eyes widened as if struck by a revelation. "Most extraordinary."

"What is?"

"You, miss. I could be mistaken, but your resemblance to the general's late wife is . . . most remarkable."

I pursed my lips. He remembered after all.

"Quite remarkable," he reiterated.

"Good night, Mr. Morris." With a polite smile, I hurried to Betsy, who munched on the foliage as if she had just arrived.

"Wait, miss, you haven't told me your name," he called from behind the iron bars, turning a large key in the lock. "How rude of me not to ask."

"Florence, Mr. Morris. Florence Sterling."

Shock rippled across his face.

Though I had tried to keep things quiet, the gossip was sure to spread like wildfire. Not only did I resemble Alex's first wife, but I also shared her name. No doubt people would pity me, convinced he'd married me because I reminded him of the love of his life. If only they knew. But how could anyone ever believe such an extraordinary truth?

Don't stop now. Keep reading with your copy of ALIVE available now.

Don't miss part two of *Shadows of a Forgotten Past* with ALIVE by Marcia Armandi available now.

Florence Sterling should be living a perfect life, but dark memories of her past still haunt her.

She and her baby were murdered, but now, after a miraculous second chance at life, Florence struggles with the fear that her happiness with Alex may be fleeting.

When Alex is called away on a perilous WWII mission to secure America's support in the war, Florence's anxiety grows. Seeking answers, she embarks on a desperate investigation into the truth behind her son's death, and to her shock, she uncovers evidence that suggests he might still be alive. But as Florence digs deeper, she finds herself drawn into a deadly game with her most dangerous enemy yet—the twisted woman determined to destroy her.

As the war intensifies and Alex goes missing in action, Florence must find the courage to face her deepest fears. If Alex is lost to the war, will she open her heart to love again and build the family she's always longed for? Or will the scars of her past keep her trapped in loneliness and despair forever?

Alive combines romance, mystery, and suspense in a heart-wrenching WWII saga. If you love emotional, character-driven stories filled with twists, danger, and a powerful second-chance romance, you'll love this story!

Please sign up for the City Owl Press newsletter for chances to win special subscriber-only contests and giveaways as well as receiving information on upcoming releases and special excerpts.

All reviews are **welcome** and **appreciated**. Please consider leaving one on your favorite social media and book buying sites.

Escape Your World. Get Lost in Ours! City Owl Press at www.cityowlpress.com.

ACKNOWLEDGMENTS

My deepest gratitude to Lisa Green. Thank you for your patience, hard work, and priceless advice in bringing *Awaken* to its best version.

And a huge thanks to the entire team at City Owl Press for believing in me as an author. It is my pleasure to work with such fantastic people.

ABOUT THE AUTHOR

MARCIA ARMANDI was born and raised in Argentina. She is a soccer fanatic and loves listening to tango. Marcia studied International Family History Research and Writing.

After decades of compiling personal histories, she has developed a profound gratitude for the strength that can be found in families. So it is that through her fiction, Marcia explores the meaning of love and loyalty in times of fear, war, and finally, death.

facebook.com/ArmandiMarcia

x.com/MarciaArmandi

instagram.com/marciaarmandi

ABOUT THE PUBLISHER

City Owl Press is a cutting edge indie publishing company, bringing the world of romance and speculative fiction to discerning readers.

Escape Your World. Get Lost in Ours!

www.cityowlpress.com

facebook.com/CityOwlPress

x.com/cityowlpress

instagram.com/cityowlbooks

pinterest.com/cityowlpress

tiktok.com/@cityowlpress

www.ingramcontent.com/pod-product-compliance
Lightning Source LLC
Chambersburg PA
CBHW060612030726
47498CB00005B/1648